The Tiger Cruise

The Tiger Cruise

One

Port of Odessa, Ukraine

Andrei Kobiak stepped out of the car almost before his driver came to a complete stop. The dark gray misty morning, all too familiar to those in these parts, did little to interrupt his train of thought. The smell of diesel, welding torches and bilge stench was one he had awakened to for the last two years. Although he was slated for promotion to a high command in the CinC-Northern Fleet, his love for the sea and Russia forced his hand in renovating the old sub.

The K-387 sat at its moorings almost as if the inanimate object knew what was about to take place. Andrei's early morning ritual of boarding her before the first dawn, and inspecting the previous day's work efforts was one he had done for the last two years without fail. Although she had been mothballed some time ago, she was now plenty seaworthy. Soviet shipyards rarely fit a ship in such short a time. The crumbling Soviet bureaucracy sees to that. Paperwork alone delays ship renovations at Odessa an average of 18 months beyond scheduled start dates. And yet, the K-387 was completed well ahead of schedule. Andrei's daily routine of walking from stem to stern on the sub to make sure the work met his standards, ignoring mundane and useless paperwork, and his determination to see this project to completion, resulted in an overhaul at Odessa that was unmatched in Soviet history.

The overworked yard workers knew his reputation and most had volunteered to work on this project. Not out of any great admiration for this naval Captain but because he saw to it they were paid above average wages and, more importantly, always on time.

"Morning, Comrade Captain," a welder yelled. Andrei would always return the gesture with a nod, never a spoken word.

His inspection this morning was his last, and most important. Trial runs had proven the submarine capable of performing at sea in the most trying of conditions. All of the required reports to Soviet authorities had been carefully filed and documented to ensure no last minute snags. More importantly, they had been altered to conceal the special enhancements that had been personally ordered by Andrei.

The official reason for restoring the K-387 was to provide the navy with a new training submarine. The project had been initiated at Andrei's request, and quickly approved, although no one really knew why. The last thing this inept navy needed was another training ship, but that didn't matter. Once official government papers expressing the critical need for a superior training submarine for the Black Sea Fleet found their way to the proper approving authority, the project became the number one priority at Odessa.

Andrei calmly walked onto the submarine and went directly to control. He walked over to the navigational table, opened the pouch he was carrying and laid the blueprints on the table. Before heading to the bowels of the submarine for the final inspection, he carefully calculated the dimensions one more time and checked the wiring diagram. He folded the prints carefully, placed them in his back pocket and left control. Down one more deck and he was in the diesel room. Slightly to the left was the hatch only he had access to. He quickly keyed the code into the panel and entered.

The circular hub was clearly visible. Only two feet in diameter, it was the most critical enhancement to the K-

387. On the left and right, directly opposite each other, he turned the connection levers counter clockwise and opened the door sealing the hub. Looking at the water beneath him, he pulled the blueprints from his pocket. The engineering specifications the French supplied were critical to the design of the hub and must be followed exactly or the fitting seal installed just beneath the hub door would not ensure an adequate connection. He carefully measured the dimensions of the seal for circumference. They were perfect. Reaching over and just behind the opened door, he lifted a small tool clamp and removed the volumetric calculator he would use to test the density of the seal. It too matched specifications. Satisfied, he replaced the tool, closed the hub and went topside.

Tomorrow the K-387 would leave for "training." He had arranged for the harbor tugs to arrive before the shipyard opened. At his command, the tugs would gently move the submarine away from its moorings and turn the sub to the southeast. Once the sub cleared the dock by only several feet, Andrei would take control, release the tugs and slowly move in the direction of the Bosporus Strait. When they cleared the Strait, he would spend little time in the Sea of Marmara and proceed to the Mediterranean. He would then steer the K-387 toward the Suez Canal and into the Red Sea.

Catonsville, Maryland

There is nothing like the smell of Maryland steamed crabs. Covered with Old Bay seasoning, JO Spice, rock salt, red peppers, for those preferring the spicy variety and a beer just for good luck, the smell of steamed crabs permeates the air like nothing else. And then comes the feast. Eating crabs is more than just, well, eating. Crab feasts are a social event. The hammers, knives, picking and, of course, beer drinking all go together in one glamorous social happening that isn't rivaled anywhere else in the world.

David grabbed the hammer and the feast began. The beer was next and the cycle of crabs, beer, and more crabs seemed endless.

"These are great. I could eat these things every day of the year."

"Oh for God's sake, you say the same thing every time we eat crabs which seems to be almost every day. I swear this man is part crab. I really believe he had claws when he was born," Kim said.

Paul laughed and continued breaking claws and downing the beer. Crabs with the Spencer's for Paul and Bridget, a tradition for well over 20 years, was always an adventure. This was no exception. The men drank the beer and stuffed themselves silly with crabs and the ladies drank iced tea and seemed to talk incessantly while still managing to eat an ample amount of crabs.

"You know, I think the crabs this year are some of the best we've had in a long time. Seem to be nice and heavy and full of mustard. Pass the shells this way," Paul said.

Paul loved the yellowish mustard that hung in the corner of the outer shell of the Maryland Blue Crab. No one really knew what it was or for that matter where it came from. But one thing for certain, if you were a real crab eater you ate that yellow stuff with as much gusto as the delicious lily-white back fin.

"How can you eat that stuff? It's not even meat. It's just some yellow gunk that looks awful. Might even be crab shit for all you know." For the last 20 years, without fail, when the first clump of yellow crab fat found its way into Paul's mouth, David said the exact same thing.

"Come on, David, try it. You'll love it. Best part of the crab." Of course, Paul always had the same response and so it went as the hammers and knives and beer and laughter and friendship continued.

Kim, sipping tea and leaning across the crabs, broke a few seconds of silence. "David has a chance to go on an overnight cruise on a nuclear submarine and is not going."

"You have a chance to do what?" Paul yelled almost dropping his beer.

"I'm not going on any cramped-up submarine for two days with no beer. Anyway, I'm not sure if I can get off. I do have a job you know." David knew he was going to get it now from the crab crew.

"Let me get this straight. You have a chance to go on a nuclear submarine and you're not going. David, this is a chance of a lifetime, how can you turn it down?"

Paul gave David the chance he needed to defend himself and end this conversation now! "Yea right, and you'd go I'm sure."

"Damn right I'd go, in a heartbeat. Think about it! This is a chance that you might never get again, a chance to do something really out of the ordinary. You're damn right I'd go."

Paul was taking the bait — hook, line and sinker. "Ok wise guy, I'll tell you what. I'll call George right now and ask him if you can go. If he says OK, then I'll find the time to take off and go on the damn submarine."

George Owens, Commander USN, was the Captain of the USS Woodbridge. George just also happened to be David's brother-in-law. When George called David and invited him on a two-day tiger cruise, David never gave it another thought. He just turned him down saying he couldn't get off from work.

Paul, waving a crab in David's face, almost as if the poor damn crab had something to do with the conversation was getting excited now.

"David, you call George and if he says I can go, I'll go. Hell, the last time I was near a Navy yard was in 1968, when I got out of that man's navy. Swore up and down that I'd never go back again. But, this really is a chance of a lifetime. Hell, you're talking nuclear submarine here and all that goes with it."

Damn, David thought, that is not the reaction I was looking for. I was sure he'd back down when I put the pressure on him. Actually, they're probably right. I'm sure riding on a submarine would be exciting. It certainly would be something to tell the grandkids about.

"Where's the phone?"

USS Woodbridge, Norfolk

USS Woodbridge (SSN-349)
Christened: 14 April 1992
Commissioned: 15 March 1993
Length: 300 Feet
Beam: 33 Feet
Armament: 28 Mark 48 ADCAP Torpedoes
12 UGM-109 Tomahawk Missiles
Scutter Torpedo Decoy System
Crew Complement: 14 Officers
14 Chief Petty Officers
111 Enlisted Men

George Owens routinely looked at the boat's statistics. Even though he'd been the CO for almost 3 years now, he just liked looking at those damn statistics. Strange the things we do, he thought. Somehow looking at the stats gave him the courage and confidence he needed to command one of the Navy's finest fighting nuclear submarines.

She was more than just a submarine. Woodbridge was a member of the elite class of improved Los Angeles Class fast attack submarines. These fast attack subs are the Navy's newest nuclear submarines. They are versatile, capable of anti-surface and anti-submarine strikes and other warfare missions. Because of their versatility, they also play a vital role in covert intelligence gathering.

George was looking forward to the tiger cruise next week. The tiger cruise is a Navy tradition that began so fathers could bring their sons along for a cruise to experience, first hand, the Navy in action. Over the years, as the age of naval personnel got younger, the Navy began inviting fathers, brothers, cousins and friends to become

"Tigers" for two days. David had called and said he'd like to come and asked if he could bring a friend. George wasn't too keen on the additional body to take care of but he enjoyed his brother-in-law's company, so he agreed. Also, David was just, well, sort of crazy and always had a good time and those around him as well. George thought this would be good for the cruise and help keep things hopping. Normally, a tiger cruise was routine business for George and the crew of the Woodbridge. They had to accommodate up to 24 guests ranging in ages from 10 to 72 years of age, serve above ordinary meals to make an impression and leave a third of their crew behind to allow for living space for the guests.

On this tiger cruise, however, the Woodbridge was also testing sonar that had just been developed. So, it would be somewhat less boring this time, George thought. The tiger cruise provided an opportunity to test the sonar before their next deployment, which was less than two weeks away.

The Navy was still using the more costly AN/SQS 53C sonar. Woodbridge had just been equipped with the most up-to-date LAF/72 Series Active sonar. The LAF/72 series satisfies the Navy's need for smaller footprint sonar and, at the same time is less costly than the older 53C series. In addition, the LAF/72 sonar supports open architecture implementation and was designed for a family of systems using the same software. Specifically, the LAF/72's main objective is the detection of submarines over great distances.

George was looking forward to the sonar test. He knew what this meant to the Navy. The new sonar had proven components, which minimized risk and maximized reliability. The low active frequency of the sonar enabled it to reach over greater distances with sustainable accuracy. It could be reconfigured to meet unique situations and requirements to accommodate individual ship's needs. It was modular and could be easily updated with software and hardware improvements and its compact design minimized weight and offered increased performance.

It was somewhat unusual, he thought, that the Navy would combine a tiger cruise with a sonar test but time frames were short. The Woodbridge was due to leave on an extended five-month tour of duty and they had not as yet completed the annual tiger cruise. And, so it was, that George would have to accommodate a dozen or so civilian guests and also perform functional testing on the Navy's newest and most critical sonar implementation to date.

George didn't hear the knock on his stateroom door. This was not unusual for this CO. Whenever he found himself deep in thought, especially when it came to the Woodbridge, George became almost trance-like. That's what made him the excellent CO that he was. He would focus on the job to be done and, nothing else, nothing, would interfere with that objective.

"Here's the flyer you wanted, Captain. Let me know if there's anything else you want and I'll just update it." Chief Francisco Carlos was his right-hand man. You could count on the job being done right, on time and always damn near perfect.

"Thanks, Franky. Appreciate it. I'll check it over."

Franky knew he would approve. He knew how this CO thought. He knew what he liked, didn't like and what not to say or do. Without a doubt, this was the best CO he had ever served under.

Things were different before George Owens arrived. The old CO wouldn't even take the fish on a steep dive because he was always afraid of getting seasick. Franky just couldn't imagine how a guy could wind up being CO of a nuclear attack submarine when anything greater than a 3 degree roll resulted in the old man throwing his guts up until they tied back up.

When George relieved as the new CO of Woodbridge, the crew was skeptical at first. The first cruise quickly resolved the skepticism. They were hardly out of the harbor and George ordered a 25-degree dive to 600 feet. Almost instantly the morale improved.

George reviewed the planned activities for the tiger cruise. As usual it was what he wanted. He guessed they probably wouldn't be able to do half of them, considering the testing that was necessary for the sonar, but he knew his crew would do their best to complete it.

Baghdad

They rolled out the pontoon boat in total silence. The trucks were almost loaded and soon they would be on their way. It was critical they start immediately. Daylight was quickly approaching and if they didn't arrive in Jordan before then, the chance of one of the last international watchdogs catching them was even more likely. This was Iraq's last chance to get even with the Great Satan. It was for Allah! Once the weapon was transported to its position in Jordan, chances of the operation surviving would be much better.

Mashire knew that if he failed he would be put to death. He relished the thought of giving his life for Allah but in this instance he wanted to succeed. He was a member of the elite Republican Guard Forces Command. Sometimes referred to as the "shock troops" of the Iraqi military, the Command consisted of tank brigades, infantry and Special Forces. Mashire was a member of the Special Forces and one of their best.

"Move on! Hurry, you must go faster. We must load the trucks and proceed in order to arrive before sunrise. I will whip the first to slow down. I insist we move faster," Mashire said.

They would proceed along the Wadi El Murbah highway until they reached the safety of Jordan. Once in Jordan, the cargo that was so precious to Iraq's revenge would be moved to the submarine as quickly as possible. When the time arrived, Iraq would move quickly to implement devastation on the United States the likes of which had never been witnessed before. The satanic free giant would suffer tremendously at the hands of Iraq. Saddam would have his revenge.

The canisters were next. It was most important to load them carefully and with great respect. With this weapon, Iraq would achieve its goal; it was with this weapon that Iraq would shock the world; it was with this weapon that Iraq would conquer the great Satan.

"Be careful. We must use extreme caution. Make sure you label them correctly and secure them with the utmost of care," Mashire said.

Mashire was worried! He knew what had to be done, but the crew he had left a lot to be desired. Most were leftovers from the war living a life of squander and hopelessness. But, it was all he had and he swore he would achieve his mission. This was more important to Mashire than anything he had ever done. He would do anything to succeed.

The caravan of three trucks began its journey on the highway towards Jordan. Once in Jordan, they would move as quickly as possible to transfer the canisters to the submarine. Once the canisters were aboard the submarine, Iraq would be one step closer to achieving its ultimate goal. REVENGE! The attack would shock the United States and the world. No one would expect Iraq to wield such devastation on the world's last super power. Iraq would once again be the leader of the Middle East. Iraq would finally win the Gulf War that had never ended. Iraq would prove once and for all its superiority over the United States.

The trip was slow at first. They had to be careful. The United Nation forces had missed the canisters. They had destroyed most of the Scuds and most of the chemical weapons but Iraq's defense forces had taken great pains to avoid the discovery of the canisters. Mashire could only laugh when he thought how stupid the UN forces had been to miss such a weapon. They were truly inept. When the Iraqis allowed the inspection teams to search an area, it had already been cleaned of its most precious cargo. Always the inspection teams would wait until Iraq allowed entry and always they would arrive too late.

Lieutenant Brad Jeffrey was one of the last inspectors left in Iraq. And it was a good thing too because he was damned tired of this assignment. He was fed up inspecting for hidden Iraqi weapons, most of which were so antiquated it didn't make a damn bit of difference whether they had them or not. Mostly, he was tired of the bullshit! Going through the motions looking for crap that was always moving from place to place. Hell, he thought, the Iraqis always cleaned out the damn places anyway before they arrived. Finally he would be heading home. After making his latest delivery to Jordan, the United Nations Special Commission (UNSCOM) had been ordered out of Iraq. He was heading back to Baghdad to pack it up.

At first he didn't give it much thought when he noticed the trucks moving slowly down the only highway between Iraq and Jordan. In almost two years on this lousy job, he had never seen an Iraqi vehicle on this highway at this time of night. He traveled this road frequently, at all hours, back and forth between Iraq and Jordan making supply runs for the Commission. And, in all those boring trips he had never run across an Iraqi vehicle.

"Mashire, we have a visitor." Ifram knew this would not sit well with the leader. Instantly, Mashire slowed to almost a crawl.

Why were they moving so slowly, Jeffrey thought? His orders were explicit. Do not interfere with the locals. It was not his responsibility. But instinct told him differently this time. After all, if he uncovered something worthwhile on his last trip, he'd be a big hit with the Commander. In an instant, he pulled his jeep across the road and waited.

"What the hell is this"? Mashire shouted. Mashire almost tried to go around the jeep but decided that would be too risky. He could not risk damaging the cargo. "Ifram, when we stop, stay in the truck. I'll do the talking. We can't take any chances."

15

Jeffrey approached the truck with caution. "I am Lieutenant Jeffrey with the United Nations inspection team. I am authorized to inspect Iraqi vehicles on this highway." Jeffrey knew this was a load of crap. He was clearly overstepping his bounds but what the hell, maybe the dumb bastards won't know the difference.

Mashire spoke perfect English. "We are only farmers, sir. Just delivering some produce to market."

"And what market is that?" Jeffrey knew of no market in the area.

"The one at Karbala. Must be there by daybreak."

"I will need to look in the truck, sir. Only doing my job, you understand. Won't take but a minute and you can be on your way."

Mashire was a professional, but this was something he had not counted on. "We only have fresh produce, Lieutenant, nothing of importance."

"I understand, but I only need a quick look and you can be on your way." Jeffrey, sensing they were moving more than produce, felt for the 45 in his holster and moved to the back of the truck. "If you don't mind, I'll take a quick look."

For a moment, Mashire felt a sense of remorse for the young Lieutenant. So young and surely has a family. Probably has a pretty, young wife. Maybe even a couple of kids. But quickly he remembered the enemy. Quickly he remembered the war.

Mashire opened the back of the truck. It was dark and hard to see. "OK Lieutenant, take a look."

Mashire pulled the stiletto silently and quickly. Jeffrey, leaning in the back of the truck, strained to see what looked like something covered with a tarp. The stiletto entered at the base of the brain and, with a quick turn, severed the spinal column at the first vertebrae. Almost in slow motion, the young officer slumped over the rear gate with an icy glare that even unnerved Mashire for a brief moment.

Ifram, startled by the sudden and deadly actions of his leader, made a fatal mistake. "Mashire, I am concerned this will interfere with our journey to Jordan. We never said anything about killing anyone and, for that matter, a member of the inspection forces."

Mashire knew Ifram was right but he would not allow his authority to be questioned in front of his men. He quickly picked up the young Lieutenant's pistol and placed it on the forehead of Ifram. Without saying a word or any display of emotion, he pulled the trigger.

The Iraqi Border Guard forces were well aware of Iraqi law and how it was administered. Mashire's message was loud and clear.

Mashire placed the stiletto in Ifram's hand and the revolver in Jeffrey's hand and fired the 45. He then put them both in the Lieutenant's jeep and pushed it to the side of the road. He removed Ifram's uniform and replaced it with peasant's garb. Inside Ifram's shirt pocket he placed Kurdish papers of identification. He then emptied Jeffrey's wallet on the floor of the jeep. If everything went as planned, this would be treated as just another robbery attempt by the Kurds.

"Let us continue our journey. Hurry, we must arrive before daybreak."

USS Woodbridge

Woodbridge was almost ready. The crew from the Darrich Corporation had been working feverishly around the clock installing the new sonar. Installations such as this go in either one or two directions; smooth and easy or difficult and tedious. This one was somewhere in between. The equipment installation went well but they were still unsure of the software. That would have to wait until they deployed. Testing new technology such as this could really only be done at sea.

"Captain, here's the list of guests for the cruise."

George almost never answered on the first call. That's how he was. Whenever they got this close to a cruise, even a tiger cruise, the old man just engrossed himself to the point where he focused on nothing else but the Woodbridge.

"Excuse me Captain, the guest list is ready for your review."

"What's that?"

"The list sir! The guest list you wanted to see. Not too bad this time. Looks like we're only going to have 14, not counting the Darrich employees."

"Thanks chief. Just lay it on the desk."

He was something all right. Walked around almost in a daze. But he was the best damned CO this Navy has seen for some time. George had checked everything on the Woodbridge except the nuts and bolts. He was satisfied that all looked OK. His main concern was the sonar. The Navy was eager to test the new technology and Woodbridge would be the guinea pig. He only wished the tiger cruise were some other time. He would like to concentrate his efforts on the sonar without having to entertain a group of civilians at the same time.

The guests arrived early. Some had duffel bags, others suitcases and some, just the clothes on their backs. Boarding a submarine can be a challenging experience. You must first enter through a small hatch and climb down a skinny ladder through a narrow tube. After somehow managing to navigate the entry tube, the guests then proceed through a very narrow passageway with very little headroom. Once on the submarine the newcomers seem to adapt quickly. Some do anyway. There are always a few who experience almost immediate claustrophobia. After only a few minutes of trying to adjust, it's up the ten-foot ladder and back on the pier. Meanwhile, the others start exploring the submarine as soon as they hit the deck. This can be a harrowing experience for the crew assigned the job of rounding up stray tiger cruisers, especially the younger variety who seem to disappear almost instantly. After fifteen minutes of roundup, the guests are seated in the crew's mess to begin indoctrination.

USS WOODBRIDGE (SSN-349)
TIGER CRUISE
GUEST LIST

NAME	AGE	SPONSOR	RELATIONSHIP
Randy Geshire	15	Chief Geshire	Son
William Carlos	12	Chief Carlos	Son
Michael Owens	16	Captain Owens	Son
Matthew Owens	10	Captain Owens	Son
David Spencer	49	Captain Owens	Brother-in-law
Paul Jamison	51	Captain Owens	Friend
Scott Schneider	59	Chief Tanandra	Brother-in-law
John Archibald	72	Lt. Archibald	Father
Joseph Warfield	65	HM1 Warfield	Father
Gerry Bothsire	43	ET2 Bothsire	Brother
Chris Conway	28	RD1 Conway	Brother
Thomas Kahl	63	RD3 Kahl	Father
Kevin Dunn	68	LT-CDR Dunn	Father
Sean Berlin	32	Lt. Berlin	Brother

"Gentlemen, I would like to welcome you aboard the USS Woodbridge. The Captain will be with you shortly, but before he arrives I would like to go over a few things to help you with your stay aboard the Woodbridge. My name is Bill Dunn. I am the Executive Officer of the boat. The Captain would like to welcome you aboard one of the finest attack subs this side of the Mississippi. I take that back, the finest attack sub anywhere.

"The crew of the Woodbridge hopes your stay with us for the next two days is enjoyable and exciting. Feel free to ask any question at any time. I assure you, you will find the crew aboard this submarine more than willing to answer your questions.

"For your own safety, there are a few things I need to point out before we get started with a brief tour of the boat.

"Be careful walking the gangways. As I'm sure you've already noticed, we have stored cans of food throughout the submarine in almost every gangway. As a result, ceiling height has been reduced requiring you to walk in a bent over position or suffer the consequences of a bruised head. Woodbridge is embarking on a five-month cruise when we return from the tiger cruise and, because of short time frames, it was necessary to load up food supplies early. We regret the inconvenience.

"Any compartment on the submarine identified with a radiation insignia like the one I am holding up is strictly off limits. As I'm sure you can understand, this is necessary for your safety. Also, the radio room is off limits. Otherwise, you are free to go anywhere on the Woodbridge that you please.

"Corpsman Warfield will now go over a few health and welfare criteria with you and shortly the Captain will be here to officially welcome you aboard. Again, we hope you enjoy yourself and find cruising aboard Woodbridge a truly rewarding experience."

"Welcome aboard the Woodbridge everyone. I'm Greg Warfield, Chief Corpsman. Before we embark, I need to discuss a few things with you and also ask if you would please fill out the questionnaire that came with your welcome package. This is just to make sure we don't have any unforeseen problems after we leave port. Submarine service can, at times, cause some minor health problems so we want to make sure your trip is as enjoyable as it can be. After you complete the questionnaire and I have a chance to review them, I might call some of you to my office for further consultation.

"First, is there anyone here who is prone to seasickness? If so, I can supply you with some Dramamine.

Taken before we sail, Dramamine can practically eliminate any motion sickness. So, if you're in doubt, I recommend taking it.

"Also, does anyone have any problems with claustrophobia? We will be operating in rather tight quarters so if you are subject to claustrophobia, I recommend that you not take the cruise. We will be gone for two days and you could get somewhat uncomfortable in tight living conditions."

Two

American Embassy, London

Knox Jones had been working for the CIA for over 25 years and still loved the work. For the last four years, he had worked out of the embassy in London. His official title with the embassy was attaché but everyone knew his real occupation. One nice thing about being a professional snoop, sneak, spy, whatever you wanted to call it, the work was always exciting, never boring or monotonous. This day would be no exception.

"Knox, we've got some interesting data out of Station 3 that I think you should take a look at. Not sure what's up but there is definitely some unusual movement going on in and around the Red Sea," John said.

John Edward Lee, although only with the Agency for a short three years, was one of the best. He had risen rather quickly through the ranks and was now Deputy Director of Eastern Operations. Knox didn't know how he had gotten along without him before he arrived but one thing for sure, he was invaluable to the Agency.

"What's up John?"

"We've got some satellite photos of the Red Sea time lapsed over the last month showing a Russian submarine acting rather strange. She submerges twice a day almost like clockwork. From what we've been able to determine so far, she looks like one of the K Series class subs. I'm expecting more detailed data this afternoon at which time we should be able to pin down the sub's identification."

"Well I guess I better take a look see. Might just be some kind of training exercise they're doing over there," Knox said.

Knox looked at the photo and almost instantly knew what it was. He had seen reconnaissance photos of this submarine hundreds of times during his career.

"It's the K-387. Seen it many times. One of their earlier class nuclear subs but still plenty seaworthy." Knox walked over to his file cabinet and quickly produced the information they needed. "The K-387 was built by the Krasnoye Sormovo shipyard in Gor'kiy in 1982. The Russians originally planned to build 94 of these submarines to replace their more expensive Project 935/JUNO class."

"Knox, you are amazing. If you ever leave the Agency I'm quitting for sure. How in the hell can you come up with info like that in a blink of an eye?"

"John, when you've been around as long as I have you'll be amazed how this sort of stuff sticks in the back of your mind." Knox reached into his file cabinet and pulled out a data sheet. "Here you go, old buddy. Everything you'll ever need to know about the K-387."

John, still in amazement, looked over the stats. Knox waited to see how long it would take for John to pick up on the obvious.

"This is nice Knox. But this can't be the submarine we're looking at in the satellite photos. This baby was decommissioned in 1995."

USS Woodbridge

Greg finished going over the questionnaires and only needed to interview two of the guests. John Archibald checked out OK but Greg wanted to talk to him anyway because of his age. Not that 72 years of age is indicative of any immediate problem, but simply because they would be sailing on a submarine that could cause unforeseen problems with some older persons. Also, he needed to see Sean Berlin who indicated on his form that he was diabetic. No real problem here either. Greg just wanted to cover all bases before they embarked.

"Captain, I don't see any real medical problems with our guests, with the exception of one of the Darrich employees. It doesn't look like one of the two sonar technicians from Darrich is going to make the cruise with us. Steve Harmon, the software engineer for them tells me he suffers from claustrophobia. Christ, as I was talking to him, the poor guy had trouble breathing. He's scared to death Darrich will fire him if he doesn't go on the cruise. There's no way this guy will make it at 500 feet. I advised him to leave and he agreed. Hope he'll be all right. Here's my report."

"Thanks, Greg. Tell Bill I'd like to see him before I come down to speak with our guests."

"Aye, sir."

The report on Mr. Harmon was not good. If they had any software problems with the sonar, just what in the hell were they supposed to do to resolve the problem? As far as George was concerned, the hell with the damn tiger cruise. They should be concentrating their efforts on the sonar shakedown. The Woodbridge was scheduled to go on a five month Mediterranean cruise in five days and, quite possibly, they would be leaving with sonar that might be defective.

"Captain, you wanted to see me?" Bill asked.

"Bill, we've got a problem. Greg just informed me that Darrich's computer whiz won't make the cruise. Apparently the guy has claustrophobia. Get a hold of Command and see if we can delay the tiger cruise until we return from the Mediterranean. We could use those two days to wait for a replacement. I'd like to get a good test on the sonar before we leave for our extended cruise."

"I'll get on it right away. I agree, it seems silly to go ahead playing hosts to a bunch of civilians out in the Atlantic for two days when we could be using that time to concentrate our efforts on the sonar," Bill said.

George walked aft to talk with his cruise guests. He regretted they might have to delay the tiger cruise but his first priority was the sonar.

"Attention on Deck!"

"At ease, gentlemen."

"It is my pleasure to introduce to you our Captain, George Owens."

"I would like to welcome each and every one of you aboard the Woodbridge. By now I'm sure you've been briefed about our two-day cruise and had a chance to talk with the doctor. Actually, Greg is our Corpsman but we like to refer to him as Doc.

"Before I go over a few things about the cruise, I would like to let you know that something of importance has come up and it is possible we might not be able to embark on the tiger cruise at this time. I realize this would be disappointing for you as well as the crew, but sometimes these things happen.

In addition to using the next two days for the tiger cruise, the Woodbridge is also scheduled to test new sonar technology for the Navy. I've just been informed that one of the technicians familiar with the sonar cannot make the cruise. As a result, we might have to postpone the tiger cruise in order to wait for a replacement technician. If that

26

is the case, we will need to wait at least another day before we leave and with our tight time frames because of our upcoming Mediterranean cruise, the tiger cruise might have to wait."

George heard a few moans, which was to be expected. Some of these folks had traveled across the country to make the cruise and wouldn't be real pleased if it were canceled.

Before George could finish Bill returned from control. "Excuse me, Captain, I've got a response from Command."

The two senior officers stepped out into the gangway to talk. "They want us to go out and get the cruise out of the way. They are concerned for public relations since we had to cancel the last tiger cruise. They tell me they checked with Darrich and they don't think we'll have any problems with the software. They said the software has been tested repeatedly and everything is working just fine. So, it looks like we're going to be taking a few folks sailing for a couple of days," Bill said.

"So be it. I'm going back in and let our guests know we're still sailing. While I'm in there do me a favor and get copies of the schedule of events."

George knew what the answer would be before he even asked Bill to check with the Commander of the Submarine Force U.S. Atlantic Fleet (COMSUBLANT). You would think common sense would prevail, he thought, but that's how things go in this man's Navy sometimes. Maybe he was worrying too much anyway. Hell, if the damn sonar didn't work they'd just have to put the old stuff back in before the Mediterranean' cruise. No big deal...

George walked back to the crew's mess where the guests were eagerly awaiting the outcome of the tiger cruise decision.

"Well, I've got good news. The cruise is on as scheduled. We get underway at 1030. That's about 45 minutes from now. Here's a copy of our schedule of events for today. I would like to point out that at 1930, we are scheduled to do some high-speed maneuvers and some pretty sharp angle diving. When we do the sharp dives and angles it can, at times, be difficult to maintain your footing. Don't worry, we'll make an announcement before we do any fancy stuff. We won't ambush you. So, when you hear the announcement for the exercise, be aware of your surroundings.

"Also, at times during the cruise, each of you will get a chance to steer the submarine, view sonar readings and man the periscope. When we are on the surface, for those who don't mind climbing up through a twenty-foot tube, you can visit the bridge.

"Well that's about it. I hope everyone enjoys cruising aboard Woodbridge, and if there is anything I can do to make your stay with us a pleasant one, please don't hesitate to ask. Any questions?"

"Yes sir, I have a question. Are we going to get a chance to see the torpedoes? I hear they're really big. I sure would like to see one."

Willy Carlos couldn't wait to actually sail with the Navy. His father, who was a Chief Petty Officer, had told him all about riding in a submarine and how much fun it was. Especially how big the torpedoes were.

"By all means, young man, you'll get a chance to see them. And you're right. They are big. Even I was surprised to see how big they were when I first came aboard the Woodbridge. I don't think we'll be shooting any off though.

"OK then, Chief Carlos will hand out the schedule of events while I get ready for the ship's departure."

USS Woodbridge (SSN 349)

TIGER CRUISE
SCHEDULE OF EVENTS

0900 LIBERTY EXPIRES ONBOARD FOR ALL HANDS.
0930 TIGER CRUISE INBRIEF
0930 STATION THE MANEUVERING WATCH
1030 SHIP IS UNDERWAY
1200-1300 LUNCH
1230 SECURE THE MANEUVERING WATCH
1700 DINNER
1845 DIVE, DIVE
1930 ANGLES, HIGH SPEED OPERATIONS
2000 TIGER CRUISE EVENING MOVIE
2300 MIDRATS

SECURITY COUNCIL RESOLUTION 68791, APRIL 1991

As a condition of the cease-fire agreement between Iraq and the coalition forces in the Gulf War, UNSCOM was formed to supervise, in part, the destruction of Iraq's NBC weapons.

UNSCOM was created to carry out on-site inspections of Iraq's biological, chemical and missile capabilities and to destroy weapons of this nature, if discovered. The Commission initially inspected those Iraqi sites that had been declared stockpile locations by the Iraqi government and ultimately inspected additional sites identified by the Commission itself. UNSCOM would continue this mandate indefinitely or until such time it was decided that all weapons had been destroyed.

From the beginning, the UNSCOM tasks that had to be carried out to remove and render harmless all weapons of mass destruction, all stocks of agents, any related subsystems, all research and development and the manufacturing of such weapons, were substantial, time consuming and practically impossible. In addition, the Commission was also responsible for the supervision of the destruction of all ballistic missile sites with a range greater than 150 kilometers. The problem here was the Commission was not tasked with destroying the sites. They merely had to supervise the Iraqi destruction of the sites. No small task, indeed considering that trying to supervise Iraqis doing anything, much less the destruction of their own missile sites, was damn near impossible.

Moreover, the Commission was also supposed to assist the Secretary-General in implementing the plan for the long term monitoring and verification of Iraq's compliance with the Security Council Resolution. The problem with the plan was that it wasn't executable. Whenever inspectors would plan to visit a site, the Iraqis would clean the site before the inspectors arrived or make them wait until "the site was ready for inspection."

The final Commission task was to assist the Director-General of the International Atomic Energy Agency in the carrying out of on-site inspection of Iraq's nuclear sites. All of this, of course, was to be accomplished based on Iraq's declared locations and any areas so designated by UNSCOM.

UNSCOM was destined to fail from the beginning. It had neither the resources nor the wherewithal to carry out its objectives. For over eight years now inspectors had been running around Iraq checking this and checking that only to wind up where they started. The latest Iraqi act of defiance to the Security Council's resolution would be its last. The President had had enough. Again the bombs were dropping to try and convince the Iraqi government that the Commission meant business. The President's announcement that Iraq had the capability of producing nuclear weapons in four short months confirmed the dismal failure of the UNSCOM mission.

Sam Richardson, director of the International Chemical Weapons group, advised the Council earlier this year that Iraq's "continued refusal to cooperate in any activity involving investigation of its chemical weapon program would result in renewed bombing."

Captain Will Harrison had read it and seen it over and over again. And now, Sam's predictions had come true. The bombs had started dropping again over Iraq and UNSCOM was apparently leaving for good.

"Sam, we have a report that one of our last inspectors left in Iraq didn't show up this morning to be transitioned home. He is Lieutenant Brad Jeffrey from the southern command post. He was supposed to arrive in

Baghdad early this morning but didn't show up. He was last assigned to the supply run along the Wadi El Murbah highway. We have a crew out there looking now," Will said.

"OK Will. Let me know what you come up with. He'll probably show up later. Won't be the first time one of the boys went out on the town and showed up late."

Will left to see if they had anything back yet on Jeffrey. Sam was probably right, he thought. Jeffrey probably did a little too much partying last night.

Sam was behind in preparing his weekly report. He hated that more than anything about this lousy job. The report always had to be politically correct and was always supposed to reflect the great job the Commission was doing in finding and destroying Iraqi weapons. As he began the routine laborious chore, Will burst back into his office.

"I've got some bad news Sam. They've located Jeffrey's jeep on the side of the road. I'm afraid he's been killed. Looks like some sort of robbery attempt. There was a body of a Kurd lying next to the jeep. Jeffrey's wallet was lying on the floor. It looks like the Kurd stabbed Jeffrey and apparently the Lieutenant shot him. Damn shame. He was a fine young man. They're doing the autopsy now. As soon as I get the results I'll let you know."

"Goddamn it! We have never had anything like this happen over there. After all the crap we've been through at least we can say we haven't had any casualties. Not until now at least. Have we contacted the next of kin yet?" Sam asked.

"Yes, sir. We called the Navy and they're sending over someone, as we speak, to tell his wife."

Sam Richardson didn't like the sound of it. Why would some poor Kurdish refugee be wandering around a deserted highway somewhere between Iraq and Jordan and somehow manage to commandeer Jeffrey. Something just didn't sit right about the report. He couldn't help but think there was more to this story than just a burglary attempt. It looked too easy.

"Will, I want a full report on my desk in the morning. I want a list of all traffic on that road for the last 24 hours. I want the full autopsy report as well. I smell a rat here. Something tells me this was no robbery attempt. If it wasn't robbery, then we need to find out why the Lieutenant was killed. The Iraqis have never been real friendly over our presence in their country but there has always been an unwritten rule with the Iraqi government that no harm was to come to any of the inspectors.

"Who's doing the autopsy? I want our best medical team on this. Make sure they understand to use a fine toothcomb. Tell them not to assume anything; leave no stone unturned. I want to know exactly what happened out there. I don't want them dragging their feet on this. Also, if anything unusual shows up, I want to be notified immediately. I don't want to wait around for any damn paper work or get caught up in any bureaucratic shuffle."

"Got it. I'll get the message over to them immediately," Will said.

"One more thing. Get a Navy chopper out to that highway now. Tell them to stop any and all traffic traveling on that road. I don't care what they have to do, but impress upon them that ANY traffic they see is to be stopped and searched. Understood?"

"Yes, sir!

Three

Eastern Tech Seismological Observatory

Stephen Jensen never realized Eastern Tech would be this difficult. Hell, the only reason he came here was to get experience and hopefully work one day at the National Earthquake Information Center (NEIC). This was just a stepping stone to bigger and better things. He had been here three years already and had yet to see even a quiver on the seismographer. In this region, what do you expect, he thought, but it sure would be nice to get some real experience at this stuff. The lab work was interesting, but after three years of walking around this room looking at nothing, he was bored shitless.

"Stephen, Professor Wilkens is coming over. Says he wants to show us something interesting," Jeff said. Jeff Barnes was his best friend, colleague and always seemed to line him up with the best blind dates.

"Oh that's just great. Just what I need to make my day in this cramped-up excuse for a seismo lab. What's he going to show us, his etch-a-sketch?"

"Ya got me, just called and said to meet him over in the lab. And when the Prof says jump, I jump."

Professor Harry Wilkens was one of the best in his field. For years they had been trying to recruit his services at NEIC. And, for years, Harry had steadfastly refused to leave his beloved Eastern Tech.

"Fellows, you'd better take a look at this. I think you finally might get to see some real interesting data and, what's more, it's in this area. We have activity in the Tennessee seismic zone extending as far north as Virginia

34

Beach. Data just received is showing unusual pressure build up for the entire region. In all my years here at Tech, I've never seen anything quite like it. I've seen crustal movements similar to this before but the stress gradually accumulating in this region is highly unusual. It's essential for us to determine the state of any earthquake generating stress within the area associated with these movements. Once we do that, we need to monitor the crustal strains, look at any abnormal deformations on the fault planes, and check the stress concentrations in some of the weaker zones. Then we should be able to get a good idea of the relationship between these crustal movements and any potential earthquake occurrence in this area."

"Earthquake occurrence? Are you serious? Around here?" Jeff could hardly contain himself and wanted to stop Wilkens right there but the old professor didn't hear a word he said.

"We will have to carefully monitor the data with monitoring chains along the East Coast. In addition, we need to carefully look for any noise reduction in the crustal movement observations especially with respect to any ground deformations or any rerouting of groundwater. Hopefully, our observations will detect any wide scale movements from plate motions to local ground movements. In addition, I plan to request assistance from the Global Positioning System (GPS) team and use any electro-optical measurements they are using for research. They have a network of 250 GPS receivers that continually measure the constant, yet physically imperceptible, movements of earthquake faults."

GPS is a constellation of 24 Earth-orbiting satellites, arranged so that several are "visible" from any point on the surface of the Earth at any time. A user on the ground with a GPS receiver can determine his or her precise location by measuring signals from the GPS satellites. The continuous, earthquake-related measurements from the GPS allow seismic networks to make a high-precision survey of the area. Information from the network of receivers are then used to create maps of strain accumulations along fault lines and are used to evaluate future probabilities of regional earthquake hazards, and develop earthquake scenarios for specific faults.

Currently, the network has 40 GPS receivers up and running, with the remaining 210 receivers scheduled to be installed over the next three years. The receivers are placed about six miles apart, usually in open fields.

GPS measurements are also useful during and after earthquakes. Seismic labs can measure ground motions from earthquakes, identify the fault that ruptured, and help evaluate regional deformation and stress changes in near real time using an automated system. The network also monitors important structures. GPS receivers placed on or near dams, bridges, and buildings allow off-site detection of probable damage to those structures. GPS can also evaluate extended crustal strains using time interval data obtained over several months. By evaluating this data, any errors encountered due to atmospheric refraction are then studied elaborately by using water vapor radiometers. Finally, any changes to the physical properties of the crust can be analyzed using observation of earth tides.

Stephen leaned over looking at the charts in disbelief. "Professor, I'm still not sure what all this means. I've been walking around this room for the last three hours and have yet to see anything."

"We're not sure. It could be nothing. But then again, every time we've seen this kind of data at the San Andreas fault, we usually have some sort of occurrence within 60 to 90 days. I've already sent the data to the folks at the National Center for verification and alignment. In the meantime, I want you guys manning this center at all times.

I don't care if you have to sleep here. I want someone in this observatory 24 hours a day."

"Professor, why didn't I detect anything here at the observatory? The computers still show no unusual activity in the area."

"You wouldn't have noticed anything on the graphs, Stephen. The data that we obtained could only be picked up with a High Resolution Digitizer (HRD). The HRD is designed for short period, broadband seismic monitoring and is used in fast micro-earthquake networks. The digitizer connects directly to most accelerometers and seismometers without requiring any additional amplification. It receives the input signal and formats the data in time-stamped packets for transmission over satellite or telemetry links. So, since no real measurable occurrence has yet to happen, you wouldn't have noticed the data on the seismograph. The digitized data was sent over by one of the members of the Eastern Cooperative Network."

"You mean to tell me some amateur picked this up on their computer?" Stephen asked.

"That's right! It's not unlike your amateur astronomer detecting a new comet. Happens all the time.

"I'm expecting a report back from headquarters any minute now. As soon as I get the data, we need to sit down and come up with a probability chart for the region. If the data holds true, we might be issuing our first earthquake alert for the East Coast of the United States, ever!

"I'm also going to go back and look at the historical data we have on the Giles County, Virginia earthquake that hit on May 31, 1897. That shaker was the third largest quake to hit the eastern U.S. in the last 200 years and was felt in twelve states. At that time, of course, they didn't have the equipment we have today but based on the magnitude of that quake, I should be able to simulate the pressure data and compare it to what we are getting now.

That might give us a better idea of what we are dealing with. As soon as I get the computer data, we'll sit down and do the analysis."

After the professor left to see if the report had arrived, Stephen and Jeff began going over every piece of information they had recorded at the observatory over the last 36 hours. There must be something recorded here that would give them some indication as to what was going on, they thought. Even though they didn't have any HRD equipment, it seemed like they should have detected something. As they looked over the graphs from the seismographers, the phone rang.

"Wilkens called. He's on his way back. The data he was waiting for is back already and he wants to show it to us. He really sounds concerned. Do you really think this stuff could amount to something? For some reason, I still can't get real excited over what probably will turn out to be nothing. I'm not hoping for an earthquake, you understand, but a little excitement every now and then wouldn't hurt," Stephen said.

"Man, that was quick," Jeff said. Jeff couldn't get over how Stephen always complained about something. Jeff was just happy to be where he was. Having grown up on a tobacco farm in Georgia, he didn't care what it was he was doing here as long as it wasn't picking tobacco. In his wildest dreams he never thought he'd wind up here at Eastern Tech researching earthquake data for one of the smartest minds he had ever met.

The professor, running back into the room, almost tripped over the seismographer.

"This is looking interesting my friends. Remember the comparison I made to the Giles County, Virginia earthquake. I simulated the pressure data and compared it to our data and let me tell you, if this baby hits, it should be something else. Assuming the data are correct, if the quake would strike today, we're looking at a major earthquake somewhere around 8 on the Moment-Magnitude Scale," the professor said.

"The what Scale? Sir, don't you mean the Richter Scale?" Jeff asked.

"Scientists have abandoned the Richter Scale and have gone to using the Moment-Magnitude Scale. Look at the scale."

The Scale and how the numbers compare:
Note: each number is 10 times as powerful as it goes up each number
1. Detected by instruments only
2. Felt by some people (10 times #1)
3. Felt by many people (100 times #1)
4. Felt by everyone; pictures fall off the wall (1,000 times #1)
5. Minor damage--may cause walls to crack (10,000 times #1)
6. A destructive earthquake in populated areas (100,000 times #1)
7. A major earthquake causing serious damage (1,000,000 times #1)
8. A disaster--a great earthquake, destruction (10,000,000 times #1)
9. Catastrophic (100,000,000 times #1)

"Are you kidding me? A quake that size on the East Coast would be equivalent to a 12 or higher on the West Coast. That would be so devastating it's almost beyond comprehension. I just can't imagine what something like that would do around here. All this time I have hoped for some action, just a little action, but I must admit Professor, this is just way too much to handle. I sure hope your figures are wrong," Stephen said.

So did the professor. He was sickened when he actually stopped and considered what he was saying. The possibility of a quake of this magnitude seemed almost incomprehensible. The devastation to an area that is totally unprepared for such an event would be terrible. If they issued an earthquake alert what good would it do, he thought? People in this area wouldn't have the slightest idea what to do anyway.

"I hope so too, Stephen. We are giving the data a real hard look. Remember it's still possible all this stuff means nothing. But we have to treat it objectively. If we were looking at the same data on the West Coast, we would be issuing some sort of warning by now. Just because we are in an area that is not prone to earthquakes, shouldn't keep us from doing the very thorough job that is expected of us.

"The pressure data has remained unchanged now for several days. It's not an anomaly. This is something that is real and could be a warning sign for things to come. Frankly, I am extremely concerned. It worries me that if I attempt to issue an earthquake warning it won't be taken seriously. I haven't slept very well the last several days. Every day I get up I hope the data just goes away. I hope for equipment failure as an explanation. But it just doesn't happen. I pray to God that what we are looking at here is some sort of, well, false reading. If we don't do anything and this thing hits, I'll never forgive myself; on the other hand, if we go out on a limb and issue what amounts to be a panic-causing warning and nothing happens, we'll be the laughing stock of the scientific community."

USS Woodbridge

Few modern institutions can rival the nuclear submarine for complexity and absolute self-sufficiency. It is the only man-made structure that can duplicate the amazing oxygen-producing capabilities of the Earth. The often inhospitable environment of the sea only intensifies the need for these marvelous machines. The keystone of the submarine is the Commanding Officer. The responsibility for each operation of the submarine and the responsibility of each individual aboard converge at the command level and create the Commanding Officer's obligation: to successfully carry out any and all missions assigned.

The boatswains whistle almost stopped Paul dead in his tracks. It had been almost thirty years since he'd heard that sound. It was almost surreal, he thought. It was as if for a brief moment he hadn't even left the Navy. It never ceased to amaze him how the more things changed, the more they stayed the same. Strange, that with all the computer wizardry we have today and the advanced electronics, that in thirty years one would expect to see a big difference in the way the Navy operated. But it wasn't much different. The same old whistle and the same old announcement over the 1MC (PA system on a naval vessel) system of the ship's departure.

So here he was some thirty years later back on a naval vessel. Actually, it was kind of nice, he thought. In a way, he could appreciate his surroundings much better now that he had a few years on him. Back in 1968 he was so insecure and scared to death that he really couldn't appreciate and notice just what the hell was going on. This time was different. Paul was sailing on a submarine. Back in '68, he sailed on a top heavy cruiser that did nothing but go up and down the East Coast waiting for any emergency that would necessitate the President of the United States to take up residency on board. At least that's what they told us back then, he thought.

"There will be a brief orientation in the crew's mess in fifteen minutes for all guests. The Captain requests your presence," someone shouted over the 1MC.

Damn, Paul thought, almost sounds like an order. Oh yes, the 1MC system. It was like it was a part of you. Something you lived with day in and day out. That feeling had never left him. After all these years, somehow the 1MC announcements you hear almost constantly onboard ship seemed as though they had always been there.

"Hey Paul, you going down for the orientation? I thought we already had one but hey, what the heck, not much else we can do anyway," David said.

"Might as well, David. It might help us find our way around the boat."

Paul and David left for the crew's mess to hear yet another speech. The Navy loved telling you what you could and could not do, Paul thought.

"Hi gang, remember me. I'm Chief Carlos, Chief of the Boat. I know we already talked to you earlier but the CO thought it might be a good idea if we went over the command structure of the submarine just to give you a better idea of day-to-day living aboard the Woodbridge.

"Second in command is the Executive Officer. The XO coordinates the administrative and training activities of the boat. The remainder of the boat's force is comprised of five departments: Navigation-Operations, Weapons, Engineering, Supply, and Medical. Divisions are the smallest organizational units onboard and consist of groups of enlisted specialists organized according to their skills. The most senior, experienced technicians onboard are the Chief Petty Officers. Their expertise is the backbone of the Woodbridge. Every piece of material on the boat, from the propeller to the paint job, is assigned to a division and finally to an individual technician for its care."

And so, after what seemed like an eternity, Chief Carlos proceeded to tell everyone how the sub was organized. Paul noticed a few of the guests nodding off every now and then, after what seemed like an endless litany of naval bullshit.

"How far out in the Atlantic are we going, Chief?" someone yelled.

The question broke the monotony and ended the command structure lecture for good.

"Good question. We'll be going out past the continental shelf so we can make some deep dives. We should be about 300 miles off the coast, at which time we will dive to about 600 feet. I suspect we'll stay there overnight, surface the next day, and head back into port later tomorrow." Now he had their interest. The part about the 600-foot dive was really all he had to say.

"600 feet. What does it feel like at that depth, Chief?" another guest quickly asked.

"You won't even know you're under the ocean. Unless of course we have an undersea earthquake."

Carlos could sense that not too many picked up on his little joke and quickly let on that he was teasing. "When you are under the sea, you don't feel the normal wave action that you would feel on the surface. It's very calm. Only when we make a steep dive will you have any sense of real movement and then it's just like riding in an elevator. You'll love it."

American Embassy, London

"Knox, the detailed data from the satellite images just came down. Looks like our decommissioned submarine is still commissioned. We have contacted the Russian embassy and they have assured us the sub is just being used for training purposes. I've instructed our agents in the area to look into it further. Also, I've contacted the FBI and the National Security Agency (NSA) to see if they have any additional data that might steer us in the right direction. Our collective officers here at Central all agree on one thing; they're up to something sneaky," John said.

Knox knew the answer before John ever received the new data from imaging. He knew the sub was the K-387. What he didn't know was the "whys" and the "whats" of this latest Russian escapade. After looking through all the data the Agency had on the K-387 he still hadn't come up with anything unique or special about the sub. Why then had the Russians taken great pains to go through the ritual of decommissioning the submarine and then resurrecting it again?

"John, I'm not sure what we have here, but I suspect it has something to do with Iraq. The Russians have been against the embargo for some time now. Perhaps they're just sneaking in supplies to their old buddies. What we need to find out, if this is the case, are the supplies military in nature, or, perhaps just some raw materials the Iraqis need but can't yet buy on the open market?

Call a meeting at 1500 hours with all Station Chiefs working on the region. That will give me enough time to hopefully come up with more than we have right now. Also, check with Israeli Intelligence and see if they have anything on the Russian submarine, and then get in touch with our Jordanian contacts and see if they have any information about the region that might be helpful to us.

Finally, look over recent data on unusual movements, or any strange or out of the ordinary occurrences in the area that could somehow have connections to the sub. Our Russian friends are up to something over there and it's our job to find out what it is."

Knox sat down at his desk to review everything they had come up with to make sure they weren't missing the obvious. He had learned over the years that sometimes the answer was right in front of your nose. This time it didn't appear to be. The question kept popping up in his mind over and over again. Why have the Russians been cruising around in the Red Sea for almost a month now in a training submarine? It just didn't make sense.

And then it hit him. Of course, he thought, they're waiting for something. Why else would they be just sailing up and down the Red Sea? If they really were doing some sort of training exercise they certainly wouldn't stay in the same area. No, they were there for a purpose; they were there waiting for something. Either they were scheduled to rendezvous with another vessel, or whatever it was they were waiting for simply hadn't arrived yet.

Knox picked up the secure phone and made a call to the Israeli embassy. He then called the embassies in Jordan, Kuwait and Egypt.

None of the station contacts had any data on unusual movements in the area. In fact, not one of them had anything to report at all that could possibly shed some light on the Soviet submarine and the reason for its presence in the Red Sea. Almost an hour had gone by and still he had nothing to go on.

"Knox, they're waiting in the conference room for you," John said.

"Thanks John, tell them I'll be right down." Damn, he thought, either he was slipping or the Russians had done a damn good job of covering their footsteps on this one.

Knox walked into the conference room somewhat subdued. He didn't like going into meetings with little or nothing to go on. Usually when this happened, the meeting never really got off to a good start; instead, everyone would sit around waiting for the first person to put their foot in their mouth. Knox decided he would be the first. One thing Knox knew for certain. Don't try and bullshit anyone in this Agency, and be as honest and forthright as you can.

"Gentlemen, a Russian K-387 submarine has been cruising up and down the Red Sea for the last 30 days, and I don't have the slightest idea as to why."

John came to the rescue. "Knox, I just spoke with Scott Peterson over in Central just a few minutes ago and he's come up with something that might be related. It's a long shot, but it's the only thing we've got right now.

They found one of the UNSCOM weapons inspectors dead on the Wadi El Murbah highway about 120 miles southeast of Jordan. The circumstances surrounding his death raised a red flag with one of the UNSCOM officials. UNSCOM is leaning in the direction that someone tried to make the inspector's death look like a robbery attempt. The last we talked with them they were intercepting all traffic on the highway in an attempt to find out just why the inspector was killed. They're concerned he might have inadvertently stumbled across something nasty along the highway, and they want to find out what it is."

"And we damn sure want to know what it is too. Gentlemen, my suspicion is that whatever it is the inspector stumbled across is right now heading for a rendezvous in the Red Sea. Get me UNSCOM on the phone!" Knox said.

Wadi El Murbah highway, Iraq

They were making good time now. After the incident with the American inspector, Mashire had done a good job keeping the caravan on the move. The caravan was now well past the halfway point and only twenty miles from the border. Soon they would be in the safe confines of Jordan where Mashire could breathe much easier. As a Special Forces agent, Mashire had participated in many subversive activities over the years but he had never done something like this before.

When he told Rajel the reason for checking in late, his contact in Jordan wasn't pleased, but he was relieved that everything was OK. They both knew how important this mission was to Iraq and they would do anything to insure its success. Mashire had assured Rajel that no one would suspect anything. He had carefully made it look like another Kurdish robbery attempt gone wrong.

Once they reached the Jordanian border they would proceed to Tilal Al-Ashaqif. There they would rest and prepare for the trip to Aqaba. Rajel had assured him that the caravan would easily pass through the Jordanian border guards. I'm sure Rajel paid them off handsomely, Mashire thought. Mashire's orders were explicit. Upon reaching the border, he was to present his Iraqi identification card to one Shasif Ula Turdam. Mr. Turdam would then let them pass immediately without going through any customs search. Rajel had assured him that he had taken great pains to ensure that passage through the border would be smooth and easy. It had to be. The cargo they were carrying was so lethal, so destructive, no Jordanian official in his right mind would ever let it enter their country. It was essential that no inspection be made at the border. The cargo must enter Jordan untouched and unseen.

The Iraqi border guards had been unusually quiet after the little incident with Ifram. Mashire knew this would settle them down and would ensure no more insubordination the rest of the way. What he didn't know is that this fear would also prevent them from saying anything. When the last truck in the caravan noticed the low flying helicopter heading right at them, not one of them even attempted to notify Mashire.

At first he didn't notice the noise. The poor condition of the road and the constant clatter of the caravan prevented him from realizing what was happening until the chopper was almost on top of them. But then he saw the American flag on the tail of the chopper and instant panic settled into a man that had ice water in his veins. He looked back at the rest of the caravan and screamed as loud as he could.

"Faster, faster. The border is close. We must continue without interruption."

The chopper was directly overhead now. A soldier, leaning out of the right side, was yelling into a loud speaker but Mashire couldn't hear a word he was saying. The precious cargo they were carrying was in the first truck. As he slowed down and came to a complete stop, the chopper settled down about 30 yards in front of the lead truck. Three soldiers, with weapons drawn, walked slowly toward them.

Mashire jumped from the first truck and ran back to the truck immediately behind him. He grabbed the driver, pulling his head next to his and gave the order.

"Drive around me and ram the chopper. Now!"

The driver looked at him and didn't move. Mashire pulled his gun, placing the barrel on the driver's left temple and shouted again. With this, the driver began moving forward and around Mashire's truck. Mashire quickly ran back and jumped in the lead truck.

"You are ordered to halt immediately," the soldiers yelled.

Mashire hoped he had enough time before they started shooting. UNSCOM inspection teams rarely used force unless provoked or threatened. Perhaps they would not perceive the threat until it was too late. As the truck behind him passed on his left, the soldiers raised their rifles in defiance. He heard them shout again. The truck continued to move toward the soldiers and the chopper. The soldiers looked somewhat dazed as if they couldn't quite understand what was going on. The truck had passed him now and was picking up speed. Mashire prayed to Allah that the driver would follow his orders.

Mashire started moving, slowly at first, while the diversion in front of him continued. The soldiers started shooting. The driver continued toward them and the chopper. Mashire jammed his foot on the accelerator. The soldiers, still shooting at the other truck, suddenly realized what he was doing. When they took aim on him Mashire knew his plan would work. It was just enough time for the second truck to reach the chopper. When the pilot of the helicopter revved his rotors in attempt to lift off, the soldiers turned back again to the second truck. The chopper was almost airborne when the truck suddenly veered to the left and struck the chopper in the rudder. The chopper swayed, violently at first and then settled back down.

Mashire kept the accelerator floored all the way. Looking to his left, he saw the soldiers run toward the chopper and then suddenly turn their weapons in his direction. The diversion worked. He was out of range. Mashire had only a few more miles to go before reaching the border. He had saved the canisters. It would be difficult without the other supplies, especially the pontoon boat, but, thanks to Allah, the canisters would arrive safely in Jordan.

Mashire, continuing to pick up speed, heard the noise again. Looking in the rear view mirror he saw the helicopter flying in what appeared to be an erratic pattern. It had been damaged but the pilot was trying desperately to catch up with him. The chopper swayed violently back and forth but was still gaining on him. For the first time, beads of sweat suddenly appeared on his forehead. He looked ahead and could see the border. He couldn't be any more than a half mile away. He had to make it.

The first shot hit just to the left of the truck. Mashire was now only a few hundred yards away from safety. He could see the Jordanian border guards looking at the scene that was unfolding in front of them. The second shot didn't miss. This one pierced the rear window splattering glass shards into the cab and the back of his neck. Mashire continued forward. If necessary, he would ram the border gates.

A hail of fire suddenly riddled the truck. Mashire didn't know from what direction it was coming or even if he'd been hit. But one thing for sure, he was still moving. They were shooting at him from both directions. Suddenly, as he approached the border, he saw someone run towards the guards and instantly they stopped firing. The guards quickly opened the gates.

The chopper took one more last chance shot and then veered off to the left wobbling crazily. As Mashire entered Jordan he screamed in ecstasy and pulled the truck to a stop.

"We've been expecting you, my friend." Extending his hand, Shasif Ula Turdam welcomed Mashire to Jordanian soil.

"Mr. Richardson, we just received the pathologist's report on Jeffrey. He died from a stab wound to the base of the brain. The knife severed the spinal column killing him instantly. The autopsy team all came to the same conclusion. Jeffrey wouldn't have had time to blink an eye much less pull the trigger at the forehead of his attacker. This was no robbery attempt, sir. We haven't as yet received all of the lab work. I expect it any minute. They're rushing it through for us," Will said.

"I knew it. Why in the hell did they kill the poor son-of-a-bitch. Christ, he was to go home as soon as he reached Baghdad. Jeffrey must have stumbled onto something really big in order for them to take such drastic measures. I think we better contact CIA and let them know what's happened."

"That won't be necessary, sir, they've already contacted us. They are aware of what happened. Apparently they are tracking something else in the region and suspect the attack on Jeffrey might have something to do with whatever they are looking at."

With that, Will handed Sam the phone. "I have a Mr. Knox Jones from CIA on hold. He would like to speak with you."

Sam was amazed how efficient the boys at CIA were. They didn't miss much. I'll bet they knew before we did what the hell happened out there, he thought. "This is Sam Richardson. What can I do for you?"

"Mr. Richardson, my name is Knox Jones. I am Director of Eastern operations for the Agency. I am speaking to you, sir, on a secure line, so I'll be frank. First, what I am about to tell you is not to be repeated. You are not to mention anything, whatsoever, to anyone. Is that understood?"

For a minute, Sam felt like he was back in grammar school and if he didn't obey, he'd be sent to the principal's office.

"Go ahead, Mr. Jones."

"We have been tracking a Russian submarine in the Red Sea for almost a month now. To be honest, we have been beating our brains out trying to figure out why they are there and what it is they are doing. Yesterday, when we received word of the death of one of your inspectors and a report of your suspicion that it might have been murder, we began to suspect that the two are tied together somehow. It's my understanding that you have dispatched a…"

Will ran into the office and almost fell over the center coffee table and Sam. "Excuse me, Sam, I think you better take a look at this."

"Mr. Jones, can you hold on for a second. My associate demands my attention at the moment." Sam gave Will an icy stare. He hated being interrupted like that.

"Sam, the Navy chopper you ordered came across a caravan of three trucks on the highway heading toward Jordan. The chopper tried to stop them but they rammed the chopper with one of their trucks. We killed the driver of the truck that hit the chopper and got the third truck without incident but the lead truck in the caravan made it to Jordan before we could stop him. The Navy searched the trucks and came up with supplies, lanterns and a pontoon boat. Here's the report," Will said.

Sam looked over the report as he spoke. "Mr. Jones, I have some additional information here that might interest you."

Knox cut him off. "Mr. Richardson, did the Navy find anything out there?"

"That's what I was about to tell you Knox. May I call you Knox?"

"Yes, by all means."

"The Navy discovered a caravan of three trucks on the Wadi El Murbah highway. The chopper tried to stop them but they managed to hit the chopper with one of their trucks. We have two of the trucks but the lead truck apparently crossed into Jordan before we could apprehend him. In the two trucks that were captured, we found numerous supplies and a pontoon boat. There were no weapons of any kind."

Will interrupted again. He knew how Sam hated that, but he also knew who he was talking to and was sure he wanted to see the report.

"Sam, excuse me again, here's the full autopsy report."

Sam looked at the report. It supported the findings of murder. Then he looked at the toxicology report.

"Thanks, Sam, you did a good thing getting the Navy out there as soon as you did. I'll contact them and get their report. We'll need to know what time that truck crossed into Jordan," Knox said.

"Knox, I was just handed the full autopsy report on Lieutenant Jeffrey. I'm reading it as we speak. It confirms my suspicion that he was murdered. From what I can see, there's nothing other than the knife wound…Hold on a minute." Something caught Sam's eye at the end of the toxicology report:

A complete analysis of the decedent's blood and tissue samples reveals no anomalies with the exception of a minute residue located on the decedent's middle two fingers of the right hand. Chemical analysis of the residue revealed minute traces of bacteria commonly associated with molecular biology. This bacterium is a byproduct of the production of Anthrax.

Eastern Tech Seismological Observatory

The professor didn't look happy. When he walked into the observatory, he didn't say a word. Just kept walking past the instruments, ignoring his two students as if they were invisible and sat down at his desk. After what seemed like an eternity, Stephen broke the silence.

"Professor, are you OK?" Still no reaction. "Professor, what's going on? You look like you just saw a ghost."

"I just left a meeting in the Governor's office. I didn't want to bother you guys with the details. The meeting was set up rather hastily after I contacted headquarters and presented them with our data. I think the data is sufficient to warrant some sort of warning to the public that we are in imminent danger of having a major earthquake on the East Coast. The head honchos in the front office agreed with me and contacted the Governor's office and requested the meeting.

"I presented them with all the data and my conclusions as to what we might be up against. I told them we could be looking at a Deep Focus earthquake."

"What's a Deep Focus earthquake?" Stephen asked.

"Deep Focus Earthquakes are the most disastrous ones, Stephen. They are short in length, yet very deep. A typical Deep Focus quake is about 50 miles long and 650 miles deep. Oceanic trenches are associated with these types of earthquakes. They also occur along subduction zones. They can cause significant damage because of their depth. I've done my calculations over and over again, and what's really disturbing with the pressure data we are looking at is that, if we have a quake, it has the potential of being much longer and much deeper."

Stephen and Jeff just stood there with their mouths open in total silence. The Professor was scaring them.

"My calculations indicate that if we were to have a quake today, based on the pressure readings we now have, it would more than likely be a Deep Focus quake. In addition, the quake would be approximately 75 by 825. For example, let's assume my calculations are correct. If we have a quake centered somewhere around Washington, DC, the shock will be felt from Bangor, Maine, to Orlando, Florida. The major damage will be primarily within 500 miles of the epicenter, in all directions.

"I told everyone at the meeting exactly what I just told you. One of the Governor's cronies insinuated that I was some sort of crackpot. Do you believe that? Right to my face. I felt like nailing the little twerp right between the eyes. At any rate, after much discussion, the same jerk jumps up and says, "perhaps we should wait for additional scientific data before issuing any kind of alert or warning. We don't want to cause any undue alarm to the general public."

"I couldn't restrain myself any longer. I told the Governor that I thought this was bigger than a state matter and that we should contact the federal government, perhaps even the President, with our findings. If we are looking at the possibility of extensive damage up and down the eastern seaboard, it seemed to me that this should be a federal matter."

Stephen and Jeff both jumped in at the same time. "And what did the Governor say?"

"He said, he thought we were jumping the gun a little bit, and that he would take my advice under consideration, but at this time he was not prepared to make any kind of announcement or notify the federal government."

Stephen and Jeff just stood there and didn't know what to say. They both were in a daze. Finally, Stephen spoke up.

"Professor, to hell with the goddamn Governor. Why don't we just contact the feds ourselves? There must be some way we can get to them and let them know the risks involved and the potential danger. Let's send them an e-mail from the observatory."

There was a quality in Stephen that Harry liked. He wasn't a quitter that's for sure. "Don't think I hadn't thought of that. I'm not sure they'd take us seriously. In addition, I don't know who in the hell to even contact in Washington."

"Let's send the damn e-mail everywhere! If we notify every congressman, senator and the White House, someone might take notice and do something. We can't just sit here and do nothing."

Stephen's right, Harry thought. But it would be a mistake to run the risk of sounding like flakes by sending mass emails all over the country. He knew something must be done, but it must be done in a levelheaded manner that was convincing enough to get someone's attention. Harry knew they were running out of time. He sensed that something was going to happen sooner than later and that people had a right to know what might take place. Standing there, going over and over the situation, Harry didn't hear the phone ring.

"Professor, it's the Governor's office," Jeff said.

DIVE, DIVE!

The announcement over the ship's 1MC system was loud and clear. At first they couldn't feel anything. Just a slight jerky movement and then a feeling of leaning forward.

"Take her down to 150 feet Mr. Dunn and level off. We'll stay there for one hour and then proceed to the steep dive exercise. Meet me in the sonar room."

Bill Dunn gave the order, repeating what the Captain said to the exact word. Always the order was repeated exactly to ensure no misunderstandings would occur. The Officer of the Deck (OD) issues the orders. The OD is the only person who can issue an order to the crew.

The control room is the heart of the submarine and is most impressive. In the center of the room, which is about 45 feet long, are two periscopes. It is in this area of control, referred to as the conn, that the OD stands his watch and issues orders. Central to all operations, control is located close to the Captain and XO's staterooms so each can have quick access to the boat's day to day activities. Directly behind the conn and to the left are the plotting tables used by the navigator and quartermaster for navigation. Toward the front of the room are two seats, each with steering wheels. It is here where the sub is driven. The plainsman mans the port steering wheel. By pushing or pulling on this wheel, the stern planes are moved up or down and control the angle of the submarine. The helmsman mans the starboard steering wheel and operates the boat's rudder and sailplanes. On the left or port side are the depth instruments and on the right or starboard side are the fire control stations. A small room forward and on the right of control is the sonar room.

If control is the heart of the submarine, then sonar can be considered the eyes and ears of the ship. Constantly monitoring ocean waters, sonar provides the only outside contact with the sub's surroundings when submerged and is critical to each and every movement the submarine makes.

"65 feet, 75, 90, leveling off, sir. We are at 150 feet," Mr. Dunn said.

"Maintain current speed and heading." The Captain ordered.

"Aye, Sir."

And so, as each order was given, and repeated again and again, the crew of the Woodbridge did their jobs almost effortlessly.

"Captain, we have the new sonar up and running and so far everything looks real good. It's amazing what we can pick up with this stuff. Not only is the detection capability much better but the range is phenomenal."

That was music to George's ears. He was not about to do any steep diving or maneuvers unless the sonar was working perfectly. They were only about 150 miles off shore and already it looked like the new sonar was going to be OK. The technician from Darrich sat there observing the crew and had little to do other than make a few simple adjustments.

"Thanks, Chief. Glad to hear it. Now, give me an idea what this stuff can do."

Chief Robert Fowler walked over to Dennis, the sonar technician sitting at the computer screen and had him enhance the image. A quick move of the mouse and immediately the monitor reflected images on the screen produced from sound waves. "Captain, take a look at this. Here we have a school of fish 35 yards dead ahead. With the older sonar, all we could really determine was that there was a school of fish. With this stuff, we can actually count them if we want to. Now look at the screen in the upper right- hand corner. You see that blip at 2 o'clock?"

George leaned over to look. "I see it Chief. What am I looking at here? Seems to be quite a distance away from us."

"You are correct, sir, it's about 150 miles away. And what you are looking at is a fishing boat that is no bigger than your average tug. We can easily determine its bearing and range. This stuff is amazing."

George was impressed. The older sonar's range was 65 kilometers or approximately 40 miles. He turned to the technician and nodded a job well done. He had read the reports on the new sonar, but seeing it in action was truly impressive.

"Chief, what is our maximum range?"

The technician spoke up almost immediately. "Sir, the sonar is rated at 724 kilometers or roughly 450 miles. That, of course, would be in ideal situations with minimal interference. The best we're picking up now is about 250 miles."

George was somewhat surprised at the dead honest answer from the technician. Usually these industry guys immediately started out on a litany of bullshit and hype that made you feel like wringing their necks. But this response was refreshing indeed and George appreciated it.

"Good job, men. I appreciate the quick test. When we get to our cruising depth, I'll be back to see how we're doing. So far we're looking real good. If it continues to perform like this, we should be able to get most of the tiger cruise activities completed. Let me know if there are any changes. I want around the clock testing until we are satisfied we've got no bugs."

George started toward the gangway heading back to control to give the order for the steep dive to 400 feet and then to 600 feet. They would level off at 600 for the night, surface in the morning and head back to Norfolk. As he started walking, George felt a slight vibration in the handrail and had a sensation of lateral movement for a brief second.

"Chief, did you just feel any movement?"

"No, sir. What type of movement?"

Knox finished looking at the fax they received from UNSCOM. He now knew what the Iraqis were up to, or at least what had crossed over the border in that truck. And he knew it was heading for a rendezvous with the Russian submarine. But he didn't know why. And that is precisely what scared the dickens out of Knox Jones.

When the Agency received the fax over the secure line, they immediately started the ball rolling to try and determine just what the hell was going on. To be specific, their immediate concerns were twofold: Find that truck in Jordan before it reached the Red Sea, and what did Iraq plan to do with the anthrax?

Knox ordered satellite telemetry for the area for the last two years. He wanted to make damn sure they did not miss a thing. Every movement in the area would be scrutinized to see if they could come up with something, anything that might help them determine where the target was and when it was supposed to occur.

In addition, Knox requested all data the Agency had on anthrax, any new strains that might be in existence, where the major manufacturing sites were located in the world and how the Iraqis managed to get their hands on one of the most lethal biological weapons known to mankind.

His first instincts centered on Kuwait or Saudi Arabia as possible sites for release of the weapon. Or perhaps somewhere in Israel? But then again, the Russian submarine would not fit into this scenario. Why in hell would they be moving the anthrax to a submarine if they intended to attack Israel, Knox thought. It was so lethal, all they had to do was shoot another Scud in their direction. It didn't really make a damn bit of difference where the thing hit. Anthrax would do the job and quickly.

What was really disturbing is that the damn Russians were helping them. Cold war over my ass, he thought. Those bastards know full well what anthrax can do and how devastating it can be. Knox could not help but think that once they caught them red handed, some sort of retaliation would be in order. The Russians would need to be taught a lesson.

John walked in just as Knox was picking up the phone.

"John, you must be psychic. I was just calling you. Get a list of our experts on anthrax. I want the best we have. I need to know everything we have on the crap from A to Z. I want a list of all studies we, or anyone else for that matter, have done on anthrax. In addition, find out what vaccines we've got on the table, how much we can get our hands on and how quickly we can ship it to the Middle East. I want to know the current delivery systems that are available, and whether or not the Russians and the Iraqis have access to these delivery systems. Don't forget to contact the Department of Defense and find out what we've currently got over in the area. We need to get over to the Red Sea as quickly as possible to keep a close eye on that sub. I don't want that damn thing moving anywhere. If it does, we need to eliminate it. Finally, get me the latest data on that damn sub."

John didn't say a word. Just turned around and walked out. Knox knew he could depend on him to do everything he requested, and quickly.

Knox turned his attention back to the autopsy report. He had read it twice already but he wanted to make sure he hadn't missed anything. In what seemed like only minutes, John was back.

"Knox, here's our latest on anthrax," John said.

Knox looked at the report.

Anthrax – A New Strain

Russian scientists have developed a new strain of Anthrax. Evidence suggests that the new strain could be resistant to current vaccines. The United States needs to identify this strain in order to test it and immediately start to develop a new vaccine. The U.S. needs to understand how this new organism reacts and the specific relationships it might have to the current strain.

The new organism is resistant to all known vaccines in the world today. In the course of their development, the Russian's apparently mistakenly genetically engineered a strain that's even resistant to their own vaccine.

The U.S. is currently working through diplomatic channels to persuade the Russians to share their research papers on the organism in the hope that we can together develop a new vaccine.

The new strain, considered more lethal than the Ames strain, the most virulent strain to date, apparently attaches itself to white blood cells preventing the immune system from protecting the body against natural diseases. The immune system breaks down rapidly resulting in a rather painful death not unlike that from Aids but only much quicker. Experts are unsure if the current vaccine can be altered to provide protection or whether it will be necessary to develop a new vaccine altogether.

There is great concern in the scientific community that the Russian strain, which contains two new genetically engineered anthrax organisms, cannot be readily identified.

Knox read the report again. Was this the strain that was on the Iraqi truck heading for somewhere in the Middle East? Or even worse, could the Iraqis have some master plan for delivery to the U.S.?

Knox could not help but think how this ordinary day was turning out to be anything but ordinary. The satellite photo of the submarine and the discovery of the dead UNSCOM inspector were coming together to form a dismal scenario. And now Knox was faced with the reality that the CIA would be required to unravel the mystery and hopefully save thousands of innocent lives.

In all his years with the Agency, Knox never felt like he couldn't handle the pressure. And believe me, he had been in some real pressure cookers. But this one was shaping up to be a real beauty. For the first time Knox found himself questioning his ability. He knew this was not a good sign. Once an agent lost his or her edge; once they lost confidence in their abilities they faced a good chance of botching up the job or losing their life.

John walked back into the office. "Knox, here's the report you wanted listing our biological experts."

Four

Mahattat al Jufur, Jordan

Mashire was well past the border now. As soon as he crossed into Jordan, he ditched the truck. Mr. Turdam had been most accommodating. Mashire knew that since they sent the chopper out looking for them that the killing of the inspector had been detected. They hadn't fallen for the robbery setup. Damn, he thought, they usually weren't that bright. He had been certain they would have just passed the young inspector's death off as just another crime statistic to be filed away. Now that the caravan had been discovered, Mashire had an additional worry that he didn't particularly need at this time. He had counted on the trip through Jordan to be a relatively safe and easy one. But now, they would be looking for him. Jordan was friendly to the US and this would greatly complicate matters.

His cover was a good one. Turdam had supplied him with, of all things, a taxicab. A run-down rusty cab that sounded like it was on its last legs; a cab that squeaked with every turn; a cab that looked like it had gone through a demolition derby. And it was perfect. This was all he needed. He was only carrying the clothes on his back and, of course, the precious canisters.

He suspected the Americans would be concentrating their efforts along the major highways. After all, they knew he was in Jordan, but they didn't know where he was headed. And what's more, they didn't know what he was carrying. I'm sure, he thought, they were extremely concerned but as far they knew, he could have been stealing Iraqi weapons or supplies.

More than likely the Americans would assume he was headed in the direction of Israel or even Syria. It was unlikely they would suspect he was ultimately headed for the Gulf of Aqaba. Mashire was sure this was to his advantage but he wasn't about to let his guard down now. He would not take anything for granted.

When he ditched the truck, he had called Rajel to inform him of the problem they encountered leaving Iraq and that he had changed vehicles. Rajel wasn't pleased that he'd lost the pontoon boat but understood the circumstances. He would get another boat before Mashire's arrival. What was important was that Mashire had managed to get the canisters out of Iraq.

Mashire decided to travel by day. They would probably assume he would be traveling by night and concentrate their efforts accordingly. He would move as quickly as possible but, in order to help prevent detection, he would pick up customers in his cab ferrying them back and forth and then quietly leave for his next destination. He would do nothing to raise suspicion.

He would proceed from here to Hafif with stops in Shishan, Jafr, and finally Aqaba. At each stop he would check in with Rajel.

He had even driven his first customer to the airport at Jufur passing Jordanian authorities along the way, without even the slightest inclination that they suspected he was anything but just another cab driver. After leaving the airport, he headed toward Hafif. There he would spend the night.

As he approached the city limits, he noticed traffic was becoming increasingly congested. This was highly unusual, he thought, since he had left well before the normal rush hour traffic. As if Jordan could have rush hour traffic? Most Jordanians still did not own a car and most used public transportation. So he could not understand what the holdup was. Traffic slowed almost to a standstill when he finally realized what was happening. He was looking directly into what appeared to be a roadblock. Jordanian soldiers were stopping each vehicle and were even searching some. At first Mashire thought of turning back and trying one of the back roads, but he didn't want to cause any undue attention in his direction. He was only about ten cars away from the stop and any sudden movements at this time would surely be the wrong move. He decided to stop like everyone else. After all, he was just a cab driver trying to earn a living.

As he approached the roadblock he quickly retrieved his Jordanian credentials that Turdam had given him. He even had a Jordanian driver's license that identified him as a cab driver.

He was only about three cars away now. He could almost read the lips of the soldiers as they abruptly opened doors and looked into the backs of trucks. Mashire was uneasy. He was carrying Iraq's most precious cargo and he faced the possibility it could all end here.

"Where are you heading, my friend?" The Jordanian soldier asked.

The soldier seemed friendly, almost courteous. In his anticipation of coming to the roadblock, Mashire had not even thought of a destination he could give them if he were asked. The obvious question for a cab driver. Mashire didn't even know any of the street names or local avenues to come up with a name. Again, his instincts took control.

"I'm going over to Hafif to visit some friends for the night and will return tomorrow. Need to make a living you know. Cab drivers don't make the salaries you soldiers do."

The soldier laughed and waved him on. As he started to move forward, another soldier quickly ran up to the one who had stopped him and seemed angry. Mashire continued forward as if he didn't notice what was going on next to him. The second soldier was yelling something and then blew his whistle. Mashire came to a stop.

"Is there a problem, sir?"

"My supervisor has instructed me to look in your trunk. We have been searching vehicles all day, mostly trucks though, but he wants me to look in your trunk. He can be a real pain in the ass sometimes. Will you open your trunk please?"

"But I am just a cab driver, sir. What on earth are you looking for anyway? All I have is a suitcase."

The soldier became agitated. "What I am looking for is none of your concern. Just open the trunk and you can be on your way."

Mashire decided now was not the time to argue. He got out and walked to the back of the cab. He slipped in the key and opened the trunk. The soldier quickly looked inside and removed the suitcase.

"Open it please."

Mashire started to lift the suitcase when the other soldier started yelling.

"That's good enough. Let him go. We're holding up traffic."

Mashire put the suitcase back in the trunk and pulled away. As he moved down the road toward Hafif he now realized this trip through Jordan would not be an easy one. But he had covered all bases. The canisters were not in the trunk. He had carefully hidden them under the back seat of the cab.

American Embassy, London

Knox reviewed the list of agents who had been identified as experts in chemical warfare. He was pleased to see that the agents had just returned from visiting the JBD chemical plant in Baltimore for training. But, their visit also indicated the Agency's lack of knowledge about the manufacturing of biological weapons. The agents were sent there to study the intricacies of chemical production and how facilities designed to produce agricultural pesticides might be converted to make chemical and biological weapons by countries such as Iraq.

The CIA wanted to visit a functioning chemical plant close to Washington that could give them some guidance about what they might see in rogue states. The Agency was well aware of the risks involved regarding chemical weapons and had already taken the initiative to explore possible production techniques. Specifically, they were very interested in how a seemingly harmless chemical plant could easily be converted into a biological weapons factory.

At JBD they got their answer. Officials demonstrated how any efficient chemical plant could easily manufacture chemical weapons almost as a routine product during day-to-day activities. The biggest problem any chemical plant would have in trying to make biological weapons was insuring the purity of the product. Therefore, it might be necessary to build a new and separate line in order to manufacture a reliable biological weapon that was free of contamination. It was estimated that a company equivalent in size and capacity to JBD could manufacture a biological weapon in as little as two weeks from start to finish. Knox had almost finished reading the report when John walked in.

"Knox, I've got the information you requested concerning anthrax. From what I've been able to gather, we have numerous studies on the effect it would have if it were ever released into the general population. I'll lay them on your desk. Also, here's a list of the vaccines we have available that are currently stockpiled in Atlanta. The final report I have for you is one the Agency did last year on the Soviet biological delivery system. If you want me…"

Knox cut him off. "Let me see the report on the delivery system."

Soviet Delivery System:
Biological Weapons
The Soviet Union has developed a sophisticated biological delivery system. Russian engineers have devised a way to mount biological warheads, each earmarked for a different target, atop a missile. As many as 12 warheads can be mounted on a single missile. The warheads can be armed with several different biological agents thereby releasing various forms of destruction on its target. When detonated over a specified area, the warheads are designed to explode at different altitudes releasing the agents in patterns that quickly become invisible.

In addition, Russia has also developed a hand-held model that is capable of delivering a dose of biological germs just as lethal as the larger models but on a smaller scale. The hand-held missile can be discharged by one individual and has a range of 45 miles. The delivery is much the same. The warhead simply breaks apart at a predetermined altitude and location.

"Knox, here's the current data on the sub. I'm afraid she hasn't done much. Still in the same basic position she's been in for over a month now. The Russians don't seem real concerned that her location can easily be picked up. Also, we've got every available agent and contact looking in Jordan for the truck. The Jordanians have set up roadblocks at every major city. We even have them looking in the direction of Israel, Syria and Saudi Arabia just in case the sub is some sort of diversion. They have been very accommodating to say the least," John said.

"What did you just say?" Knox asked.

"They've got roadblocks at every…"

"No, not that. You said something about a diversion."

"It's possible, Knox, the sub is diversionary."

Damn, he hadn't even thought of that. Maybe the sub was just a decoy. "John, I hadn't even considered the sub might be a decoy. I knew I hired you for a reason. Good job. Make sure we keep close tabs on those roadblocks. I want to find that Iraqi truck before it reaches its destination, wherever that might be."

USS Woodbridge

The Captain gave the order for the 600-foot steep dive. They would only be diving at about a 20-degree angle. The submarine was capable of much more than that but the old man didn't want to cause any undue hardship for his guests. The announcement was made to the crew to prepare for a steep descent. All hands were to secure any loose items in preparation for the dive.

Paul and David were in the crew's galley drinking a soda when the dive was announced. They could have used the wardroom if they wished because they were guests of the Captain. At the indoctrination all guests of officers were informed that they had access to the wardroom and would sleep in the officer's quarters.

Paul had assumed that the officers' staterooms would be equivalent to the Waldorf Astoria. When opening the door to the stateroom, there is open floor space about three and a half feet wide and six feet long. On the outside wall of the sub, there are three bunks stacked up. The bunks are only about three feet wide and about six feet long. Getting in out of the bunk takes some practice. You must first crawl into the center making sure you're facing in the proper direction. This is extremely important, because once you are in, there isn't enough room to turn around and barely enough to roll over. Along the open space there are storage areas and a fold down desk. Behind the door, is a fold down sink. Outside at the end of the hall is the "head" and at the other end is the wardroom.

Paul couldn't help but think about his navy days some thirty years ago. He remembered the cramped sleeping conditions, mattresses so thin that they weren't much thicker than the sheets. He remembered standing in long chow lines. And now here he was a guest of the

Captain on a nuclear submarine. And, he got to eat in the wardroom and sleep with the officers.

But David and Paul were sitting in the crew's galley munching snacks and drinking sodas. They just felt more comfortable there. Some of the crew even reminded them that they could eat in the wardroom. It was almost as if the crew felt uncomfortable having them there. Guests of officers somehow became officers. Strange, Paul thought.

Suddenly the sub tipped dramatically forward bringing with it the sensation that you were falling. In fact, had they been standing, there was a good chance they would have fallen. They were really moving now. You could feel it. It was almost like a fast moving elevator, only at an angle instead of straight down.

"Now this is something. Man we're moving fast. I wonder how deep we are?" Paul said.

David was up, leaning forward, playing around and didn't respond at first. "Yea, this is really neat. I never thought you would notice the steep dive this much. This is really dramatic. I love it."

Almost as soon as the dive started, the sub seemed to level off. They announced that they were now at 600 feet and would remain there for the night. In his wildest dreams, Paul never imagined that he would ever sleep 600 feet under the ocean. There was almost total silence and no movement.

Another announcement invited interested guests to control for those wishing to observe the sub in operation and assist in steering the sub. In addition, the navigator would be giving a brief demonstration of navigation using oceanic charts and instruments.

Paul, having served on a heavy cruiser during his short navy career remembered how the navigator seemed to be one of the most demanding jobs on the ship. While everyone else was standing around, the navigator was constantly examining charts and coordinates and never really seemed to be able to take it easy. After all, he was the person who determined where the ship was going. Based on his calculations, the OD would issue the orders for the ship's course.

As they walked toward control, Paul chuckled at how much fun it was walking on top of tin cans through a skinny gangway. You had to walk bent over in order to keep from bashing your head on the bulkhead. You adapt quickly especially after hitting your head numerous times. Everyone looked like they had severe posture problems. Everywhere you went you passed bent- over people nodding hello, except of course for the kids onboard. They just ran around as usual having a great time. Kids adapt much quicker than the old fogies do. Kids always do, Paul thought.

When they reached control, they were relieved to see that the cans were not stacked there and you could actually stand without stooping. Funny, Paul thought, as he glanced around the room, some were still standing in the stooped over position, not realizing they could stand up.

Control was packed with people. With the crewmembers on watch and the guests getting in the way, you pretty much had to pick your way around very carefully in order to get a decent view of the good stuff. Paul noticed the two periscopes.

"Are we going to get a chance to look through the periscopes, sir?" someone blurted out.

"By all means. We are going to surface in a few minutes and be on top for a short time. Everyone will have a chance to look through the scopes. We will also surface in the morning before we head back to Norfolk. So, anyone who misses out on a chance today will have their opportunity tomorrow," the OD said.

"I thought we were going to stay down here for the night, sir."

"We are, but the Captain just decided to do a few more maneuvers before we settle down for the night. I think he might be thinking of doing an Emergency Surface or 'blow' routine sometime this evening."

Paul was the first to ask the OD what an "Emergency Surface" was.

"The Blow is an exercise that enables us to surface at a fast rate of speed. When the order is given, compressed air will be forced into the ballast tanks quickly forcing the water out of the tanks. The result is an exceptionally rapid rise to the surface. The sub will actually blast through the surface with the bow extending up as much as 20 feet before we settle down topside."

"Why are there two periscopes?" one of the guests asked.

"One scope is used for surface searches and the other is used as an attack scope. One scope is connected to a computer monitor and the other is connected to what looks like an old black and white television. In addition, we can photograph everything we see with the surface scope. The surface scope, equipped with a digital camera, provides us with a good way to document our exercises and any combat situations we might encounter."

The questions were almost endless. Paul noticed that, even though the officers and crew seemed very busy at all times, they always took the time to answer any questions the guests had and in a pleasant manner.

While his crew entertained the guests in control, George sat in his quarters going over the most recent sonar data. He was pleased that everything was working perfectly. They had done a good job on this one. Usually when they go out on test runs like this, they encounter numerous problems with either the software or the hardware. In this case, however, both were working properly.

One thing bothered him though. He could not stop thinking about that slight little swaying movement he had felt earlier as he was leaving the sonar room. Sonar had not picked up any unusual wave movement or at least they hadn't noticed it and yet something moved the submarine. He was sure of it. George Owens had been sailing submarines for the last eight years and had seen or experienced just about everything you could imagine. There was always an explanation for any unusual movement in a submarine. What he felt earlier was slight but he felt it. Apparently no one else had.

"Captain, we're ready to surface. Our guests are getting anxious to try out the scopes," the OD said.

"Bill, did you feel anything unusual with the sub about fifteen minutes ago?"

"Like what, Captain?"

"Like a slight swaying motion that lasted only a few seconds. I swear I felt the sub move laterally."

"Sorry, Captain, I can't say that I felt anything like that. Maybe you just lost your balance for a few seconds or perhaps your equilibrium was just a little off. You know, sometimes that can happen out here."

"I guess you're right. I seem to be the only one onboard that felt it, so I guess it's just me."

Bill went back to give the order to surface. George was always worrying about something. I guess that comes with the territory, he thought.

American Embassy, London

John walked into Knox's office with the new data they had just received. This might be the break they had been waiting for, John thought. Seems like the Iraqis that they detained after capturing the two trucks in the convoy did a little talking after some gentle persuasion. They now had an ID on the driver of the first truck that was somewhere in Jordan.

"Knox, I've got good news. We've got a positive ID on the driver of the truck we're looking for. We believe he is the only occupant of the truck that made it through. His name is Mashire Al Jebred. He is a high-ranking Republican Guard and apparently one of their best. The boys did a good job on this one. They came up with a photo and it is recent. I've already sent it over the wire to our representatives in Jordan and they are quickly getting it out to all the roadblock areas. I think we've got a good chance of picking up this clown before he does any damage."

"How are the Jordanians holding up?" Knox asked.

"As you know, initially they were somewhat hesitant about setting up road blocks throughout their country. But when we told them what it was the Iraqis were transporting, they became extremely cooperative. They are just as eager to catch this fellow as we are. So, they didn't object when we asked them to distribute the photograph to all the sites. I doubt that Mr. Jebred is aware we are onto him. It's just a matter of time before we nab this guy."

Knox, although pleased with the update John had just given him, was still concerned. He had been in this business too long to get overly excited about, what appeared to be, good news. Not that it wasn't good. But his instincts told him not to get too optimistic.

"John, have we considered the possibility that our man is no longer driving the truck? My suspicion is that one of his first moves would be to ditch the truck. He didn't exactly cross the border undetected. Check with the Jordanian authorities for all reports of stolen vehicles since our man crossed over the border. I want a report of every make and model that has been reported stolen. We need to make sure the guards at the roadblocks are not just looking for a truck. They need to search every vehicle moving between cities in Jordan.

"We are searching every vehicle. I issued that order at the beginning, Knox."

Knox should have known. John was fast becoming one of the best. He needed very little direction and had that sixth sense an agent needed to be successful.

"Nice going, my friend. We'll grab this guy shortly. I'm sure of it!"

"There is one more thing, Knox, that perhaps we should consider. Let's assume that you are correct and Mashire is driving another vehicle. It's possible he has already passed through one or more of the roadblocks. Perhaps we should alert the Jordanian authorities to this possibility and have them track each vehicle to see if they get any repeats. In other words if they detect the same vehicle passing through consecutive roadblocks, especially if that vehicle is heading in one direction and not just back and forth, it might just be our man. The Jordanians are under orders to shoot to kill. They aren't taking any chances. I told them we didn't object to this approach. Any problems with that?"

"Not at all. Our first objective is to prevent him from delivering his cargo. Once we've done that, we can deal with the Russians."

After John left Knox sat down to digest the latest data John had just given him. As any good agent, he would assume the worst and hope for the best. He needed to plan what their next move would be if the Iraqi wasn't caught. What was his destination? Was the submarine a decoy or were the Iraqis planning a drop-off at the sub? If the Russians were involved in transporting the anthrax for Iraq, Knox knew that this would have serious consequences. The Cold War had ended. Russia was moving toward a free market and, ultimately, democracy. Why then would they risk provoking the U.S. with biological warfare? It didn't add up.

Was it possible the Russian government wasn't aware what was going on? The thought was a scary one. Could it be that the Russian's truly thought the submarine was being used for training purposes when in fact it might be part of a sinister plot against the U.S.? It's possible, he thought, that a faction of Russian zealots had convinced their government to re-commission the submarine for training purposes concealing the real reason for its use.

Knox picked up the phone and immediately his secretary was on the line. "Madge, connect me with the Russian embassy please."

Jafr, Jordan

Mashire had passed through Hafif and Shishan without a hitch and was approaching his next stop in Jafr. A pleasant smile crossed his face as he drove with patience. He seemed calmer, more relaxed. It was almost as if he didn't have a care in the world.

The cab was holding up well. Even though it looked like it was ready to fall apart, it was in good mechanical condition. For that he was thankful. He noticed the roadblocks were just about everywhere now. He had been stopped as he entered Shishan and he had been stopped when he was leaving. Each time they searched the trunk of the cab and each time they came up empty. At the last stop, they even went through his suitcase, finding nothing of course.

As he approached Jafr, he noticed the long line at the roadblock. The stops were taking more time now. The Americans were hell bent on catching him, he thought. Mashire just smiled as he approached the roadblock. He noticed the soldiers were carefully looking at something as they checked each vehicle. After what seemed like an endless wait, there were only four vehicles in front of him now. He was close enough to see what was going on. The soldiers were looking at a photograph as they checked the vehicles. Now he knew why it was taking so long. Not only were the soldiers searching each vehicle, but they appeared to be asking each occupant to get out of the vehicle so they could make a comparison with the photo.

Mashire was next. He reached over underneath the front seat and pulled out his revolver and placed it under his shirt. He pulled the cab up to the line and kept the engine running.

"Please turn off the engine, sir, and get out of the cab," the guard said.

Mashire did neither. Without a word, he pulled his revolver and fired point blank into the soldier's face. At the same time he jammed the accelerator to the floor crashing through the flimsy gate. Now he would see what the old cab could do. As he pulled away, he could hear the shouting above the gunfire, which was surely coming his way. He approached an intersection, which was nothing more than an old dirt road and quickly turned right. Looking in his rearview mirror he could see they were gaining on him. He pushed harder on the accelerator that was already on the floor. Through it all, he seemed unusually calm. He was almost serene. He continued down the road passing a farm surrounded by barbed wire. Inside were a few cattle and some sheep. As Mashire jerked the wheel of the cab crashing through the wire and into the field, the animals panicked and started running in different directions. The old cab was holding up well, he thought. It would not be much longer now. He was prepared. He was ready for his great sacrifice.

As he approached what appeared to be a small hill, they shot out his left rear tire. The cab suddenly jerked violently to the left and then the right. It was all Mashire could do to straighten up the cab. Somehow, he thought, he was still managing to keep up a decent speed considering he was riding on three tires and one rim.

As the fatal shot entered the rear of the cab striking him in the head, the hill that he had been climbing suddenly came to an end and the cab became airborne. For a brief moment the cab appeared to glide silently forward and then, suddenly, it pitched into a nose-dive. The cab fell into the rocky gorge below, ending its journey in a violent explosion.

Five

Aqaba, Jordan

The storage facility was small but practical. Iraq could not risk detection by the Jordanian authorities. The cargo was too precious. The Iraqis were well aware of the consequences if they were discovered. It was a risky enterprise but one worth taking. The payoff was worth the risk of an international crisis if the cargo were discovered.

Once the canisters arrived in Aqaba, they would be placed in a small boat in the Gulf of Aqaba and quickly moved to the K-387. At the proper time, the canisters would be transferred to the mini-submarine that would proceed towards the target area somewhere off the coast of America. This would be chosen carefully to prevent detection, and would come at the most inopportune time for the United States.

Only a few selected Iraqi officials had been told of the nature of the weapon they would unleash on America. Not even Saddam's closest advisors were aware of the mission.

Once the plan was implemented fully, the world would soon learn the true power of the Iraqi people. Then and only then, could Iraq declare victory. The naïve Americans would then find out who had won the Gulf War; the war that had never really ended. Saddam was still in power. The bombs dropped on a poor defenseless country did nothing but strengthen the resolve of the Iraqi people to defeat America.

Rajel was very organized. He had obtained the small building to store the canisters while they were waiting transit to the submarine. He filed the necessary papers with the United Nations and Jordan for a permit to store the food obtained by the "Oil for Food" fiasco. He could not help but think how naïve and just plain stupid the rest of the world was to actually believe that Iraq was buying food and medicine during the embargo. The embargo that had been going on now for over eight years and for eight years Iraq had managed to purchase just about anything they wanted on the open market.

Mashire was late reporting in. He was supposed to check in at every scheduled stop. This worried Rajel. He considered breaking radio silence but that was too risky. He'd wait a little longer and if he didn't hear from him within the next hour, he'd make contact with their liaison in Azraq. Rajel was not about to take any unnecessary chances with the radio or cell phone at this point unless he considered it absolutely necessary. While he waited, he decided to take another look at the plan for delivery. Rajel was a cautious man and very meticulous. He wanted to make damn sure everything was in order.

The Internal Security Forces and the Republican Guard had been working on the plan for some time now. Not long after the Gulf War started, the Council of Ministers started planning the assault that would save Iraq. Although the Russians had long ago abandoned them as an ally, Iraq still had some very important Russian friends in the Soviet Union. It took careful planning but with some rogue KGB agents sympathetic to the Iraqi cause, Iraq had pulled it off. The agents had devised a plan to pull a Russian nuclear submarine out of mothballs to be used for training. What the Russian government didn't know was that the crew on that sub were sympathetic to Iraq, disdained the current Soviet government and would do anything to ruin the current friendly relationship with the United States. It was a great scenario. Iraq would devastate the U.S. with terrible destruction and America would undoubtedly assume the Russians were involved in the

Iraqi conspiracy, and again become bitter enemies. Iraq's Soviet helpers would achieve Russian solidarity and ultimately the Russia of old.

Iraq would no longer engage in silly terrorist attacks or downing airliners. This tactic, although destructive and impressive at the time, never really did any damage to the United States. But this endeavor would show the world that Iraq was capable of fighting back and on a major scale. Iraq would show the Arab nations that it was capable of inflicting devastating damage on the great super power.

Timing was critical for its success. Only when the United States was most vulnerable would the plan work. So, Iraq must be patient. It must wait for the most opportune time to implement the attack. Iraq had learned from experience that deployment tactics must be developed in a timely manner. The Iraqi endeavor must be appropriate, executable and powerful.

The mini-submarine had actually been designed in France as the Experimental Submarine Observatory (ESO). The sub was small, easy to use, could easily avoid conventional sonar and, above all, was nuclear. This was most important if they were going to get close to the shores of the United States and deliver the payload of destruction. The ESO was the smallest nuclear ship afloat.

The plan was simple but would be difficult to carry out. The mini-submarine, which attaches to the bottom of the mother submarine to avoid detection, would be released at the proper time. Once released, the sub could travel great distances. In addition, it could easily maneuver to the shoreline in as little as 15 feet of water. When the proper disbursement point was determined, the sub would anchor itself quite easily with two anchor lines, one extending from the stern and the other from the bow. The two-anchor system on such a small submarine provided for increased stability in shallow water. Once properly anchored, the Iraqis would leave the submarine using the exit chamber located directly beneath the control room. It would then be a simple matter of swimming the short distance to shore and using the hand-held missile launchers to release the spores into the air. Airborne anthrax was so lethal it didn't really matter where it was released. Within a short amount of time, the results would be devastating. The Americans wouldn't have any idea what was going on or where it was coming from until it was too late. Revenge would be sweet for Iraq.

After release from the mother submarine the mini-sub would be on its own and would not be retrieved. When the mission had been accomplished, the sub and the three highly trained Iraqi Republican Guards that operated it were dispensable. The guards were under orders to destroy the sub by detonating explosives they had stored near the reactor core, resulting in widespread radiation contamination in America. This most assuredly would be done with the three guards inside. It would be their sacrifice for Allah.

American Embassy, London

Knox had been on the phone with the Russians for what seemed like most of the day. He could not help but think that they were sincere. He was sure they were under the impression the old submarine was only being used for training purposes. He had raised some suspicions in Moscow, he was sure, with his call. They seemed perplexed as to why the Americans were so interested in a sub that was doing nothing but floating around in the Red Sea. Without letting on why he was asking, Knox had grilled just about every contact he knew in the Soviet Union and not one of them let on that the submarine was doing anything but training.

This concerned Knox greatly. He had hoped that at least someone in Russian intelligence would have let on as to what they were really doing over there but not one of them budged. It was looking more and more like the Russians were in the dark and unaware that one of their own submarines was possibly being used in some sort of covert plan involving biological weapons. Knox knew that, if in fact that was the case, and it was looking more and more like it was, the Agency would eventually have to let them in on the little escapade in Iraq and what was currently going on in Jordan. Knox knew, of course, that if their intelligence gathering was worth an ounce of salt, they were already aware that something was going on. You don't set up dozens of roadblocks in and around Jordan without raising a red flag in the international intelligence community.

If Knox was correct, that the Russians were unaware that one of their submarines was being used to wage biological warfare against the US, they would be just as anxious as the Americans to prevent it. The deadly strain of anthrax, that was now somewhere in Jordan and possibly heading for a rendezvous with the submarine was most lethal. Moreover, to the best of his knowledge, a vaccine had not as yet been developed. Knox was quickly coming to the realization that they might be faced with a terrorist action that could be as deadly as a nuclear attack. The virus would spread unabated and without warning.

As Knox continued to contemplate the scenario that was unfolding a half-a-world away, he did not hear the knock on his door. John walked in carrying the latest information they had on the situation in Jordan.

"Knox, we've found our man!" John said.

Knox jumped from behind his desk and was momentarily speechless. "You've found Mashire? Is that what you just said?"

"We've found him alright. He was driving a cab. At the roadblock in Jafr, he shot and killed a soldier. Shot him point blank and smashed the gate. The chase was on. The Iraqi turned off onto a back road and ultimately attempted to drive through a local farm. During the pursuit, the soldiers were sure they scored a direct hit. They must have been right. The cab climbed a hill on the other side of the farm and fell over a ridge down a thirty-foot embankment and burst into flames.

The Jordanian officials, who knew the cab might contain anthrax, panicked. They didn't know how to handle the situation and, quite frankly, I'm not sure we would have either. Jordan is not equipped with environmental clean-up equipment like we have and, as a result, they refused to get anywhere near the wreckage. They're very concerned about the anthrax and just what might happen as a result of the accident. I can't say that I blame them. The cab was burned beyond recognition. Our agents should be on the scene within the hour so I should know more shortly. Right now, it appears that everyone is just standing around trying to figure out just what in the hell to do."

"Where in the hell did the son-of-a-bitch get a cab? How do we know the driver was Mashire?" Knox asked.

"The guards at the roadblock made a positive identification based on the photo we sent them. In addition, they found the truck he had when he crossed the border. They are positive the driver of the cab was Mashire."

"Well, I'm not positive. Before we come to any conclusions here, I want a positive ID on the driver."

"We're moving as fast as we can sir. The body was burned beyond recognition."

Knox picked up the phone. "Madge, get me FEMA on the phone please."

"I'm sorry, sir, what was that?" Madge asked.

"The Federal Emergency Management Agency. I need to speak to someone who is knowledgeable about anthrax. Tell them it's an emergency."

FEMA, the government agency responsible for the Nation's emergency management system has over 2,400 full time employees. In addition, the Agency has at their fingertips 7,000 additional temporary disaster assistance employees who can be called to help when a disaster occurs. FEMA's primary mission is to ensure the continuation of governmental functions during an emergency. The Agency also coordinates the government's response to disasters that might be more than state and local governments can handle. When a disaster occurs, the Agency implements its Comprehensive Emergency Management (CEM) program that immediately takes action to reduce the risk to the population, conducts emergency evacuations, assists in the providing of food, water and shelter and ultimately helps in the rebuilding of the communities affected by the disaster. Finally, FEMA participates in risk assessment with other government agencies in the hopes of prioritizing those potential hazards most likely to strike the country. The most recent list included nine potential threats or hazards most likely to occur and the prioritization of each, in the order of importance. Number eight on the list was the threat of biological hazard as a result of the consequences of terrorism...

Within seconds Madge buzzed Knox back and said the Director of Emergency Hazards was in a meeting and would get back to him shortly. John knew when Knox was angry. You could see it in his face. His eyes would bulge and his complexion turn a bright red. John was sure his blood pressure was sky high.

Knox picked up the phone and dialed FEMA.

"This is the CIA. I don't give a damn what kind of meeting the Director is in, I need to speak to him now! Listen lady, you can tell him anything you want. Tell him I'm the President of the United States. Just get his ass on the phone now."

John and Madge started to crack a smile.

"This is Walter Nacchio. I am the Director of Emergency Hazards at FEMA. To whom am I speaking, please?"

"Mr. Nacchio, my name is Knox Jones, Director of Eastern Operations at CIA. We have somewhat of an emergency on our hands. I need some information on anthrax. Specifically, I need to know how quickly the virus attacks. How long after exposure does one become symptomatic?"

"Mr. Jones, I'll need to know what exactly it is you're talking about. I'm not sure..."

Knox cut him off! "Mr. Nacchio you don't need to know the specifics. Sir, I am dealing with a national emergency. That's all I can tell you. How long, sir, before the symptoms appear?"

"If it's a national emergency Mr. Jones, we at FEMA need to get involved. That's our job you know."

Knox lost it. "I don't care what your job is, Mr. Nacchio. I don't have time for bureaucratic bullshit. I need an answer and I need it now!"

Nacchio got the message.

"Anthrax is tiny, fast-moving and deadly. Microscopic amounts can kill many people in a short amount of time. Without vaccination, anthrax spores can cause death in a matter of days from massive pneumonia and breakdown of blood vessels and organs. Within minutes of contamination, the germ spreads through the skin, mouth, nose or lungs. A common symptom is a skin lesion or sore, which may appear in less than an hour. Anyone within a one-mile radius would more than likely become infected. This, of course, depends on the wind direction and speed. As time goes on, the spores would quickly move through the atmosphere and infect a much larger area."

"Thank you, sir. I appreciate your help. I assure you the CIA will officially contact your office regarding this matter."

Knox hung up and looked ashen.

"John, how long has it been since the cab crashed?"

"I guess it's been about 45 minutes since I first received the report. By now, I would guess it's been almost two hours since it happened. Our agents should be there by now. Be right back."

John ran out before Knox could say another word. Knox just sat there looking at his desk. If they were right and the cab contained the anthrax, right about now a major catastrophe was developing in Jordan.

John was back with the information Knox wanted.

"From what they tell me, Knox, they're all still standing around the area just looking. Our agents removed the charred body and are in the process of determining if it's our boy Mashire. So far, there is no report of anyone feeling sick or any signs whatsoever of anyone with lesions or sores. We should have equipment there within the hour that can detect biological contamination. We should know for sure then. But as of this moment, it doesn't appear that anyone is complaining or displaying any symptoms of infection."

"Then there's a good chance our friend Mashire wasn't the driver of the cab," Knox said.

"You think the cab might have been a decoy?"

"I'm leaning in that direction. It seems to me that if Mashire was driving that cab, we would have seen some sort of infectious reaction by now. Since we haven't, I fear that our Iraqi friend might have given us the slip. That would be good for Jordan, but I'm afraid not so good for us."

"Mr. Jones, we just received word from our agents in Jordan regarding the body recovered from the wreckage. They're holding on line 3 for you," Madge said.

Knox picked up the phone. It was the station manager in Jordan.

"Knox, we have positively identified the remains to be that of one Mashire Al Jebred. No sign of anthrax, however."

Eastern Tech Seismological Observatory

At first they thought the Governor's office was calling back with good news. Perhaps they'd come to their senses and realized the professor's assessments were legitimate. That was not the case. They had simply called back to remind the professor that any official word concerning this matter must come from the Governor and not Eastern Tech. Harry was beside himself. Here he was looking at what could just possibly be a major catastrophe for the eastern seaboard and the idiots at the State House just passed it off.

Stephen noticed it first. As he walked around the room thinking how or what they should do to possibly alert someone about what might happen, he routinely passed the seismographers. He had made the same walk-around so many times and always there was nothing. He almost missed it. Funny how you can look at something and not see it, he thought. It reminded him of the term "muscle memory" that golfers used. Their muscles were conditioned to the point that they made the same swing all the time without thinking about it. Only for him, it was "mental memory." As he glanced at the graphs he first saw nothing but as he started to turn away, there it was.

"Professor, look at this!" Stephen said.

Harry walked over and looked at the graph. He immediately started doing calculations. It was small but it was there. It looked to be no more than 2.1 on the scale, which in most regions, might not even be noticed. But Harry suspected it was a sign of things to come.

"We need to determine its origin," Harry said.

Harry went on to explain how they could locate the epicenter of an earthquake.

"We need to examine seismograms recorded by three different seismic stations. On each seismogram we have to measure the different time intervals in seconds." Harry decided for the sake of expediency not to go into too much detail. Training could come later. He continued.

"The procedure is relatively simple. We will guess a location, depth and time, and then compare the predicted arrival times of waves from our guessed location with the observed times at each seismic station. Then we move the location a little in the direction that reduces the difference between the observed and calculated times. We repeat this procedure, each time getting closer to the actual earthquake location and fitting the observed times a little better. When our adjustments have become small enough that the observed times fit our adjustments, we've got the location."

This is simple, Stephen thought. Somehow he couldn't get over how archaic this all seemed. Hell, they were approaching the millennium and we were still determining earthquake locations using guesswork.

No sooner had the professor finished his dissertation on locating earthquakes, they started receiving the data from other stations around the world. They quickly loaded the data into the computer and within seconds, they had the location.

"Professor, I thought this would take longer than it did," Jeff said.

"I forgot to mention that all our calculations are now done on the computer. In the old days, it would have taken at least an hour to determine the exact location."

Harry printed out the data and laid the location coordinates on the table. The quake was centered at 35°45N′, 70°3W′ or about 320 miles due east of the Outer Banks of North Carolina.

"Professor, what does this all mean. Could this be the result of the pressure data we've been reviewing?" Stephen asked.

"No, Stephen, it's only a prelude of what's going to happen. It's a warning sign so to speak. In a way, it justifies our concerns for a large earthquake in this area. Normally, small quakes precede the larger more destructive 'main' quake. Considering the location of this quake and because it was so small, I doubt it was noticeable unless you were right on it."

"Well, considering that it occurred out in the ocean, I doubt anyone noticed it," Jeff said.

"That's right Jeff. It might cause small wave action or swells that would not alarm anyone on the surface. Perhaps if you were below the surface near the epicenter you might notice something unusual but even then I doubt anyone would pick up on it."

"Professor, are we going to report this?" Stephen asked.

"You bet we are. This should help us persuade the Governor to do something."

Aqaba, Jordan

Rajel continued looking over the details of the plan all the time wondering why he hadn't heard from Mashire. It was not like him to miss a contact. Mashire was well organized and, above all, punctual. Something must have gone wrong. Mashire was now over two hours late in reporting. Rajel decided it was time to try and make contact. If Mashire had been caught, it wouldn't make much difference anyway if the transmission were intercepted. On the other hand, he thought, if Mashire had not been caught but just ran into a problem which prevented him from making contact, any move on his part at this stage might be picked up by American or Jordanian intelligence. He decided to make the call.

He walked over to his small office and started to pick up the phone. Before he could begin dialing, he heard a car pull up in front of the storage building. Rajel immediately dimmed the light and walked to the front of the building. Looking out the window he noticed what appeared to be a military jeep. It was not likely that any vehicle would just happen onto this location. Rajel stopped and listened. He waited for what seemed like an eternity and then there was a knock on the door. Rajel pulled his revolver and walked to the door. His first thought was to ignore the knock hoping his visitor would leave. But he was sure they had noticed the light as they pulled up.

Rajel slowly opened the door, revolver ready. It was dark and he could hardly make out the figure that was standing before him. As his eyes adjusted to the darkness, Turdam spoke.

"Rajel, I'm sure you remember me. It's Shasif Ula Turdam. I have something for you."

Turdam sat down and immediately started telling Rajel what had happened. "Mashire was worried that he would be discovered before making his delivery. He was very concerned about all of the roadblocks. In Shishan, Mashire contacted him and asked if he would deliver his cargo to you. He promised you would pay handsomely once I arrived. I tried to persuade him to continue in the cab I gave him, but he insisted that I transport these canisters to you. So, he loaded them in my jeep, gave me detailed directions and this note."

Rajel opened the note.

"My dear friend. If you are reading this note, then I have succeeded. My journey through Jordan had become most precarious. I pay homage to Allah and the mother country, for it is with their guidance that I made the decision to trust Turdam with our precious cargo. If I do not arrive before the mission begins, then I will have made the ultimate sacrifice for Allah. For that, I am thankful. Mashire."

Rajel put the note down and walked over to Turdam.

"You have done well, my friend. Your safe passage here will enable us to achieve our goal. The people of Iraq are indebted to you. Come, help me bring the canisters inside."

Rajel followed Turdam to the jeep. Turdam lifted the tarp revealing a wooden crate. They picked it up, carried it inside and opened the crate. The canisters were carefully packed inside and in perfect condition.

"Come, join me in a celebration drink. You have earned it my friend."

Turdam removed his coat and started walking toward the table in the corner of the room.

"I will get the glasses. If you would be so kind to hand me the bottle on the shelf behind you, we can begin our celebration," Rajel said.

Rajel was an experienced Iraqi agent. The invasion they were planning would succeed only if secrecy was maintained. The Jordanian had done well. Allah would welcome him into his domain most assuredly. His knowledge of the canisters sealed his fate.

As Turdam turned reaching for the bottle of bourbon sitting on the shelf, Rajel reached around him with the garrote and pulled with all his strength. Turdam twitched violently forward waving his arms and kicking wildly. The force of Rajel's grasp briefly lifted the Jordanian off the floor almost decapitating him. Rajel released his grip as Turdam slowly fell to the floor.

USS Woodbridge

The OD issued the order for the emergency blow. The chief of the watch, who is seated off towards the left of the stern plainsman, initiated the ballast blow that would force water at a rapid rate out of the ballast tanks replacing it with air. At the same time, the plainsman pulled on the ship's steering wheel to move the stern planes upward. The helmsman or sometimes called the bow plainsman, also pulled upward on his wheel thereby changing the position of the sail or bow planes. All of these operations resulted in what some describe as one of the most dramatic maneuvers a submarine can make, the emergency blow. Within a matter of a few short minutes, the sub went from a depth of 600 feet to the surface, exploding out of the water and violently hitting the surface when it settled back down.

At the time of the blow, several of the guests were in control and witnessed the exercise that brought them to the surface.

"Ain't the beer cold!" Paul yelled. Funny how you repeat things you haven't heard for years Paul thought. He had heard the announcer for the old Baltimore Colts, Chuck Thompson, repeat this phrase many times during the broadcast when the Colts would do something great on the field. And now, here he was using it to describe another truly remarkable experience.

"You've got that right. That was something. Really quite extraordinary," David said.

The OD issued the order for "up periscope" and within minutes there was a scramble to look through one of the two periscopes. The seas were calm and the sky a bright blue. The OD turned to the navigator and announced that he was moving to the bridge. Once the OD is on the bridge, the navigator then became the contact coordinator or officer in charge of the conn. Everyone took turns looking through the scopes and a few even got a chance to snap a few pictures with the digital camera on the surface scope.

After a while, George came back into control and announced over the 1MC system that the sub would dive in 10 minutes. The Woodbridge had been on the surface for about 45 minutes when the OD asked the Captain for permission to dive. The OD then gave the order to the chief of the watch who then announced over the 1MC system, "Dive, Dive". The plainsman pushed on his wheel until the gauge read a 10-degree dive reading. Woodbridge dove to a depth of 200 feet and leveled off for a buoyancy check. The ballast tanks were adjusted so that the ship was buoyant and the angle of the boat zero. The chief of the watch reported to the OD that Woodbridge was stable. After a few minutes, the OD issued the order to dive to 600 feet. The dive exercise was repeated with the plainsman until the sub reached the 600-foot depth.

The OD reported to the Captain that the Woodbridge had reached its dive depth and that the ship was again stable.

As he was leaving, George turned to the OD and asked for a final ship position report. The OD relayed the order to the navigator, Lt. Charles Newsome, who in turn relayed it to the quartermaster. As the QM prepared the report, Paul looked over his shoulder. He moved so fast, Paul could hardly keep up. Although he was busy doing what seemed to be many calculations, the QM, sensing that Paul was not picking up everything he was doing, offered the answer to Paul's question before he could ask it.

"Once the sub is positioned for the remainder of the day, we prepare a ship position report, record it and send it the skipper. Let me show you what I'm doing."

The QM went on to explain that the report would contain the time of day, date, latitude and longitude. In addition, he would also indicate compass and drift readings and stuff like, last azimuth, gyro errors and last fix, that didn't make a whole lot of sense to Paul but sounded interesting.

As George headed back to his quarters, his son Matthew and Willy Carlos almost knocked him down as they raced through the gangway.

"Did so," yelled Matthew. "Did not," yelled Willy.

"Whoa' fellows, better slow down before you get hurt. What's all the commotion about?"

"Dad, can submarines move sideways?"

"Not really Matthew. We can move up and down, left and right, but we really aren't equipped to move sideways."

"Told you it didn't happen. My father's a Chief and said we can't. Mr. Owens, Matthew said he felt the submarine move sideways and I told him we can't do that."

George told Willy that he needed to talk to Matthew and that they could play again in a few minutes. Matthew, sensing that something was wrong, began to squirm.

"Dad, am I going to get punished or something?"

"No, Matthew, of course not. I just need to ask you something, that's all."

American Embassy, London

Knox told John to call a meeting to discuss all the events that had transpired over the last 24 hours. After hearing that Mashire had been positively identified and they had not discovered any sign of anthrax, Knox was extremely concerned about where all this was going to end up, especially since they did not have the slightest idea what happened to Mashire's cargo. In addition, he had decided they had reached a point where they needed to advise the White House about all that had transpired. Earlier he had called the Director with his recommendation and was waiting for the phone call that would connect him with the Oval Office for the meeting he knew was sure to come.

John came in with the news and before Knox could get a word out, John started. "Knox, the sub has moved. The last contact we have shows they entered the Suez Canal heading for the Mediterranean. They should be there by now and I suspect they have submerged. It's a good bet they're heading for the Strait of Gibraltar and open seas in the Atlantic."

Knox didn't say a word. He just sat there staring and was completely motionless. After a few minutes, he finally moved toward the wall map hanging in his office.

"How long before they reach the Atlantic?" Knox asked.

"Assuming they are moving at max speed, we anticipate they'll be there in a little over two days."

"Damn it John, we've got technology that can detect the movement of an ant from orbit. I'm sure we can pin their arrival time down a little better than that. Maybe I should call the damn Russians and ask them."

John got the message. He knew Knox was upset after the latest incident in Jordan, but he also knew there really wasn't any way to be more specific about the sub's arrival in the Atlantic.

"Knox, we're doing the best we can. You know as well as I do that when a submarine is submerged they are literally out of contact with the rest of the world. As long as they stay down, there's not much else we can do but come up with a best guess. If they come up for air, we'll pick them up right away."

Knox knew John was right. He was just so damn frustrated over losing the cargo in Jordan. Iraq had done a good job eluding them and making their delivery. And that really made Knox mad. The son-of-a-bitches had more on the ball than he had given them credit for. It was a serious mistake on his part. Never underestimate your enemy, he thought.

"John, have we contacted the Navy to see what they've got over in the Med?"

"We have, Knox. They were quick to point out that most of their heavy hitters were stationed in the Persian Gulf. They said they'd get back to us."

"Get back to us? John, do they realize the seriousness of the situation? Do me a favor and…

"I'm on my way, Knox," John said.

As soon as John left, Knox picked up the phone and Madge was there immediately.

"Madge, you better get me the Director. I'm afraid our time is running short."

Within minutes, Madge buzzed Knox. The Director was on the line.

Russell Trelinko had been Director of CIA since the new administration took office six years ago. Knox liked him. He was honest, straightforward and smart as a whip.

"Mr. Trelinko, this is Knox Jones. With regards to our most recent operation in Jordan, I believe we have reached a point where it is critical we meet with the President's staff. The sooner we brief them the quicker we can get the military moving. I'm afraid the Navy might be dragging their feet a little, primarily because they don't understand the severity of the situation."

"Where do we stand at the moment, Knox?"

"As you know, sir, the Iraqi gave us the slip. He was definitely one of their best. I was sure we'd grab him before he reached his destination but we underestimated him. Our latest satellite data reveals a contact with the sub. It was apparently a small boat that dropped off the cargo in the early morning hours. As soon as the contact was made, the sub left the Gulf, entered the Red Sea and submerged. The next contact we made was when they transgressed the Suez Canal. At this time, the sub is somewhere in the Mediterranean. They are submerged and probably will remain so."

"Have we contacted the Navy?" Trelinko asked.

"Yes, sir, we have. Their response was they'd get back to us. Sir, we need to know immediately what kind of craft they may have in the area, so we can at least keep close to that submarine. Once they reach the Atlantic, it will be that much more difficult to make contact. Also, I'm leaning towards asking the Navy to order the Atlantic fleet on full alert. If we lose this submarine now, we'll need those naval resources on an as-needed basis."

"Good work, Knox. I'm waiting now for the boys over at the White House to get back to me. If I don't hear anything within the next half-hour, I'll call the Joint Chiefs and apprise them of the situation. I'm sure we'll grab our Iraqi and Russian friends before they can do any harm. What are the Russians saying about all this?"

"I called them earlier. They insist the submarine is there strictly for training purposes. As soon as I get off the phone with you I'm going to call them again. I want to see what their reaction is to the sub's movements."

"Excuse me, Mr. Jones, I'm sorry to bother you but I have the Russian embassy on the phone," Madge said.

"Russell, Madge just advised me that the Russians are on the other line. I'll get back to you as soon as I get off the phone."

When Knox answered the Russian call, he didn't have to mention the sub's movement. They already knew the submarine had left the Red Sea. It's difficult to read the Russians, Knox thought. You want to believe them. You want to think they are sincere. But always in the back of your mind you know you are talking to, what used to be, a cold war enemy of not too long ago. This time, however, Knox suspected they were telling the truth. They were concerned that the submarine had moved. The sub was under orders to remain in the Red Sea for training exercises and ultimately return to the Soviet Union in two weeks. Since they had not received any contact from the Commanding Officer, they did not understand why the submarine appeared to be returning to its Soviet base in Sevastopol two weeks early.

When Knox advised them that he didn't think they were headed toward Russia but rather toward the Strait and ultimately the Atlantic, the Russians reacted understandably.

"Why on earth would you think that, Mr. Jones? I'm sure they are headed towards the Bosporus Strait at Istanbul and the Black Sea," the Russian official said.

"Sir, we have reason to believe your training submarine is carrying biological weapons. We captured an Iraqi caravan leaving Iraq, but the lead vehicle managed to escape into Jordan. Chemical analysis of an American naval officer killed by the Iraqis revealed a residue commonly associated with the production of anthrax. In spite of our best efforts, we fear that the anthrax was ultimately delivered to your sub."

There was a long silence at the other end of the phone. Knox decided to inform the Russians of the true nature of their training submarine. Based on the reaction he

104

received, he would be able to determine if the U.S. was dealing with an Iraqi operation or an Iraqi/Russian operation. He got his answer almost immediately.

"Mr. Jones, the Russian government will do anything it can to assist you in commandeering that submarine. I would like to assure your government that we were unaware of this situation. I'm afraid it might be more dangerous than you realize.

"You might not be aware that our government has developed a new strain of anthrax that is resistant to any vaccines in existence today. This new strain is most lethal. For example, previous strains had an incubation period of one to six days. The new strain has an incubation period of only an hour or two. It is swift and deadly. A five pound bag spread airborne could easily destroy the population of New York. If that strain has found its way onto that submarine, then it is extremely important we capture that submarine immediately."

Knox knew, that as soon as the Russians divulged the existence of the anthrax strain they had developed, they were telling the truth.

Six

Port Said, Mediterranean Sea

As soon as the submarine exited the Suez Canal, it submerged immediately. It was crucial that they give the appearance that they wanted to hide as quickly as possible but also not appear too eager. They did not want to raise any suspicions with the Americans at this point. The operation had gone well and thus far, the Americans were doing exactly what they anticipated. They were falling into the Iraqi trap just like Andrei said they would.

They headed due west and would stay submerged until they passed the point just south of Iráklion, on Crete. Then they would surface intentionally to draw attention, refresh their air supply and submerge again and remain submerged as they passed through the Mediterranean. They were also aware that now they would have the Russians looking for them as well as the Americans. As soon as the sub moved into the Suez, the Russians would realize the K-387 was not returning to its homeport. They also anticipated that the Americans would ultimately tell the Russian government what it was they suspected the sub was carrying. Once Russia realized the payload was the new anthrax strain, they and the Americans would be hesitant to shoot them out of the water. The cargo they were carrying was far too dangerous. If an attempt were made to sink the submarine with a torpedo, depth charge or even a missile, the K-387 could easily release the spores into the air with one of their projectiles. The risk of contamination would simply be too great.

As they were passing through the Suez, they took pride in the fact that they had managed to smuggle the anthrax safely to the ESO right under the noses of the Americans. The Americans surely knew by now that they were dealing with a formidable foe. Iraq had them running scared. By now they were certainly aware how lethal their weapon was and must be wondering where it would be deployed. So far, they had managed to stay one step ahead of American intelligence. And if everything went as planned, the attack on the U.S. would be successful. They no longer referred to what they were doing as the Operation. They were now declaring a full-scale attack on the only super power left in the world. The super power that would be brought to its knees by the country they had indiscriminately bombed over the last eight years.

Their enemies knew what they were carrying on the submarine. They knew it was anthrax. But that's all they knew. They didn't know where they would deliver the lethal blow and they didn't know about the mini-sub.

Andrei Kobiak was the Commander. He could trace his lineage all the way back to Ivan Kobiak who was a Moscow Ambassador in 1511. He was a Russian. His disillusionment with the current state of affairs in the Soviet Union led to his defection and ultimate decision to command this submarine. He had been a Captain in the Black Sea Fleet for almost 15 years when he decided to defect. Even though he was about to be promoted to Vice Admiral in charge of the First Deputy CinC-Northern Fleet, Andrei decided to risk everything he had worked for to help return the Russia of old.

They would travel the length of the Mediterranean to the Strait of Gibraltar, a distance of over 2,100 miles. Andrei knew the Americans would be in close pursuit and attempt to prevent them from passing the Strait into the Atlantic. It was his job to do just that and extend the chase as long as possible.

"Captain, we have a sonar reading. Bearing two-six-nine; range 650 yards and closing," Sergio said.

"OK Sergio, let me know when they get within 400 yards. When they do, order all-ahead full and then dive to 200 feet. Once we reach that depth, I want an emergency blow. Let's scare the hell out of them. Once we're on the surface and we find out what they're sending at us, we'll know better how to handle the situation."

Sergio Serkiz was Andrei's right-hand man. On this mission he was serving as Executive Officer, Navigator, Sonarman, you name it. They were operating with a bare-bones crew. They had just enough to ensure the proper operation of the submarine.

Sergio gave the order. When the submarine reached 200 feet, they stayed there for only a minute or so and then went to the emergency blow. This was somewhat risky, Sergio thought. The ship that was on the surface was dangerously close. They risked the possibility of the submarine crashing through the surface into the ship. Andrei knew this. That's the type of Captain he was. He was well known for doing unexpected, dangerous maneuvers. He was daring and bold and it paid off. Rarely did his enemies predict his movements or exercises.

The K-387 crashed through the surface 150 yards in front of the American Naval vessel.

"Up Scope!" Andrei ordered.

As they observed the ship through the scope, Sergio and Andrei could almost make out the shocked look on the faces of the crew aboard the ship. People were running everywhere. Andrei looked at Sergio and they both laughed hysterically.

"Control, radio."

"Control, aye."

"Captain, we have a message from the American ship," the radioman said.

"Read it to me," Andrei said.

"Aye, sir."

"THIS IS THE UNITED STATES NAVY. YOU ARE ORDERED TO HALT IMMEDIATELY! WE ARE UNDER ORDERS TO BOARD YOUR VESSEL. COMPLIANCE REQUESTED WITH INTERNATIONAL COLORS."

Andrei looked over at Sergio and they started laughing again.

"Hey Sergio, where did we put our international colors?"

"Well Captain, I think we must have forgotten them."

"Take her down to 200 feet Mr. Serkiz. Let's show them our international colors."

American Embassy, London

As soon as Knox got off the phone with the Russians, Madge came in with the information from the Navy.

The Navy has one ship in the Mediterranean. It wasn't good news. The ship was the USS La Salle (AGF-3) stationed at Gaeta, Italy. The La Salle was a Command Ship. Its armament consisted of the Phalanx weapon system, four machine gun mounts and two saluting guns. The La Salle was in the Mediterranean doing good-will cruises and was under orders to look for the submarine.

Great, Knox thought. We've got a nuclear submarine stock full of the worst strain of anthrax known to man that we need to prevent from entering the Atlantic, and we're going to have to do it with a Command ship that doesn't have enough armament to stop a tug.

John broke his train of thought. "Knox, the La Salle has contacted the submarine. The Navy got right on it after the Director contacted the Joint Chiefs of Staff. Here's the report."

Knox looked over the report. The sub had apparently surfaced within earshot of the La Salle and quickly submerged again.

"John, get me the Captain of the La Salle on the phone!"

In less than a minute, Knox was talking to the CO.

"Captain, my name is Knox Jones and I'm with the CIA. What can you tell me about your encounter with the submarine?"

"Well sir, it was the strangest thing. In all my years in the Navy I've never seen anything quite like it. The damn sub surfaced within 150 yards of my ship. Scared the living hell out of the Brass onboard not to mention half the crew. As soon as they surfaced, they went down again.

We've got them on sonar and are tracking them as we speak. It was almost like they were toying with us."

"Where are they now, Captain?" Knox asked.

"Currently they are about 750 yards off our bow heading due west at 10 knots. Our orders are to maintain contact but under no circumstances are we to fire upon them."

"No offense Captain, but if you did, what would you fire at them with?"

Knox was out of line and he knew it but he couldn't resist the little dig. Shit, what would they do, shoot the sub with their machine guns?

"Mr. Jones, I see you fellows in the CIA are familiar with our armament. What's on paper that is. In addition to our machine guns we are also carrying depth charges. Does that answer your question?"

"Sorry, Captain, it's been a little hectic around here lately. I stand corrected. Did I hear you to say the submarine was doing 10 knots?"

"That's correct, sir. She's maintaining that speed. Just seems to be cruising right along."

"Captain, it's imperative we keep that submarine from leaving the Mediterranean. I'm afraid your ship will have to go it alone. You will need to do whatever it takes, short of sinking her, to keep her contained. Is that understood Captain?"

"Mr. Jones, I was not under the impression I was taking my orders from the CIA. I will check with my superiors to receive further instructions. Until then, I will continue to remain at bay, which are my current orders."

Knox put the Captain on hold and picked up on the other line. When the Director answered, Knox briefly filled him in on the situation and requested he be given full authority. He didn't have the time or the patience to deal with the chain of command in the Navy.

"Sorry, Captain, for the brief interruption. I understand your situation but I'm afraid we are dealing with a national emergency here. It is, therefore, imperative we eliminate as much of the middleman as we can in order to speed things along. I'm sure you understand."

"I do understand, Mr. Jones, but I cannot and will not follow orders from anyone other than my immediate superiors. The Navy is capable of issuing... Mr. Jones, can you hold for a moment please?"

Knox anticipated why he had been placed on hold. After only a minute, the La Salle's captain returned.

"Mr. Jones, I'm at your command sir. I must say, you fellows sure do move fast. Please forgive me."

"Nothing to forgive, Captain. I would have done the same in your situation. We will need to keep in constant contact. I want to know where that submarine is at all times. I want an online feed of her current heading and speed. I cannot emphasize enough how important this mission is, Captain. I'm afraid you have been placed squarely in the middle of it."

"Mr. Jones, sir, if I could be so blunt as to ask just how we are supposed to prevent this submarine from leaving the Mediterranean without using some sort of fire power?"

"Captain, that's one we haven't figured out just yet."

The K-387 was now at 33°52N′, 25°34E′ or about 80 miles southeast of Iráklion on Crete. Andrei had not planned to surface before Iráklion but the American naval vessel had forced him to make a showing.

Andrei ordered all ahead full. He was finished playing with the Americans. From this point on he would maintain 22 knots until he reached the Strait. Once in the Atlantic he would head due west and then turn abruptly to the North in the direction of Lisbon. He would continue the northerly route indefinitely.

"Where are our American friends, Sergio?" Andrei asked.

"They're keeping up with us sir. Bearing two-four-eight, range 650 yards."

"Let me know if you notice any change in their direction or range. I want to make sure they keep tagging along."

"Yes, sir," Sergio said.

Andrei went below to his stateroom to review some charts and to catch some rest. If all went as planned, the rest of his journey would be relatively easy. The Americans were doing exactly what he suspected they would. He was somewhat surprised that the only ship they had in the area was a Command ship. He wished his pursuer was a more formidable foe instead of a spit and polish ship designed primarily to coddle navy brass. He should have anticipated this, though, given that most of their firepower was floating over in the Arabian Sea playing games with Iraq. How ironic, he thought, that what the Americans were looking for would be right under their noses. By the time they realized what was happening, it would be too late. In the meantime, he would continue his journey with the Americans in close pursuit.

113

A knock at the door interrupted Andrei's much needed rest.

"Captain, I think you better come up to control, we have a new contact you better take a look at," the messenger said.

Andrei quickly put the charts away and headed for control.

"What is it Sergio?" Andrei asked.

"Captain, we have a sonar contact, bearing one-five-three, range 800 yards and closing. It looks like we've got a submarine on our tail."

Andrei walked into the sonar room to look at the monitor. It was a submarine all right. Now, he thought, this was going to get interesting.

Andrei returned to control. "Left full rudder, all ahead one third, dive to 450 feet," he ordered.

Sergio repeated the order and immediately the submarine began its descent.

"Where's our friend now?" Andrei asked.

"Bearing two-five-six, range 300 yards and closing," Sergio yelled.

Damn, Andrei thought, they were serious. He might just get the dogfight he wanted.

"All stop. Reverse engines, full astarboard. Let me know when we're in position," he ordered.

The K-387 came to a stop as the grinding of the turbines could be heard throughout the submarine. Almost immediately, the sub turned right and waited.

"Where's our target now?" Andrei asked.

"Bearing three-six-nine, range 200 yards."

"Arm number one," Andrei ordered.

Sergio looked at Andrei in shocked admiration. "Andrei, what are you doing?"

"I'm going to sink her, Mr. Serkiz, before she sinks us."

Knox finished the conversation with the Captain. Strange, he thought, why would a submarine that was attempting to make a run for it be doing 10 knots? That submarine had the capability of doing 22 knots.

Knox called John back into his office. "John, get me the satellite reports for the K-387 for the last three days in the Red Sea. Specifically, I want to see where she submerged, re-surfaced, submerged again and how long she was down each time."

"OK Knox, just curious, where are you heading with this?"

"I'm not sure yet. Something just doesn't fit. I don't know, call it my sixth sense but I feel there's something we're missing. I keep asking myself why would they be meandering around in the Mediterranean at a measly 10 knots when they should be hell bent on getting out of there and into the Atlantic."

John left to get the data. Knox walked over to the radio and turned on some music. He needed time to think and listening to music helped him relax. Knox was sure there was something they were missing. It all seemed too easy. The K-387 passes the Suez into the Med and acts like they are on a moonlight cruise.

John returned with the data. Before Knox looked at the figures, he took a call from the Captain of the La Salle.

"Mr. Jones, the K-387 has picked up her speed to 22 knots. Also, we have company over here. There's a submarine on the K-387's tail. We think it might be Russian. Can you verify this?"

"I'll get back to you Captain."

Knox wasn't pleased that he had found out about a Russian submarine in pursuit of the K-387 from the Navy instead of the Company.

"John, the CO of the La Salle has just informed me there is a Russian submarine in the vicinity of the K-387. Did we know about this?"

"Sorry Knox, in the rush to get the data you requested, I didn't look at this morning's updates. I'll get them now," John said.

While he was gone Knox looked over the report.

John quickly returned and confirmed that they had identified a contact that appeared to be a Russian sub from their Black Sea Fleet.

"John, look at this. See anything here that catches your eye?" Knox asked, referring to the report.

They reviewed the data together. Over the past month the submarine had routinely meandered up and down the Red Sea and twice a day had submerged; once in the morning and once in the evening, almost at the same times each day. In the morning they submerged near Jeddah and in the evening near Port Sudan.

Recently, however, the K-387 submerged at the mouth of the Gulf of Aqaba and did not surface until Djibouti. It remained on the surface for about an hour and again submerged. The next time the submarine was on the surface was at the mouth of the Gulf of Suez.

"John, my friend, they're telling us something here. If my suspicions are correct, the K-387 might be a decoy. It's possible they dropped off their cargo at Djibouti and are merely leading us on a wild goose chase through the Med."

"Knox, if you don't mind me saying so, if they dropped off the anthrax at Djibouti, where did they drop it? They never reached port. They surfaced for about an hour and made no contact with any ships, so I'm not sure how they could have done that?"

"I'm not either, John, but we're damn sure going to find out. I think we need to talk to our Russian friends again."

Within minutes, Knox was again speaking with Russian Intelligence. Only this time he made a direct call to Moscow. He sensed they weren't telling everything they knew about the K-387's training mission.

"Mr. Makarovich, this is Knox Jones with the CIA. Sir, I need to ask you a question about the K-387 and to be frank, it is extremely important you be open and honest with me. We suspect the K-387's excursion into the Mediterranean might be diversionary. Our satellite data reveals that the K-387 made some maneuvers in the Red Sea, just before entering the Suez that might indicate they moved the anthrax before they entered the canal. Also, can you confirm for me that you have a submarine in the area?"

"Yes, Mr. Jones, we have assigned the SSN Leopard to the area to try and determine what the K-387 is up to. With respect to your first question, I must admit I'm somewhat confused. What do you mean by diversionary?" Makarovich said.

"Was the K-387 carrying a mini-submarine with it? Knox asked."

John looked shocked when Knox asked the question.

"Hello, Mr. Makarovich. Are you still there, sir?"

There was no response on the other end of the phone. His silence answered Knox's question.

"Mr. Jones, may I get back to you, sir. Something has come up that I need to concern myself with here. You know, local business. I'll call you back within the hour."

Knox hung up the phone and looked at John.

"John, call the Navy and tell them the K-387 is of no further use to us. While you're at it, get the most recent data on what we've got deployed in the Arabian Sea. I hope we're not too late."

Seven

Earthquake

Earthquakes come in three varieties. They can be artificially produced in the laboratory or in the field. And then there are the kind nature produces: tectonic and volcanic. The tectonic variety is by far the most devastating. When stress builds in zones containing major plates and one plate slides past another, something has got to give. In a mid-ocean ridge, where the seafloor interacts with ridges in relatively shallow depths, the undersea quake can have devastating results.

The quake struck at 33°53′N, 60°22′W or about 913 miles southeast of Norfolk. The quake was a tectonic deep focus quake measuring 65 miles long and 725 miles deep. It measured 8.1 on the Moment-Magnitude scale.

The professor came running in just as Stephen was printing off the data from the seismographs. Funny, Stephen thought, he felt only a slight shudder when the quake hit. He knew it was a big one and yet he hardly felt any shaking.

"Professor, I think the big one you were predicting is now a reality," Stephen said.

Wilkens didn't say a word. He just walked over to the graphs and studied them. Jeff stood there just watching and waiting for his next reaction.

"Professor, why didn't we feel the impact?" Jeff asked.

When the professor looked up, his face said it all. He had lost all color and was so pale, Stephen and Jeff thought he was going to pass out. He walked over to the telephone to make a call. Within minutes, the professor was speaking in tones they had not heard before. They heard him request GPS data and something else and then he quickly hung up.

"Fellows, we have just experienced an earthquake of major proportions. Because the quake was centered over 900 miles out in the Atlantic, we have been spared major damage on land, so far. Our greatest fear now is what I was afraid of if the quake occurred in the Atlantic. I'm afraid we are in for our first tsunami on the East Coast. This is a major stroke of bad luck. If the quake had struck inland, we of course would have sustained major damage with a quake of this magnitude. The damage would have been mostly structural and devastating. But I'm afraid what we are in for will be far more damaging and destructive."

Stephen and Jeff looked at the professor and said nothing. Neither one of them had done any serious research on tidal waves and were unprepared to comment. The professor, as usual, came to their rescue.

"Tsunamis can form when the sea floor abruptly deforms and displaces the overlying water. When these earthquakes occur beneath the sea, the water above the deformed area is displaced from its equilibrium position. Waves are formed as the displaced water mass, under the influence of gravity, attempts to regain its equilibrium. When large areas of the sea floor elevate or subside, a tsunami can result.

"The damage from a tsunami resulting from a quake of this magnitude can be more devastating to coastal areas than a land-based earthquake. Tsunamis differ from ordinary wind- blown waves in that they can be almost imperceptible out in the ocean. In deep water, they can move at speeds approaching 500 miles per hour, almost as fast as a jet aircraft. Traveling at these speeds, a tsunami can travel from one side of the Pacific Ocean to the other side in less than one day. Its length from crest to crest might be hundreds of miles or more and its height from crest to trough will only be a few feet or less. They cannot be felt aboard ships nor can they be seen from the air in the open ocean.

"As they approach shallower water near the coast, they are slowed down. This causes them to rise in height to 100 feet or more, depending on the size of the quake. When they arrive on shore, they can reach heights of 200 feet or more with speeds of 150 miles per hour, resulting in massive destruction. Flooding can extend inland 100 miles or more, covering large expanses of land with water and debris."

Stephen and Jeff had first assumed that the quake's distance from shore was a good sign. They were now quickly coming to the realization that what the professor was telling them would probably mean a large loss of life with major damage.

The professor continued.

"The first sign for those living in coastal areas of an incoming tsunami is often a sudden outrush of water exposing the seabed and leaving boats stranded. Shortly thereafter, huge waves will strike inland. The first is not necessarily the largest. Usually, the biggest wave will strike between the third and the eighth. Consequently, after the first wave hits, those inland often assume the worst is over when in fact it has yet to come. Since the waves are traveling at great speeds, anyone on shore will not survive to tell about it."

The boys interrupted. "When, professor, when?"

"Since the quake struck about 20 minutes ago, I would guess we have about an hour at best. I'm afraid the Atlantic seaboard doesn't have a warning system like the Pacific does. The Tsunami Warning System (TWS) in the Pacific functions as a monitoring station throughout the Pacific Basin. After I called for the GPS data, I made a quick call to their warning center in Honolulu. If we had more time I could have used their influence to convince the local authorities to issue a warning bulletin with instructions to evacuate the coastal areas up and down the eastern seaboard. I even thought about using the National Oceanic and Atmospheric Administration's Weather Wire Service satellite communications system to help with evacuation. I'm afraid we just won't have sufficient time to evacuate very many people. As it is, if the tsunami strikes multiple areas, given the short time frames we are already dealing with, I suspect we will be looking at some very heavy casualties."

The phone rang to interrupt Harry's dissertation.

"It's for you, professor," Stephen said.

Harry picked up the phone. By the expression on his face, the boys could tell something was wrong. The professor always had a way of letting you know what was going on by his facial expressions. They clearly weren't good.

"The Governor's office just called. They appear to be in panic mode. They want to issue a tsunami warning for the tidewater area immediately. The Navy is jumping down their backs wanting to know how much time they have. When I told them that they have less than an hour, I think the reality of the situation really set in. They are in the process now of notifying Washington of the seriousness of the situation. They're thinking of flying helicopters up and down the coast in the most populated areas to try and raise awareness and will, within the next ten minutes, announce over the Emergency Broadcast System an immediate evacuation of coastal areas."

"Professor, it looks like they are making a serious attempt to at least do something. Why the sad face?" Stephen asked.

"I'm afraid it's too late, Stephen. Many of the coastal populated areas only have limited access. There just isn't enough time to evacuate. Their intentions are good, but I'm afraid the result will be less than satisfactory."

ESO

Someone once said, "There's two kinds of ships in the world - subs and targets."

The ESO fell into the non-target category. In the ever-increasing game of hide-and-seek between submarines and sub hunters, the hunters usually come out losers. Although designed in France, the ESO fell into the "Quiet Soviet Sub" category. In the critical area of quietness, which is the key to survival in undersea warfare, Soviet submarines had always been deficient. The new breed of Soviet submarine, the Akula, was a stealth design that was far more difficult to detect. The ESO was designed using Akula specifications and was much smaller than conventional submarines. This made it even more difficult to detect by today's standards. Conventional anti-submarine warfare was almost rendered useless by the new Soviet design. This technology uses passive sonar to convert the pressure of acoustic waves into an electrical signal. Unless the Americans were using next generation fiber optics sonar with high-powered computers utilizing low-frequency transmitters, the ESO was in the position of sailing up to the shores of America without detection.

ESO was even capable of evading the Integrated Undersea Surveillance System (IUSS) which is comprised of fixed, mobile, and deployable acoustic arrays that provide vital tactical cueing to anti-submarine forces. IUSS provides the United States Navy with its primary means of submarine detection both nuclear and diesel. With the advent of submarine warfare and its impact on Allied forces and supply lines in WWII, the need for timely detection of undersea threats was made a high priority in Anti-Submarine Warfare (ASW). As technology progressed, it was recognized that shore-based monitoring stations were the answer to the problem since they could be made basically impervious to destruction, foul weather, and ambient self-generated noise. Since the early 1950s, the Atlantic and Pacific oceans have been under the vigilance of the Sound Surveillance System with long acoustic sensors installed across the ocean bottom at key locations. ESO, with its "quiet" design was capable of avoiding this detection. Its nuclear turbines created less noise than a 50-horse power outboard and would easily slip through the current sound detection systems of the IUSS. Even newer technologies, which have been implemented over the years, would not detect the ESO.

By the time the K-387 entered the Mediterranean, the ESO was well on its way towards America. The K-387's mission for the last week or so had been purely diversionary. After the anthrax had been delivered, the K-387 submerged and easily deployed the ESO in the Gulf of Aden near Djibouti. The trip for the little submarine would be a long one but one that would help avoid detection. The extended route around South Africa was necessary for their survival. Any attempt to reach America by way of the Mediterranean would have been way too risky. It would have been too obvious. This is exactly what the Americans would suspect since the route around South Africa is much longer, requiring more time. They had decided to drop ESO where the Americans would least expect it - where America presently had six ships deployed in the Arabian Sea. By the time they realized what had happened, the ESO would be well past Cape Town and out of reach from the American fleet. When the Americans realized that the K-387 did not contain the weapon they were looking for, ESO would be well passed Madagascar on its way around Cape Town towards America.

The ESO would travel a total distance of 8,345 miles to reach its destination. The trip would take almost 16 days. It would be an exhausting trip for a three-man crew but one that was achievable.

ESO was scheduled to surface at 8°25'S, 3°40'W or about 1,152 miles due west of Luanda, Africa. They would remain there until they made contact with the K-387. It was necessary for the small submarine to surface at least twice during the long trip in order to receive instructions from the K-387 and to replenish its air. Although surfacing was always dangerous, the only way ESO could receive its final deployment instructions - they could not communicate while submerged - was on the surface.

United States Naval Base, Norfolk VA

The Navy had 72 ships stationed at Norfolk, VA. Of those 72, two, the USS Stout (DDG 55) and the USS Klakring (FFG 42) were currently serving in the 5th Fleet area of operations in the Arabian Gulf and 24 others were deployed throughout the world. The USS Woodbridge (SSN-349) was on a tiger cruise in the Atlantic. The remaining 45 ships moored at Norfolk would be destroyed or rendered unusable. The damage at Norfolk alone would be greater than that at Pearl Harbor. In addition, the Navy would suffer substantial losses to ships stationed at Charleston, SC., Groton, CT., Little Creek, VA. and Kings Bay, GA. Only those ships stationed at Mayport, FL and two submarines currently stationed at Portsmouth, NH would survive intact.

Cmdr. Edward Raft, Executive Officer on the USS Dwight D. Eisenhower (CVN-69) was probably one of the first to notice the giant wave that struck them down. It would be the first of ten tsunamis, all over 100 feet in height and traveling at more than 130 miles per hour. His early morning routine of jogging on the deck of the great carrier would be his last.

The giant waves could not have been moving in a more lethal direction. Heading due east, they would first strike at Willoughby Bay turning slightly to the southeast heading for a direct hit at Pine Beach.

As Cmdr. Raft entered his sixth lap of the morning, he noticed what looked like, for the lack of a better explanation, a "wall" on the horizon. Strange, he thought, as he continued jogging, that cloud out over the ocean this morning almost looks like it's been shaved off at the top, almost as if it were a wall extending as far as he could see.

"Hey sailor," he yelled. "Doesn't that cloud over there look strange to you?"

The young deckhand quickly snapped to attention looking in the direction the XO was pointing.

"Yes, sir sure does. I'm out here every morning and I don't think I've ever seen a front approach from the east like that. Usually they come in from the west."

Cmdr. Raft stopped running and looked at the great wall of water that was quickly approaching. As he turned to ask the young sailor another question, the Eisenhower dropped from beneath him as if it were an elevator without brakes and the great carrier fell instantly to the seabed.

The depth of the harbor averaged 40 feet. Within seconds, the outrush of water reduced the depth to just 10 feet. Great ships moored to their piers suddenly dropped to the sandy bottom. Some sat upright for a brief moment and then fell off their keels and rested on their sides. The weight and mass of each ship's frame collapsed in a crushing blow sandwiching everything in between decks.

Almost as soon as the water rushed out of the harbor, the first wave struck filling it back up again and moving everything in its path. The pattern of outrush followed by another giant wave continued in ten-minute intervals nine more times. By the time it was over, it was difficult to distinguish what was once, just a short time ago, a completely functional naval base.

Two ships, the USS Briscoe (DD 977) and the USS Caron (DD 970), came to rest almost a quarter mile inland. The Eisenhower, which had been moored at Pier 12, collapsed on its side. The giant wave tore the flight deck off, an area of 4.5 acres, like a giant sail, sending it some 400 yards away where it finally came to rest on Powhatan Street. Three submarines, the USS L. Mendel Rivers, the USS Oklahoma City and the USS Jacksonville, all moored at Pier 23, were ripped from their moorings and thrown forward like missiles. They were then picked up in the outrush undertow with the Rivers coming to rest on Admiral Taussig Blvd., the Oklahoma City landing just inside Gate 1 and the Jacksonville, literally dragged down Hampton Blvd., finally came to rest just west of the golf course. The Chesapeake Bay Bridge Tunnel was totally destroyed between Cape Charles and Chesapeake Beach.

When it was finally over, more than 2,800 casualties in the Norfolk area would be counted. The damage on the eastern seaboard would be massive. The magnitude of the quake was equivalent to a small asteroid smashing into the ocean. The ten tsunamis that would strike the coast would move far inland. Norfolk, VA, the Delmarva Peninsula and Cape May, NJ would be engulfed.

From the moment Cmdr. Raft noticed the first wave until the almost total destruction of the Norfolk Naval Base, a little over an hour had elapsed.

In order for a submarine to kill its target, it must first find it. This was not that difficult for the K-387 since the target had found them. The SSN Leopard continually sent out sonar pings and was using her radar above the surface to help locate the K-387. In doing so, the Leopard had also given her position away.

A submarine's best defense is to avoid detection. The SSN Leopard had failed miserably in doing so. The Leopard had probably assumed that the K-387 would not risk an attack. This was a fatal mistake. Andrei Kobiak was not the type of submarine commander to hesitate when he felt threatened. When Sergio got the order to arm the torpedo bay he knew what the final outcome would be. He knew that the Leopard, once detected, had better hide and in a hurry. They did not.

The best way for a submarine to avoid detection is to remain as quiet as possible, listen for any sound and quickly attempt to identify it. Since a submarine's own noise can equally be detected by the enemy, submarines will usually lay low and as quiet as possible. It's a cat and mouse game. You find your enemy before he finds you. Other submarines, of course, use the same tactics as you do. Therefore, subs usually move around trying to find a good area of water where they can lay low and maneuver occasionally to mess up the other submarine's telemetry. Consequently, the best way to detect your enemy and not be detected is to move slowly and quietly. The Leopard had done just the opposite. And so, it was quite easy for the K-387 to attack her and kill her.

When sonar reported the contact, the K-387 got a clear signal and quickly classified the target as a submarine. The K-387's next step was to determine the target's course and speed. In these days of modern warfare, this is usually done using advanced computer technology, but good submariners still know how to do the computations manually. Sonar collects the range and bearing of the target and then compares it to its own course. This procedure is done repeatedly until changes in bearing and range showing relative movement accurately predict the target's course and speed.

The K-387 was ready for the kill. Modern torpedoes are wire-guided. A wire-guided torpedo, preset to run at a certain depth, can be maneuvered to a new depth or attack angle with the wire that trails behind it. When a torpedo is launched it locks onto its target with its onboard computer to determine the best attack angle. If a course change is necessary, a signal is sent over the wire and the torpedo responds accordingly. In addition, most torpedoes are programmed with search patterns. If the trailing wire breaks or is interfered with in any manner, the search patterns are automatically activated.

The torpedo's computer determines when the warhead will be detonated. This is usually done at the moment of impact. One torpedo will usually sink a submarine. While it's possible for a large submarine to survive a torpedo attack, most don't. It all depends on the size of the warhead that the attacking submarine is using. Although the Leopard was one of the newer Soviet nuclear submarines, the K-387 was carrying a warhead sufficient to sink her.

When Captain Kobiak gave the order to fire one, the crew could hear the distinctive swoosh inside the submarine. It took one minute exactly for the torpedo to reach its target. When it did, the outer hull of the Leopard ruptured immediately. Most of the crew died instantly as a result of the shock wave that reverberated through the submarine. As crucial parts of the Leopard began to disintegrate, the hull collapsed, resulting in the immediate implosion of the SSN Leopard.

Kobiak immediately ordered hard left rudder, a dive to 400 feet and all ahead full. The K-387 was now heading toward the Strait of Gibraltar. Andrei assumed that after the sinking of the submarine, the Americans would pursue him immediately.

"Tell me what's going on, Sergio?" Andrei asked.

Sergio was still in a state of shock. He somehow didn't think it would come to this but it had. The sudden realization of their mission and what it meant finally hit home. He realized now he would never return to Russia. They had just destroyed one of their own.

"Sergio, where's the American ship?" Andrei yelled.

"She hasn't moved, Captain. She's right where we left her. Probably scared to death she'll suffer the same fate as the Leopard."

Andrei gave the order for all stop. The K-387 slowly came to a stop. He then issued the order to surface.

"Sergio, we're going on top to take a look at our American friends," Andrei said.

Sergio knew better than to question the Captain's judgment but he was still shaken from the sinking of the Leopard.

"Captain, maybe we should wait awhile before we surface? Perhaps we shouldn't antagonize them right now. You know, so soon after the sinking," Sergio said.

"Have you forgotten, Mr. Serkiz, it's almost time for our scheduled contact with ESO."

USS Woodbridge

Temperature and moisture content determine the speed of sound in air. In dry air at 32° F, sound travels about 1,090 feet per second. As the temperature increases, the speed of sound increases. In addition, the speed of sound increases slightly in moist air because moist air contains more molecules resulting in greater speed. The velocity of sound is much faster in water. Almost five times as fast or about 5,000 feet per second at the same temperature. As the temperature increases, the speed of sound in water increases greatly. Sound velocity in water is a function of temperature, salinity and pressure. Of these three, temperature is the most important. If any of the three increase, the velocity of sound increases.

An earthquake produces sound waves that are known as bottom bounce waves. The sound waves are either beamed or bent toward the ocean bottom and then reflected off the bottom. Depending on the surface at the bottom of the ocean, the absorption of the sound waves can be substantial or none at all. If the bottom is uneven, more is absorbed and less reflected. The converse is true for an ocean bottom surface with little or no contour. In addition, the sound path that occurs in very deep water, where the effect of pressure causes increased sound velocity, the sound waves are bent upward. The stress fault that produced the quake, heretofore undiscovered, lay in an area that was as smooth as a baby's bottom. The resulting sound waves and their velocity were increased substantially.

It would take 10 minutes for the first acoustical wave to strike Woodbridge after the earthquake hit some 600 miles to the east. The first shockwave would strike with the force much more magnified than that in air. The nuclear attack submarine would move laterally almost 30 yards from the initial shock. The sound alone would be deafening. It would be the equivalent of being inside a tin can with someone banging on the outside with a metal hammer on every square inch of can surface.

George was in his rack when the shockwave hit. He was out of it after it hit. He awoke on the deck just as the sound was reverberating throughout the submarine. At first he thought he was dreaming. He quickly realized he was not. Regaining his senses, he called control.

The OD answered on the third ring. "Captain, I don't know what in the hell just happened but we've got a real mess down here," Lt-Cmdr. Dunn said.

"Have we done any damage control yet?" The Captain asked.

"We're checking that now, sir. As soon as I get the first report back I'll let you know. We did all we could do to maintain control. What in the hell was that Captain?" Dunn asked.

"I don't know. In all my years at sea, I have never experienced anything like it. Are we still maintaining 600 feet?" George asked.

"Yes, sir. We sustained minimal damage here in control. We have a few banged up heads, though. It was almost like something just picked us up and tossed us. And the sound, it was deafening. I'm sure we're going to have a few busted eardrums."

George hung up the phone and headed for control. When he opened his stateroom door, he thought he could hear some crying in the distance. Damn, he thought, why did this, whatever it was, have to happen on the tiger cruise? His first thought, as he headed for control, was that he must do whatever he could to prevent any panic with the guests. He decided that when he reached control he would get on the 1MC and talk to them. Then he remembered his two sons were on board. He quickly stopped and headed for their staterooms. As he turned the corner, he ran into Matthew.

"Matthew, are you OK?"

"Sure Dad. I'm fine. That was really cool. What did you do to do that? I thought submarines couldn't move sideways. Can we do it again?"

"Where's Michael?"

"I think he's sleeping."

George ran into the stateroom. Michael was still in his rack, as were Paul and David.

"You guys OK?" George yelled.

"Sure, we're fine. That was a heck of a way to wake us up though. Was that another emergency blow?" David asked.

George didn't answer. He quickly turned and headed for control. He was relieved his children and his guests were OK. There was an advantage, he thought, to those small racks after all. It was practically impossible to be thrown out of them.

When he arrived in control, he noticed the chief of the watch was bleeding from his left ear. Other than that, all seemed in order.

"What's the word from damage control, Bill?" George asked.

"So far, everything looks good. The engine room reports no damage. They're checking the reactor room now, but we've had no alarms go off, so I suspect we're OK there as well. The torpedo room also reports no signs of damage. I rounded up as many of the crew that I could and sent them throughout the boat to check on each guest to see if they are OK. We are getting some crazy readings on sonar, though, so I called the technician down to take a look at it. Otherwise, I think we're in pretty good shape."

George breathed a sigh of relief.

"What do you suppose that was, Bill?" George asked.

"Damned if I know, sir. We were sitting here at 600 feet and the next thing I know, it felt like my eardrums were blown out of my head. My ears are still ringing. And then, it felt like something just picked us up and threw us. We checked our bearing and we moved some 30 yards to the west. It almost felt like we were spinning."

The Woodbridge was not scheduled to surface until 0830. George, not knowing what had occurred, called a meeting in the wardroom to discuss the situation. His main concern now was not only for the welfare of Woodbridge, but primarily for his guests. If something was going on that they didn't know about that could jeopardize the boat, the only way they could find out about it, was to surface. By staying submerged, they were out of contact with the rest of the world.

"Gentlemen, whatever happened down here concerns me greatly. It appears we have minimal damage and only a few minor injuries. I'm inclined to surface immediately to find out just what is going on and get this boat back to Norfolk as soon as possible. Let's go around the table. I would like to hear from each one of you and then I'll decide," George said.

Each officer spoke starting with the XO. All agreed it would be in the best interest to surface now, make communication with COMSUBLANT and head for home. The only concern raised at the meeting was for the sonar, which appeared to have suffered some damage as a result of the sudden movement of the submarine. Since the Woodbridge was scheduled to go on an extended five-month cruise in less than a week, the opinion was they should at least attempt to resolve the sonar question before heading for port.

"Has the technician looked at it yet?" George asked.

"Yes, sir. It looks like some sort of software problem. He's not sure what happened. It was working fine before the incident. Since their software engineer didn't make the cruise, he feels the best way to try and fix it is make contact once we surface so he can have someone talk him through a possible fix," Bill said.

"OK, gentlemen, then let's take her up to periscope depth and snorkel. I want to use the diesel briefly to make sure we don't have any unforeseen problems in the reactor room. When I'm satisfied we're OK with nuclear, we'll take her all the way up and man the conn from the bridge. Once we're on top, I'll be in the radio room. Bill, I would like you and Mr. Berlin up on the bridge to take a look-see. Once we re-establish communications and find out just what in the hell is going on, I'll feel better. Let's take her up nice and slow. I'm afraid our guests are probably still a little shaken up and I don't want to upset them anymore than they already are."

Snorkeling on a submarine is a fancy way of saying they need air to run the diesel. The snorkel is simply a hollow tube that is near the periscope and is used to provide air and also allow for the diesel exhaust. It is maintained by a Chief Petty Officer, usually the Senior Chief of the Boat, and is probably the cleanest engine you will ever see. The diesel has twelve cylinders and is immaculate. The diesel is used for emergency power and for recharging the sub's batteries, which are used when the reactor is turned off. When the ship is running on nuclear power, they are on what they refer to as a quiet run. A submarine is anything but quiet when running on diesel. The noise can literally be heard throughout the boat and is deafening in the engine room.

When they left the wardroom, George went to sonar to take a look at what was going on. Damn, he thought, I knew when we left that software engineer home it was a bad sign. George wanted the sonar trials to be a success. If the damn stuff didn't work properly, they would surely be delayed in their next deployment while they waited for replacement sonar.

When George walked into the sonar room, the technician was staring at the terminal. This was not a good sign. He hoped he could depend on a straight answer when he asked if there was anything that could be done to help resolve the situation.

"Well, sir, as you know, I'm not a programmer. I work on the hardware side of the operation. Hopefully, when we get on the surface, they can tell me what to do. But I must be honest, I don't know the first thing about programming," the technician said.

George looked over at Chief Tanandra, who had been in the room since the problem was first reported.

"Chief, what kind of problem are we looking at here? Is it useable at all?" George asked.

"Sir, the low frequency readings seemed to be all screwed up. As a result, our range is drastically reduced. It's still useable but it's just not very reliable. I guess unstable is the best way I could describe it. They think some of the code was damaged when we lost power and switched to batteries."

"What about our UPS backup? Wouldn't that prevent something like this?" George said.

"Should have, Captain, but I suspect the batteries were jarred when we were hit resulting in an interruption of current."

"Thanks, chief. Let me know if there are any changes."

George went to control to prepare for surfacing. When he arrived, he made a brief announcement over the 1MC system telling his guests that they were preparing to surface and return to Norfolk. He briefly mentioned the incident and assured everyone that the submarine was just fine.

The OD gave the order to come to periscope depth and the Woodbridge slowly started moving toward the surface. As he looked around control he couldn't help but notice the concern on the faces of his crew. There was a look of apprehension that George had never seen before. Even though they had been through some tedious times during the last two years there was a feeling in the air that almost seemed foreboding. George didn't like it.

"Captain, we are at periscope depth. The radio room reports we are resuming communications. Request permission to snorkel?" The OD asked.

"Permission granted. I'm going over to radio. I'll be up on the bridge as soon as I'm finished."

When the OD gave the order to snorkel, the loud rumblings of the huge diesel could be heard throughout the boat. Bill gave the order for up scope and soon they were looking at darkness glittered by starlight on what appeared to be a perfectly calm night 300 miles out in the Atlantic.

George knocked on the radio room door. "Permission to enter. This is the Captain."

Jessie Meeker, the radioman on duty, opened the door, snapped to attention and granted permission to his CO. There are two places on a nuclear attack submarine that are restricted; the reactor room and the radio room. Both require Top Secret clearances. Out of a crew of a little over a hundred, only six possessed the top-secret clearance needed for these spaces. As would be expected, the Captain was one of them.

"What have ya' got for me Jessie?" George asked.

"Captain, I'm not sure what's going on. I attempted to contact COMSUBLANT as soon as we surfaced but I can't seem to reach them. I was just getting ready to take a quick look at the antenna leads to make sure we're still connected when you walked in. I even tried contacting CINCLANTFLT."

The Commander, U.S. Atlantic Fleet (CINCLANTFLT) headquartered in Norfolk, VA, is the U.S. Navy component of the United States Atlantic Command (USACOM). The Atlantic Fleet is responsible for the entire Atlantic Ocean, the Caribbean Sea and the waters around Central and South America extending into the Pacific (the Galapagos Islands); the Norwegian, Greenland and Barents seas; and waters around Africa extending to the Cape of Good Hope.

"Don't let me stop you. Anything I can do?"

The young radioman looked surprised that the Captain was asking if he could help. "No, sir, all I need to do is look under these cabinets to make sure none of the leads came loose last night. Be with you in a minute."

George picked up the phone and called the Bridge while Jessie checked the leads. "Bridge, radio."

""Bridge, aye."

"Bill, this is George. Take a quick look at the antenna and see if anything looks damaged. We're checking our wiring down here as well. Don't get near the damn thing, just take a quick look and see if you notice anything peculiar."

Bill shook his head as he turned to check out the antenna. He was a graduate of the Naval Academy, a Lieutenant Commander presently serving as the Executive Officer onboard Woodbridge, 35 years old, and George still felt a need to warn him about touching the antenna. I guess when you're the Captain of the boat you worry about things like that, he thought. George knew full well that Bill would never touch a live antenna but still he issued the warning.

"Everything looks OK up here, Captain. What seems to be the problem?"

"Don't know. We can't seem to raise COMSUBLANT or CINCLANTFLT on the hook. What's it like topside?"

"Dark and very calm. A little chilly though," Bill said.

George finished talking just as Jessie turned back around after checking the wires.

"Everything looks OK down here, sir. Let me try and raise them again."

The young radioman again made an attempt to contact Norfolk. Still he heard only static. He turned to the Captain to ask what they should do next when suddenly the radio came to life. The voice on the other end was not what they expected. Even so, it was heartwarming to know they had made contact with the outside world.

"I have received your transmission attempt to CINCLANTFLT and would like to be of assistance to you if I may. My name is Charles Stellson. I am an amateur radio operator affiliated with the MARS program. In case we lose contact, my call sign is XE7//WB6FCN. I live in West Palm Beach, Florida and monitor this frequency for the program."

MARS (Military Affiliate Radio System) is a program conducted by the Navy in which licensed amateur radio operators volunteer to provide communications to the Navy as an adjunct to normal naval communications. The mission of MARS is to provide emergency communications on a local, national and international basis and assist the Navy in their communication efforts during emergency conditions.

Jessie, although proficient in his field, never had an occasion to communicate with anyone but official naval personnel. It was understandable, therefore, when he looked at Captain Owens as if he had just heard his first communication with alien beings.

"Did he say what I thought he said, sir? Did I hear the word MARS?"

George wanted to laugh but the circumstances prevented that. He now realized that something terrible had happened while they were submerged that interrupted normal communications. Although he was familiar with the MARS program, he too had never actually spoken with them while at sea. Until now, he never had a need to. He wanted to explain to the young radioman what MARS was, but the urgency of the situation prevented that. He reached for the mike.

"Mr. Stellson, my name is George Owens. I am the Commanding Officer of the USS Woodbridge. We are a nuclear attack submarine presently on a tiger cruise preparing to return to Norfolk. Our position is 37°33′N, 70°20′W or about 300 miles east of Norfolk. Within the last 30 minutes we returned to the surface after spending the night submerged. Since surfacing we have not been able to reach our sub command at Norfolk. I request…"

The HAM operator cut George off. His voice was clear but a distinctive trembling was noticeable almost immediately. This was the first time Charles Stellson had the opportunity to use his radio experience in a real emergency situation. He was uneasy.

"For the record, I've noted your position sir. Mr. Owens, I'm afraid I have some rather bad news for you. While you were submerged, the eastern seaboard suffered terrible damage from what appears to be tidal waves of major proportions. Communications throughout the east are terrible. I'm not surprised you can't reach your command. The last news report I picked up indicated that an offshore earthquake was apparently responsible for what they referred to as "some of the worst tsunamis in recorded history" to make landfall. I'm afraid the Norfolk area was one of the hardest hit.

"I recommend we keep an open line at all times so I can assist you in your communication efforts. If you'd like, I'll try and patch you through to CINCPACFLT. OVER."

George looked at Jessie. The young man no longer needed an explanation of MARS. He looked like he needed to be resuscitated. George, quickly realizing the gravity of the situation, became almost fatherly. His job as CO was a demanding one that required professionalism and leadership. But, in this instance, he reached out and

140

consoled the young sailor like his own father would have. He knew in an instant that it was the right thing to do.

"Captain, I'm sorry if I appear weak. I'm scared. I just turned 20 last month and with my wedding only two months ago and my wife in Norfolk living on the base and…"

"Son, there is nothing to be ashamed of because you are fearful. You are not alone. If you were not afraid, you would not be human. Your courage will enable you to face your fears no matter what the consequences may be. I too am afraid. I am afraid for my crew; I am afraid for my family back in Norfolk. Don't ever be ashamed because you are afraid. Sometimes fear alone enables us to rise to the occasion. This time is no exception."

With that, George picked up the mike and continued the conversation with the radio operator from Florida.

"Thank you, Mr. Stellson. We will maintain this line of communication until the official lines are reopened. If you can get us patched into the Pacific Fleet Commander, I would appreciate it. I need to return this boat to shore somewhere to drop off my cruise guests. If you can, please find out the extent of the damage to the Norfolk naval base? Any information you can get for us will be greatly appreciated. I will maintain my present position until I hear from you further. OVER."

George handed the mike back to Jessie and told him he had done a good job. Any words of encouragement would surely help, given what they had just heard, he thought. He didn't let on to the young sailor but the situation worried him greatly. Never in his career as a naval officer had they lost communications with Norfolk. Damn, he thought, what in the hell is going on? He turned and told the radioman to keep the channel open with MARS and to summon him at once if communications with COMSUBLANT or CINCLANTFLT were resumed. He headed for the bridge.

The sun was just peaking over the horizon when George made the last step after the almost 20 foot climb up the ladder to the bridge. At least the world hadn't come to an end, he thought. Even though they had only been down about 10 hours, considering what he had just heard, it was nice to be topside again. The Navy requires at least two officers on the bridge and a lookout. Even with today's technology, Navy regulations still require a lookout when they are on the surface. George relieved Mr. Berlin and sat down next to his XO.

"Bill, what we experienced last night was apparently an earthquake that occurred somewhere out here in the Atlantic. It looks like we were lucky. I'm afraid the naval base was not."

"No shit, an earthquake out here? That kind of stuff is supposed to happen on the other side. How big was the goddamn thing?"

"Bill, did you just hear what I said. It looks like Norfolk sustained major damage. I'm not sure but there might have been extensive damage up and down the East Coast also. I spoke briefly with a MARS volunteer and he said…"

"You spoke with a what? George, what are you trying to tell me?"

"Will you listen to what I'm saying. The earthquake we felt last night caused several large tidal waves that struck the East Coast. As far as I can tell from the little bit of information that I have so far, the coast was heavily damaged. We can't even raise CINCLANTFLT on the horn. How many times have you been out and couldn't talk to home? It's bad Bill, real bad."

For a moment Bill was speechless. He wasn't quite sure just how to react to what George just told him. "We can't reach Norfolk!" Bill thought out loud.

American Embassy, London

Knox finally took a few minutes to relax. He sat down in his office to think about everything that had transpired over the last 24 hours. Damn, he thought, this was just supposed to be an ordinary couple of days—right! Not to be. Just when he thought things were getting on track, either John or Madge would run in his office with more bad news. His office was not opulent, as one would expect for a high official in the CIA. Knox preferred it that way.

Having grown up in Parkersburg, West Virginia, he was accustomed to the rustic look. Living within walking distance of the Ohio River, Knox couldn't remember when he wasn't outside playing in the wild and beautiful West Virginia countryside. To this day, he believed his childhood days of playing in the woods, hunting and fishing almost continuously and reading at night sharpened his instincts that would ultimately lead him in the direction of the CIA. There was no sitting in front of a television after school. There was a good reason for that. They didn't have one. Most in Parkersburg in the early fifties did not own a television. It wouldn't have made much difference if they did. The only station viewable was a local affiliate in Wheeling that stopped broadcasting in the early evening. After school was play time. It didn't matter what type of play it was. If Knox wasn't playing in the woods or fishing, he was riding the trains. They would jump the boxcars off Depot St. and simply take a ride. It didn't make any difference where the train was going. They would just ride. And when they'd decide to get off they would walk back. His favorite train ride was across the Ohio River, jumping off just before Belpre and walking to the Stones Fort Monument. There he would pretend he was Captain James Neal fighting the British.

Knox always knew he would not work in the chemical factory where his dad worked 12-hour days, six days a week. Three generations of Joneses had worked in chemicals. If you lived in Parkersburg, you either worked in the chemical factory or in the plastics factory. They were your two choices. Some traveled to Wheeling to work the coal mines but for the most part the working population of Parkersburg labored in chemicals or plastics. This, of course, was directly proportional to the average life span in Parkersburg being just a little higher than those living in Siberia.

Knox was just not an outdoorsman. He was a voracious reader. As soon as he finished his supper and daily chores, he would read anything he could get his hands on. His father would always needle him about his reading and how it wouldn't help him much when he worked at the chemical factory. Knox read anyway. He knew at an early age that reading exercised the mind just like running through the woods and swimming the Ohio or the Little Kanawha River exercised his body. He couldn't wait to go with his mother to the local A&P on Saturdays. For it was here he could buy the weekly edition of the little red encyclopedia for twenty-five cents. He read it from cover to cover. This, coupled with his daily play regimen, installed a drive in Knox that, to this day, still existed. Whatever it was he did, Knox always tried to finish first. And he usually did. He wanted to be the best at whatever it was he was doing. His mother even remarked that when Knox was just three years old, she would hear him out on the swing set betting the kids next door he could swing higher than they could. Even at that early age, Knox exhibited the fearless quality necessary for a successful CIA agent.

Knox had a way of weeding out the everyday bureaucratic bullshit that surrounded large government agencies. CIA was no exception. The Company was the premier spy agency in the world. It possessed the most sophisticated technological equipment expected of an agency that snooped on the world day in and day out. And yet, it was subject to the same bureaucratic disease suffered by most large government agencies. But somehow it all worked. Somehow, in the midst of the everyday mumbo jumbo, the Company did its job. These last two days were no exception.

His solitude didn't last long. John returned with the report on ships deployed in the Arabian Sea. "Here's what we've got in the area, Knox."

Knox looked over the report.

Aircraft Carriers: USS Carl Vinson
Guided Missile Cruisers: USS Antietam
USS Princeton
Destroyers: USS Fitzgerald
USS Oldendorf
USS Stout
Attack Submarines: USS Columbus
Amphibious Assault: USS Belleau Wood
Amphibious Transport: USS Dubuque
Landing Ship: USS Germantown
Fleet Oiler: USS Ranier
Mine Countermeasure: USS Ardent
USS Dextrous

"Where's the Columbus, John?" Knox asked.

John was prepared for the question. He knew the only ship capable of tracking down the small Iraqi submarine was the USS Columbus. He also knew what he was about to tell Knox was not what he wanted to hear.

"Her current position is 28°15′N, 50°4′E or about 147 miles southeast of..."

Knox cut him off abruptly. He knew what the coordinates meant. "Do you ever walk into my office with

145

good news? We need a break on this one, John, and so far we haven't gotten one."

John knew Knox was not voicing his anger at him. He was frustrated. John was just a sounding board. The news he had just given him placed the Columbus squarely in the Persian Gulf just southeast of Kuwait, almost 5,000 miles away from Cape Town, South Africa.

"I know, Knox. I feel the same way. It seems like every time we turn around, it's too late. I wish I had better news," John said.

"I know you do, John. Don't take it personally. Have our little friends surfaced yet?"

"Not as yet. We are monitoring the entire area very closely. As soon as they show their face, we'll get a fix on their position. It should then just be a matter of informing the Navy of their position so they can track them down. We have ample resources at CINCLANTFLT to handle the situation. In addition, I suspect the IUSS would pick them up before they managed to get too close to us. We'll nab 'em."

"Do we have any more data on the mini-sub? Have we contacted France to get the specs on the damn thing? It would be nice to know the capabilities of the little son-of-a-bitch. How in hell did the damn Russians get their hands on a submarine designed in France? Ya' know, ever since the end of World War II, those bastards have been shitting on us. Talk about ungrateful. Hell, if it wasn't for America, those sonsabitches would be...."

Madge ran into the office and ended his mini-speech. She was sobbing.

"Mr. Jones, there has been a major catastrophe in the States. Information is kind of shaky right now because communications are all but nonexistent but it looks like they were hit with tidal waves as a result of an earthquake somewhere in the Atlantic. It appears there are many casualties. This is just horrible."

146

Knox grabbed the report from her and read it out loud.

The United States eastern seaboard was heavily damaged from mammoth tsunamis resulting from a large earthquake centered in the Atlantic. Early reports indicate that one wave, striking at the mouth of the Chesapeake Bay, reached as far as the foothills of the Appalachians.

In Virginia, the Delmarva area was especially hit hard from Virginia Beach and as far north as Washington, DC. The naval base at Norfolk was said to have suffered extensive damage....

Knox had read enough.

"Well, any more 'good' news today?" Knox asked.

"I'm afraid there is sir. The K-387 sunk the Leopard!" John whispered.

Knox said nothing. He got up from his desk, walked over to the window and looked at the dreary London day that was developing. A rare sunny day would have helped his mood but it was not to be.

"John, get me the latest on the K-387. Find out if the La Salle is still in the vicinity?"

John turned to walk out of the office and almost forgot to show Knox the file on the mini-sub he received overnight. "We do have some more information on the mini-sub. I'm sorry, in the excitement over what happened with the earthquake, I almost forgot to give it to you. We received it late last night from the Russians. It looks like they decided to come clean about its existence. I think you might find it interesting. The data sheet is in the back." Without waiting for a response from Knox, John turned and left to get the update on the K-387.

Knox picked up the file and looked at the architectural drawing the French had supplied. He wasn't pleased they hadn't released the blueprints but the drawing

147

was explicit enough to give him a good idea of its capabilities. It was small indeed. Knox tried visualizing three crewmembers living in an area as small as this for such a long time. The Iraqis were desperate to travel such a great distance cramped up in a mini-sub no bigger than a large limo. The mini-sub was an unusual design. The sub's propeller was extremely large with a coating that appeared similar to anechoic coating that is used to coat the surface of a submarine. Knox also noticed the unusually large reactor area for such a small submarine. With a power plant like that, the little bastards were capable of traveling great distances, he thought. He reached in the file and looked at the data sheet.

Experimental Submarine Observatory (ESO)
Designed: Marseille, France
Commissioned: 15 June 1997, experimental
Length: 20.15 Feet
Beam: 10 Feet
Armament: 1 MK 32 Mod 14 Torpedo Tube
Crew Compliment: Three
Top Speed: 24 Knots

The ESO is the ultimate in quiet technology. Originally designed for use in ocean exploration, the design was altered using state of the art standards supplied by the Russians. In addition to its stealth design, it also utilizes a new revolutionary propeller system. The propeller rotates at a very slow speed, but provides sufficient power and emits very little noise. The mini-sub was built with an anechoic coating of eight inches. Conventional submarines have an anechoic coating no thicker than four inches. The additional four inches of rubber coating on the ESO renders it almost undetectable by conventional sonar. This, combined with the Akula specifications supplied by the Russians, enabled the French to engineer a silent and deadly mini-submarine.

In early 1998, the French, in conjunction with the Russian Navy tested the ESO off the New England coast. In doing so, the ESO evaded the IUSS. The IUSS, using fixed, mobile, and deployable acoustic arrays did not detect the ESO. Together with its propeller design propulsion and its nuclear turbines, the ESO was the ultimate in quiet submarine technology. Newer sonar technologies implemented over the years cannot detect the ESO. Three personnel man the mini-submarine. It is equipped with autopilot features not unlike those on airliners. Advanced computer technology enabled the designers to build a versatile submarine that could easily be maintained by minimal crew. The ESO is equipped with a dual anchor system, fore and aft, which provides unusually stable anchoring in high surf situations common to shallow water. After the initial trial runs and testing, the ESO returned to Russia for further outfitting.

Knox finished reading the report and walked over to the world map that lined the wall behind his desk. Staring intently at the southernmost tip of South Africa, he tried to visualize where the little sub could be at this point. He was certain now that the K-387 had dropped the ESO at Djibouti. Clever on their part, he thought. They deployed the ESO practically right under our noses. With a large American deployment in the Arabian Sea monitoring the Iraqi situation, one would have assumed they would make a run for it through the Mediterranean. It was risky indeed choosing the option that they did but an option that was paying off. We had wasted precious time, chasing the K-387, Knox thought. Knox was now faced with a situation that was looking more bleak as time went on.

The ESO was well on its way toward America and they didn't know where it was. In addition, the ESO was a stealth design making it damn near impossible to pick it up with conventional sonar. Knox was still staring at the map when John returned with the information on the K-387.

"Here's the latest, Knox, on the K-387. The La Salle is still tracking her but keeping her distance."

Knox looked at the report. As he started to read the second page, he suddenly jumped up. "Damn, what the hell was I thinking of? Damn it, I must be losing it."

"What are you talking about Knox?" John asked.

"I screwed up, John, when I ordered the Navy off the K-387. I reacted too quickly." He picked up the phone. "Madge, get me the La Salle's CO on the line immediately."

"Knox, if you don't mind me saying so, just what are you talking about. I think you did the right thing. We know now that the mini-sub is carrying the cargo and that the K-387 was only a diversion. Why on earth would we want to continue fooling around with the K-387?"

Almost as soon as he said it, it came to him. Maybe they were both losing it, John thought.

"The K-387 must continue to believe that we think she is carrying the anthrax. We cannot let on that we are onto their little secret. We will go after the K-387 in full force. And, when the time comes, we'll nab her. Right now, we need the K-387 and the ESO to continue to proceed as if their little plan has not been discovered."

Madge buzzed Knox. "I have the Captain of the La Salle holding on line 3, Mr. Jones."

"Captain, we have a change of plans. You are hereby ordered to aggressively pursue the K-387. Is your Phalanx weapon system operational?"

"Yes, sir, it is. Why the change in plans?" the Captain asked.

"Captain, it's imperative that the K-387 believe we are pursuing them to prevent their escaping into the Atlantic. You will not have to go at this alone. That I promise you."

"Excuse me, Mr. Jones but don't you think that will provoke the K-387? We just witnessed the sinking of the Leopard. I would like to keep my ship afloat."

"Captain, I can assure you the K-387 will not attack you like she did the Leopard. The K-387 will get what she deserves when the time comes. But for now, I need your ship to go after her aggressively. What's her latest position?"

"She just surfaced about 15 minutes ago. Currently she's about 600 yards off our starboard bow," the Captain said.

"Good! Maintain your current position until she starts to move. As soon as she does, I want you to arm the Phalanx and lock onto the K-387. When she realizes your weapon systems are locked on her, she will submerge. I guarantee it. Keep up the chase at close range. She will eventually surface again before she leaves the Med. I'm sure of it. And when she does, we will be ready."

"Mr. Jones, sir, please excuse what may seem like insubordination on my part, but the Phalanx weapon system is an anti-missile system. Phalanx is a fast reaction, rapid-fire 20 millimeter gun system. It is designed to engage cruise missiles and fixed wing aircraft. It was never intended for, nor has it ever been used in ship-to-ship combat."

"Yes, Captain, I am aware of that. I'm betting the K-387 is not," Knox said.

"Mr. Jones, I hope for God's sake you are right."

Knox hung up the phone. "John, find out if we have any guided missile cruisers in the area."

The K-387 had been on the surface for almost a half-hour and still the American ship had done nothing. Perhaps the sinking of the Leopard scared them off, Andrei thought. He hoped it had not. His reasons for sinking the Russian submarine were personal. His utter disgust for the new Soviet regime and its blundering attempt at capitalism was his only reason for taking the drastic action. He would show the stupid Russian bureaucrats what a real Russian was capable of. He would show them that he wasn't afraid of anyone, including them. Andrei picked up the bridge phone.

"Come right two zero degrees, all ahead one third."

"Aye, sir," the steersman responded.

Sergio stood with him on the bridge. He was unusually quiet. His reaction to the sinking of the Leopard was understandable, Andrei thought. He had not expected it. He would soon come to realize why it was necessary.

"Looks like our American friends are going to be with us for a while, Sergio," Andrei said.

Sergio, looking at the La Salle, said nothing.

"Let's see what they have in mind," Andrei said. He picked up the bridge phone and ordered all ahead full. As the submarine picked up speed, the overwash, that had been gently sweeping over the bow, now rolled in large gentle swells. Andrei looked back at the La Salle. He picked up the bridge phone and called control.

"Bearing and range of contact? He snapped.

"Bearing three-five-eight, range 500 yards and closing.

"Well, how about that. They're still interested in us," Andrei said. Still, Sergio said nothing. Andrei turned to speak to Sergio when the bridge phone rang.

"This is the Captain!"

"Captain, sir, we have detected a weapon lock on us. The American ship has initiated its laser tracking system and all indications are they have entered boresite mode. We definitely have a radar lock, sir."

The boresite mode is the first radar lock mode initiated by a weapon's acquisition system and is one of three modes. The second mode, or super-search mode, secures the first lock of the target and enters coordinates into onboard computers to expand the weapons field of view. The third and final mode is the vertical scan mode, which determines the final steering information prior to contact and detonation.

Andrei stood to look at the ship. She was indeed coming directly at them. Andrei calmly replied back. "Dive, Dive!"

Andrei and Sergio left the bridge and closed the hatch behind them. Andrei wasn't sure what the Americans were up to but he didn't like the "lock-on." Although the American ship had activated its weapon lock-only in boresite mode, Andrei must assume attack was almost certain and the Americans would carry the lock-on to its final stages. With the technologically enhanced smart weapons in existence today, it was a sign that you were only one button-push away from certain destruction.

Andrei was not pleased they had to submerge when they did. In only forty minutes they were scheduled to rendezvous with the ESO. It was important to reestablish communications with the little sub to obtain their position and to schedule their next and last communication that would provide the ESO with final instructions for the delivery of the anthrax. From the start, Andrei insisted he have full control of the operation. That way he knew it would be successful. Now he was faced with the possibility that he would have to sink an American naval vessel. This he did not want to do. The K-387's primary objective at this point of the attack was to provide diversion for as long as possible and deliver the final instructions to the ESO.

Andrei took the quick walk from control to sonar to get the latest bearings on the La Salle. When the K-387 detected the weapon lock, Andrei had ordered a dive to 300 feet, all ahead full. Fully equipped with its weapons package and a full crew complement, the K-387 was capable of doing 22 knots tops. Since they were operating with a bare bones crew and limited armor, the reduced weight increased her top speed slightly to 24 knots.

"Where's the American contact now?" Andrei asked.

"Comrade Captain, she is at bearing two-five-zero, range 500 yards."

The La Salle was keeping up with the K-387. Not bad for a ship that existed merely to ferry top naval brass to lush ports in the Mediterranean, Andrei thought. He continued his present course and speed which, if uninterrupted, would place them in the Atlantic in a little over seven hours. If the Americans continued to pace him, Andrei was sure they were not aware that the K-387 had dropped the ESO.

"Maintain current heading and speed," Andrei ordered.

He decided he would use the wait-and-see approach with the Americans. As long as they continued to pursue him and concentrate their efforts on the K-387, the easier it would be for the ESO to succeed. His main concern now was the contact he needed to make with the little sub. Once he established communications with the ESO and was satisfied they were on schedule and proceeding smoothly, he would submerge and head straight for the Atlantic. The K-387 would make one final contact with the ESO to designate the final target area in America. After that, the K-387 would exit the Mediterranean and head north.

Andrei wasn't at all concerned about communicating with the ESO. The K-387 was equipped with communications equipment that was designed and programmed to prevent interception by the enemy using the most up-to-date encryption known to mankind. It utilized a multi-function satellite-based system using standard interface units interconnected by a multidimensional database. The system is impervious to jamming, spoofing and interception. The ultimate in military communications, it was also designed to withstand nuclear-induced effects such as propagation absorption or blackouts and electromagnetic pulse (EMP), which can disrupt electronic circuitry and disable communications equipment. In layman's terms, it was practically impossible for the enemy to disable, intercept or decipher the submarine's communications. In addition, the system was capable of latching onto the closest communications satellite, using it to make contact and then disguising its transmission as a decoy. The beauty of it was, once the transmission was initiated, the message handling system would disguise the message to alter its origination site, scramble the original message and then provide a decoy message that would thoroughly confuse anyone attempting to intercept it.

The K-387 continued on its course toward the Atlantic with the La Salle close behind. Andrei looked at his watch. They would surface shortly to contact the ESO regardless of the position of the Americans. Andrei was sure they would not initiate combat. He determined the weapon lock-on was merely a scare tactic. The Americans knew they had a biological weapon onboard and they were not about to risk contaminating the Mediterranean Sea with anthrax.

Andrei turned to the OD. "We will surface in 20 minutes. I will take the conn in the radio room." He turned and walked to radio to prepare to surface and for the transmission with ESO.

Eight

The White House

The President's Chief of Staff, Charles Murphy, called the emergency meeting for 0800 hrs. in the Situation Room. The White House Situation Room is a 24-hour watch and alert center where the President, his National Security Advisor, the Foreign Intelligence Advisory Board and members of the National Security staff gather to discuss national security policy or, as in this case, a national emergency. The United States was currently in a national emergency. Also attending today's meeting was the Director of FEMA, Benjamin J. Keefer, the Assistant to the President for National Security Affairs, Joshua Stanhouse, the Deputy Assistant to the President for National Security Affairs, Admiral Randy Stetson and the Joint Chiefs.

Washington, DC had not escaped the wrath of the great waves unscathed. Although far enough inland to escape a direct hit, the force of the tsunamis had all but destroyed Andrews Air force Base, the already dilapidated Woodrow Wilson Bridge and briefly turned the district into an island. The White House Ellipse was completely under water as was Constitution Avenue, Pennsylvania Avenue east of Hamilton Place, F Street, G Street and New York Avenue. The east Wing of the White House lay just north of Pennsylvania Avenue in Lafayette Park. When the swell of floodwaters rushed over the Ellipse, it removed the southwest gate entrance to the White House and deposited it on the roof of the Old Executive Office Building. Debris was everywhere. There was no electrical power nor would there be for almost a month. The city water supply was contaminated and rendered unusable. All modern day conveniences became nonexistent. There was no trash collection, mass transit, emergency medical services or fire protection. Panic was the rule and, of course, looting was widespread. The nation's capital had been rendered a useless pit of disease and destruction by the biggest natural catastrophe to strike the country.

This was not the only national emergency to face the President this day. While the meeting had been called to address the tsunami damage and direct FEMA in its almost impossible task of emergency management, the nation was faced with a far greater threat. One with more lethal consequences than FEMA, the President or anyone had ever imagined or planned for. In direct communications with the CIA's London office, the President and his staff were working diligently with the intelligence community and the military to prevent the invasion of America. The news of the most recent Iraqi provocation was most worrisome. The most powerful nation in the world faced massive casualties from a nation it could have destroyed ten times over. A nation that had routinely ignored the international community by continuing to harbor terrorism in and outside its borders, and literally sticking its nose up at the rest of the world in defiance of human decency. Now, America was faced with the very real possibility that Iraq would inflict more destruction on the country than that of a nuclear attack. Until recently, biological terrorism had taken the back burner to other potential threats, and only now was the government realizing the gravity of the situation.

When the President entered the room, everyone stood. "Gentlemen, please be seated," the President said.

He began immediately. "I'm afraid we're in for a rather long day of it. We have two crises facing the nation that we need to address today and time is of the essence. The events of the last 24 hours, as I'm sure you are all well aware, have devastated the country. I'm afraid we will be facing a rather substantial uphill battle for some time to help bring the country to order. We are still receiving reports but the devastation to the East Coast has been massive. I've asked Ben Keefer from FEMA to brief us today on the efforts his Agency have begun and what he expects to do to help bring the situation under control. Ben!"

"Thank You, Mr. President. I wish I had better news than what I am about to tell you, but I'm afraid we were not prepared for the events that transpired. The tsunamis that struck the coast, struck almost without warning and were lethal. As you know, communications have been horrible so it has not been easy to piece together what little information we have thus far. I'll start with the most damaged areas first. As far as we can tell, we had ten large tsunamis strike the coast. The impact area ranged from Savannah, Georgia to as far north as Bridgeport, Connecticut. Starting south and heading northward, the areas that sustained the most damage were all of the coastal cities in North Carolina including, but not limited to, Wilmington, Jacksonville, New Bern, Edenton, and Elizabeth City. I'm afraid Virginia was one of the hardest hit. From what we have been able to determine so far, the Virginia Beach area doesn't exist anymore. The area is completely under water. The Hampton Roads area, including Norfolk, Portsmouth, Newport News and the entire Delmarva Peninsula were devastated. All coastal areas extending north to Atlantic City, New Jersey were literally wiped out. As we move north of Atlantic City, the damage starts to decrease proportionately but is still substantial. It appears that Long Island took the brunt in the New York area diminishing the impact for areas inland and further north. We've even had reports that the wave waters reached as far inland as the foothills of the Appalachians.

"FEMA has a sound structure that utilizes local and State programs as the heart of our emergency management system. Throughout the system, we have over 10,000 employees, including volunteers that have been well-trained in emergency management. In addition, we can tap the services of more than 30 other federal agencies to help in our effort. We have already started transporting food to those areas hardest hit. Also, we are trying our best to distribute potable water to these areas. Make no mistake about it, this disaster was a massive one, and will require a huge effort on FEMA's part as well as state and local governments. Our primary efforts at this time are concentrated on food and water. This effort, in and of itself, is a massive one considering the area of devastation. As soon as we feel we have a stronghold in the areas hardest hit, we'll begin providing assistance with medical aid, temporary housing and eventually providing generators for electric power to help keep hospitals and other essential facilities in operation.

"We have already received assistance from the U.S. Fire Administration with their efforts in coordinating fire service to the hardest hit areas. The National Fire Data Center is maintaining a database of local fire stations in each state including the volunteer departments. Where possible, when these stations have been disabled or destroyed, the Agency initiates replacement equipment and fire fighters for the area. We have volunteers from every state in the Union already heading this way. It is heartwarming, indeed, to see how Americans come together in a time of adversity."

The mood at the table was somber, more so than usual, Murph thought. Chuck Murphy had been Chief of Staff since the beginning of the President's term, some six years ago. He had called hundreds of meetings in this room, usually to discuss world events taking place outside this country. Today was different. While Ben did the briefing on the tsunami disaster, everyone at the table, including the President seemed almost catatonic. Although they had received a report weeks ago from the National Earthquake center about stress readings in the region, they had gone largely unnoticed in the everyday hustle-bustle of White House business. Even after the earthquake hit far out in the Atlantic, no one realized what was about to take place. Murph could remember a brief report that came across his desk from some university predicting the possibility of earthquakes in the region but again, it had been ignored. As a result, the country was completely unprepared for the devastation that resulted.

The second item on today's agenda was expected. The country did know about this impending disaster. They knew where it was coming from; they knew how lethal it was and they knew it would be devastating. The problem was what they didn't know. They didn't know how to stop it!

"Thanks, Ben. It is heartwarming, indeed, how this great country of ours comes together during times of adversity. If you would, please remain for our next item on the agenda. We will return to the tsunami disaster later, but I'm afraid your resources might be needed even more than you can imagine if we cannot stop our next impending disaster," the President said.

Although FEMA had been contacted by the CIA concerning the hazards of anthrax, it had not been an official contact. Consequently, the director was unaware of the situation that was developing over in the Middle East. Ben Keefer didn't have the slightest idea what the President was talking about. He had been summoned to the White House to report on the tsunami disaster. He couldn't imagine what the President meant when he referred to, "our next impending disaster." He was about to find out.

"At this time, I would like to turn the meeting over to my National Security Advisor, General Glen Alexander."

"Thank you, Mr. President. There are some in this room that are not aware of the situation we are now facing with Iraq. I will remain as brief as possible but I'll recap for those unfamiliar with the situation. Before I begin, I would like to add that we have Knox Jones from the London embassy on the speakerphone. Knox is our operative in the region and will be filling us in on the latest developments.

"For some time now, we have been observing a Russian submarine, known as the K-387, in the Red Sea that gave all indications it was simply on a training exercise. As you know, we monitor situations like this all over the globe. This particular submarine raised a red flag when we discovered it was decommissioned back in 1995. At about the same time, one of our UNSCOM inspectors was found dead on a highway in Iraq. Thanks to quick thinking on the part of an UNSCOM official, the dead inspector was quickly autopsied and identified to have residue of anthrax on his fingers. As you can imagine, this immediately raised suspicions so we quickly ordered one of our choppers out to the highway to look for everything and anything traveling that road. About 20 miles from the Jordanian border we discovered an Iraqi caravan consisting of three trucks and attempted to halt their movement. In an ensuing confrontation, two of the trucks were disabled but one was able to cross the border into Jordan. We then began to suspect that the caravan and the K-387 were somehow connected and that perhaps a rendezvous was scheduled to take place with the submarine in the Gulf of Aqaba. All indications to this point lead to the very real possibility that the truck that escaped into Jordan was carrying anthrax.

"We contacted the Russians and they confirmed that the K-387 was on a training mission and that it had been brought out of mothballs for this purpose. It wasn't until the submarine started making some unusual movements that the Russians became suspicious as well. We soon determined that the Russian submarine was a rogue warrior unbeknownst to its own government. It appears that one of their top-notch submarine commanders, who had become disillusioned with the new Russian government's attempt at capitalism, commandeered the sub to assist Iraq in a biological attack against the United States."

Alexander stopped briefly to gaze around the room. From the looks on the faces of the attendees, their reaction thus far was one of bewilderment.

"Mr. Jones, feel free to jump in at any time if I misstate any of the facts."

"You're doing just fine General Alexander," Knox said.

"Thank You, Mr. Jones." He continued. "In conjunction with the Jordanian government, we instituted road blocks throughout Jordan in an attempt to capture the Iraqi truck before it could reach its destination in Aqaba. Unfortunately, we were not successful. We managed to identify the Iraqi as a Republican Guard Special forces member, who, shortly after crossing into Jordan apparently ditched his truck and continued his journey driving a Jordanian taxi cab. The Jordanians chased him down and he was killed when his cab crashed in a fiery explosion. There was no sign of anthrax in the cab. It appears he made a switch and sacrificed himself as a diversionary tactic. Shortly thereafter, the Russian submarine started…"

The Commandant of the Marine Corps interrupted. "Where is the submarine now, General? Are we tracking it?"

"The submarine is currently in the Mediterranean and yes we have a ship on its tail," the General said.

"Well for Christ's sake why don't we just shoot the damn thing out of the water?"

"I wish it were that easy, General. The K-387 is not carrying…"

"What are we afraid of, hurting the Russian's feelings? How do we know they're not in on it anyway?" The General said.

"General, with all due respect, sir, if you'd let me continue, I'll tell you why."

"I'm sorry, Mr. Alexander. Please continue."

"The submarine is not carrying the anthrax! The K-387 was carrying a mini-sub beneath it and transferred the anthrax payload to them prior to departing the Red Sea. With respect to the Russian government and whether they are involved, I doubt it seriously. Yesterday the K-387 sank the SSN Leopard, a Soviet AKULA class submarine that was assisting in the Mediterranean effort. They are extremely upset over there, as I'm sure you can imagine. The mini-sub they were carrying is an experimental craft designed in France. It is the smallest nuclear vessel afloat and is a stealth design. We have a fairly good idea where the K-387 dropped the mini-sub but as of yet we do not have a contact. There's more.

"The anthrax strain that is now headed for America is a newly developed strain that, to the best of our knowledge, is resistant to all vaccines in existence. It was developed in Russia and they have supplied us with their research data. It is an extremely virulent form of agent that is capable of destroying large populated areas very quickly. We are currently evaluating the data but realistically it appears almost impossible to develop a new vaccine and distribute it before the anthrax reaches America.

"We have only one option, gentlemen, and that is to seek and destroy the mini-sub before she destroys us. This will not be an easy task. As I said before, the little sub is a stealth design capable of evading our current passive sonar technology. It won't be easy finding her. In addition, she is nuclear and small. So small in fact that she is capable of operating in extremely shallow water.

"At this point, I'd like to turn it over to Mr. Jones. He will fill us in on the latest information we have on the mini-sub and the K-387. Are there any questions?"

"Yes, Glen, I have a question," the President said.

"Yes, Mr. President."

"How do the Iraqis plan to deploy or deliver the anthrax on our shores? Are they just going to float up and dump it on our beaches?"

"No, sir. The anthrax they are carrying are airborne spores. Anthrax that is spread as tiny droplets in the air is much more lethal than any other form. It is tasteless, odorless and invisible. We suspect the Iraqis plan to use some sort of hand-held missile delivery system, the range of which we do not know. But any release into the atmosphere of this strain would be lethal beyond our wildest imaginations."

The President didn't say a word. He just looked around the table as if some magic trump card was out there waiting to be thrown. It didn't come.

"Mr. Jones, are you still with us sir?"

"I'm here, General Alexander. Are you ready?"

"By all means, Mr. Jones."

"Gentlemen, I'm sure by now you realize the gravity of the situation. I'll go over the latest information we have and our current plan of attack and then perhaps a question and answer session will be in order. We still do not have a contact on the mini-sub because she has not surfaced. As soon as she does, we'll be in a better position to plan our next move. The K-387 is currently about 140 miles southeast of Siracusa, Sicily heading due west at 22 knots. The USS La Salle is maintaining a 500-yard range from the submarine and will continue to do so. The sub is currently submerged but I'm betting she'll surface shortly. I suspect she is still in control and will make an attempt to contact the mini-sub. When she does, we plan to intercept the communication. Once we have done that, the K-387 is expendable and she will be destroyed. The Russians have already given us the go-ahead to do just that. As Glen pointed out earlier, they are eager for revenge.

"Our plan of attack is as follows: We have two guided missile cruisers in the area that can be of service to us and are within range of both submarines. The USS Anzio, which is currently visiting Porto Novo in Nigeria and the USS Normandy, moored at Bordeaux, France. Both of these cruisers are equipped with the MK 7 Mod 4 AEGIS weapon systems and the Tomahawk ASM/LAM long-range cruise missile. In addition, we've also enlisted the services of the Air Force and have two AWACS 707s joining the operation."

"The Airborne Warning and Control System, first deployed in 1977, is capable of providing an instant overview of more than 2,000,000 cubic miles. Housed in a rotodome on top of a modified Boeing 707, the rotodome revolves once every ten seconds scanning the area. The E-3 AWACS has several operational modes; the PDES/BTH mode which is used for land surveillance and the PDNES or maritime mode which is used at sea. The maritime mode can be commanded to vary the type of coverage for a specific area of interest thereby providing almost pinpoint accuracy in detection capabilities.

"When the K-387 surfaces and attempts communications with the mini-sub, we should be able to get an exact position on the ESO using AWACS and target both submarines. Using convergence coordinates supplied by AWACS, we can then arm Tomahawk missiles on the Anzio and Normandy and target them. Initially, we will wait for…"

"Excuse me, Mr. Jones, what is the ESO?" The Air Force Chief asked.

"The ESO is the acronym for the mini-sub. It stands for Experimental Submarine Observatory. The mini-sub, when first designed by the French, was intended for ocean research and was later modified using Soviet specifications," Knox said.

"Thank you, sir, please continue."

"When the two submarines surface we must wait for them to communicate with each other. It's imperative we determine where the ESO is headed if we have any hope of intercepting her before she reaches our coastline. We are operating under the assumption that the K-387 is unaware we are onto their plan. It is for this reason that we are aggressively chasing the submarine in the Mediterranean with the La Salle. As long as the K-387 believes we are unaware of the ESO's existence, the more chance we have in determining where they plan to deploy the weapon. Once we have that information, the K-387 will be destroyed and we will concentrate our full efforts on the ESO.

"My concern at this time is what type of support can the Navy provide us in the Atlantic? From what we've been able to determine, we have only one attack submarine assigned in the Arabian Gulf and she is currently in the Persian Gulf? What resources do we have in Norfolk that are still available?"

At first, the Chief of Naval Operations said nothing. He glanced at the President briefly and started slowly. "Mr. President, I'm afraid the Navy is not in the position to offer any support out of Norfolk. As you know sir, we suffered extensive damage from the tsunamis. I'm afraid the last report I received was not a good one. Of the 45 ships moored at the Norfolk naval base, none are operational. In addition, the harbor is not navigational. I have with me a copy of ships currently deployed in the Atlantic. We have one. The USS Woodbridge, a Los Angeles class attack submarine is currently about 300 miles off our coast on what was supposed to be a tiger cruise. I'm afraid, considering what happened as a result of the tsunamis and the scenario I just listened to that is developing, we'll be using her for much more. It is, unfortunately, a good news, bad news situation I'm afraid. Because the Woodbridge is on a tiger cruise, she left one third of her crew home to accommodate her guests. Consequently, she is severely understaffed. The good news is Woodbridge is performing a twofold mission. In addition to the tiger cruise, she is also testing a new sonar the Navy is considering installing in all class nuclear attack submarines. The new sonar is what we call the LAF/72 Series. It supports a new technology that utilizes a lower active frequency. As a result, it is capable of reaching greater distances with improved accuracy. It is, gentlemen, the most up-to-date sonar technology available to mankind. If there's a ship or submarine afloat that can locate your mini-sub, the Woodbridge is it. The last contact we had with Woodbridge indicated the sonar was working as expected. Since the tsunami disaster, communications out of Norfolk haven't existed. We are attempting to contact her now rerouting our traffic through CINCPACFLT. As soon as we do, we will issue her orders to remain onsite until such time we know more about ESO and where she is heading."

Knox could hardly contain himself. This was the first bit of good news he'd received since the episode began. We have a shot, he thought, albeit a small one, but a shot at nabbing the bastards. Knox really didn't care if the Woodbridge was missing a third of her crew. He did care about the new sonar he'd just heard about and its capabilities.

"Admiral, you've just given me the best news I've heard since this mess began," Knox said.

"Well, Mr. Jones, it won't be easy. The USS Woodbridge has a fine captain and a top-notch crew. As I'm sure you know, submarine duty can be strenuous under the best of circumstances. Missing a third of her crew will extend her to her limits, I'm afraid. We are fortunate indeed to have the new sonar aboard. We also have at our services two technicians from Darrich on board who can assist us with the sonar." The CNO was unaware that one of the technicians, the software engineer, was not on the Woodbridge.

"Gentlemen, we've been at this for some time now. Let's take a small break. Knox, please keep this line open. Give me about ten minutes and then I 'd like to see the Joint Chiefs in my office for a brief discussion before we return. When we resume, I would like to go over our final plan of attack once more, just to make sure we've got all our oars in the water," the President said.

As the President stood to leave for the Oval Office, everyone stood and waited for him to exit the room. The Joint Chiefs looked at each other but didn't say a word. They were all wondering the same thing. Who was Knox Jones and why was he controlling the situation and not the military?

ESO

The three Iraqi Republican Guards were rather enjoying their little trip aboard the small submarine. The craft had performed flawlessly up to this point and was surprisingly easy for a three-man crew to operate. They had updated the onboard computers with their current headings and the autopilot feature was turned on. In autopilot, the ESO was a pleasure. At first they were not quite sure if they could trust the automatic operation but after they had been released by the K-387, one of the first tasks they attempted was to test this feature. After almost 15 hours of continuous operation, the ESO had strayed from her course by 00.0034 degrees. A deviation that was negligible on the navigational charts. She was right on course. As a result, the three Iraqis quickly came to the realization that their mission aboard the little submarine would be much less strenuous then they had imagined. A nice consolation, they thought, considering they would not be returning. Their last patriotic contribution to Saddam and the liberation of Iraq was proceeding smoothly.

Because they didn't have to manually drive the sub, they were able to concentrate their efforts on the missile launchers they would use once they reached American soil. The launchers were the Soviet made Strela launchers that were popular with revolutionary groups. Initially designed as a surface to air missile launcher and used to shoot down Salvadoran planes during the Angolan civil war, the Strelas had been modified to launch biological weapons. The missile canisters that hold the anthrax spores consist of a fuse built into the cone of the missile from which protrude a long burster. The burster extends into the fill chamber that contains the anthrax. Upon impact, the burster disperses the agent in droplets or, as in this case, a coarse aerosol. With the use of aerosol, the weapon is extremely lethal. Anthrax in aerosol form evaporates more slowly and thus remains on target for a longer period of time. Translated, the anthrax aerosol missiles the Iraqis would launch on America would remain in the atmosphere for longer periods thereby increasing the kill ratio. The ESO was equipped with 5 launchers and 30 canisters. Each launcher was capable of launching 6 canisters before the launch rails would need replacing. Launching rails wore out quickly and needed replacing frequently. The Iraqis were not in the position to take the time to install or repair them. Once on the American shore, they wanted to launch the canisters as quickly as possible and return to the sub. The 30 canisters collectively contained enough anthrax to kill the entire population of North America.

The Iraqis entered the control room to disengage the autopilot. They were now only fifteen minutes from surfacing and their rendezvous with the K-387. They would surface precisely where they had been told, initiate communications to receive further instructions, and immediately submerge for the last leg of their journey. They knew they were really only vulnerable while on the surface. The Iraqis were well aware of American technology and what it could do. The smart weapons they used during the Gulf War on their country were devastating and extremely accurate. The Americans only needed coordinates for a target to earmark it precisely and then simply enter those coordinates into the missile's computer. Therefore, once ESO was on the surface, they knew the Americans would determine their position. But ESO had an advantage. They were not like the stationary bunkers, scud missile sites and military barracks that the Americans so freely destroyed. The ESO was a moving target and this made a big difference. On the surface, they would not remain stationary, for even one second. As long as they were moving, they had the advantage.

Unlike conventional submarines, the ESO did not have a periscope. The small bridge structure did however contain an area big enough for one man, was completely enclosed, and had what looked like a canopy on a jet. This enabled viewing from the bridge in all weather conditions but severely restricted what the ESO could see while on the surface.

The small submarine came to a stop. They slowly filled the ballast with air, expunging sea water, and the small sub surfaced. Instantly the ESO went into a zigzag formation moving at 10 knots, not fast by submarine standards, but enough to help prevent the Americans from pinpointing their exact location.

The three Iraqi Republican Guard volunteers, Mustapha Haddad, Abdulla Al-Hassan and Mahmoud Said were members of the elite Special Forces. Their devotion to Saddam and Allah would ensure their complete cooperation in fulfilling their patriotic duty. Mustapha was the Commanding Officer, Abdulla the other Commanding Officer and Mahmoud the third Commanding Officer. All three held equal ranks in the Iraqi military and would share duties aboard ESO until the end.

Mustapha was the first to look through the bridge window. Seas were calm and as best he could see, there wasn't any ship traffic in the area. Abdulla remained in control to steer the submarine and man the radio and Mahmoud assumed the duties of the navigator.

They had been on the surface for 10 minutes when Mustapha called control. "Abdulla, it is time to contact Andrei."

The Oval Office

The President returned within 10 minutes and quickly sat down. "Gentlemen, I wanted to talk with you briefly before we returned to the Situation Room. I'm sure you are all wondering why Mr. Jones from the CIA seems to be running the show. I thought it would be a good idea to brief you in here so we can discuss our plan of action once we return to the meeting.

"I have known Knox Jones since we flew together in the Navy back in '68. He is, gentlemen, one of the best we've got. He has been on top of this situation since the beginning, is knowledgeable of military strategies and above all, is one tough son-of-a-bitch. Be that as it may, it was my decision, as Commander-in-Chief, to place Knox as the watch officer for this situation. Not since WWII has this country been faced with such a precarious situation. I want to make myself very clear. The CIA is not running the show! Knox Jones is. Each and every one of you will report directly to Mr. Jones. If Knox fails then I assume full responsibility for the consequences. I do not, however, expect him to fail. I have the utmost confidence in his abilities and request you do the same.

"Gentlemen, I mean no disrespect. This is by no means a reflection on your leadership abilities. I have the utmost regard for the military, but considering what we've just gone through with the tsunamis and what we are about to face, I have decided it would be in the best interest of the country to place Knox in charge. Any questions?"

The Joint Chiefs knew this President to be forthright and this was no exception. Not one of them would raise an objection.

"OK, then, let's get back to the meeting."

They returned to the Situation Room and sat down.

"Knox, you still there?" The President asked.

"Yes, sir."

"Good, then let's go over everything one more time. Please continue, Glen."

"Thank you, Mr. President. Knox, what is the most current information you have on the situation?"

Before Knox could answer, the Marine Corps Commandant spoke up. "Mr. Jones, you mentioned earlier that you had two AWACS E-3 Sentry aircraft at your disposal. Is that correct?"

"Yes, sir, it is."

"Are you aware, Mr. Jones, of the problem the 552nd Air Control Wing had in Iraq in 1994?"

Before Knox could reply, the Air Force Chief exploded in anger. "That's a cheap shot General. Just what do you hope to accomplish by re-hashing old wounds?"

"I'm not trying to rehash old wounds, General. I'm just stating facts. We had a real problem in '94 and I'm concerned we might be relying too much on the AWACS to help us determine their positions. Positions that we will use to launch Tomahawks. It seems to me that we might only have one shot at getting the bastards and I want to make damn sure we aren't relying too much on the AWACS. I speak of course, when through a series of errors, our F-15s, supported by AWACS, shot down two UH-60 Black Hawk helicopters killing 26 people. I believe it was later learned that the mishap occurred because aircrews were either not adequately trained, were severely understaffed or suffered from poor morale. How do we know the same situation won't happen again?"

The Chief of the Air Force was not about to sit through this without further comment. "Let me assure you, gentlemen, that since that incident in the Gulf in '94 the Air Force has taken steps to avoid the situation my marine counterpart insists on discussing. First, the Air Force has new and improved aircrew training. All AWACS participants must pass stringent training that focuses on

174

academics, flight simulation and mission qualification training before they can become mission-qualified. In addition, we've increased the number of aircrews resulting in more time off. Hell, back in '94, our AWACS crews were deployed 200 days a year. We learned later that this greatly hindered their effectiveness and morale. We have learned from our mistakes, gentlemen. It won't happen again. The AWACS program is solid and trustworthy."

Knox was growing impatient with the military banter that was developing and quickly took charge of the situation. "Gentlemen, my concern at this point in time is not with AWACS reliability. I am convinced the program is sound and reliable. In addition to what the General just said, please remember that the AWACS program has been improved upon since the Gulf War. Since then, we have implemented the modified Block 30/35 E-3 equipped aircraft, upgraded four major subsystems, installed a global positioning system and improved our electronic support and data analysis. I do not foresee any problems."

He didn't say so, but the Air Force Chief was impressed with Knox's knowledge of the Air Force's preparedness.

It was the President's turn. "Knox, I am concerned what may become of the anthrax the mini-sub is carrying if we shoot her out of the water."

"That's a very real concern, Mr. President and is precisely why we need to destroy her while she is in deep water. The anthrax canisters must be detonated in order for them to disperse their content into the air. If the ESO were sunk in 25,000 feet of water, from what we have been able to determine, the threat of contamination would be minimized greatly if we could sink her without detonating their charges. The canisters would then sink harmlessly five miles deep in the ocean to lay undisturbed for centuries to come."

"And what if we don't sink her in deep water, Knox? What if she manages to get close to our shoreline? Could we take that chance and sink her in shallow water?"

"I'm afraid not, Mr. President. The risk would be too great. That's why it is imperative we get her while she is in deep water. If the ESO were to maneuver close to our coast, I'm afraid we would have to come up with some other way of disabling her before she released the anthrax."

"Then by all means, let's do everything within our power to destroy the ESO while she is in deep waters. We will keep this secure line open 24 hours a day, Knox, so don't hesitate to contact us. As soon as we determine the position of the ESO, I want to know about it."

"We just did, Mr. President. While we have been talking, we received word that the ESO surfaced within the last 10 minutes. I suspect we'll see the K-387 do the same shortly."

With that, Knox quickly disconnected from the conference and returned to the matters at hand.

Knox anticipated the K-387 would surface any minute now. Once on the surface, he was sure the Russian submarine would attempt to contact the ESO. The USS Anzio and the USS Normandy were in position and AWACS had already picked up the ESO. Knox was aware they could take the chance now and attempt to destroy the ESO without waiting for the K-387 to surface. It was a chance he did not want to take. Although the Navy was equipped with the best missile guidance systems in the world, they would still be attempting to hit a submarine no bigger than 30 feet from over 2,000 miles away. A miss would surely alert the ESO what they were trying to do and force her below the surface, perhaps for good. In order to make sure they didn't lose the ESO, Knox wanted to intercept any communication between the K-387 and ESO in the hopes of finding out where the little sub was heading. He would wait for any communication between the two and then give the order to destroy them.

The USS Normandy would target the K-387. The Tomahawk cruise missiles she would aim at the submarine had a maximum range of 1,500 nautical miles. Her current duty station provided coverage of the Mediterranean Sea from Iraklion to the Strait of Gibraltar.

The USS Anzio would target the ESO. Her position in Nigeria enabled coverage of the Atlantic from Cape Town to the Mid-Atlantic Ridge.

As soon as the K-387 surfaced, Knox would obtain the coordinates of the two submarines using AWACS and GPS and alert the two cruisers to program their Tomahawks. The satellite navigation systems were capable of providing the precise position of both submarines. Timing was crucial to obtain coordinates accurate enough to ensure a good hit. Knox would not give the order to fire until he had confirmation that any communications between the submarines had been intercepted and deciphered.

They would use the Signals Intelligence (SIGINT) satellites to detect the transmissions. SIGINT's network consists of intelligence analysis, encryption and analysis of transmission patterns over time to aid in that encryption. SIGINT is capable of intercepting communications at all frequency levels and strong enough to detect low power hand-held transmitters.

SIGINT consists of four satellites in geostationary orbit. Each satellite works in tandem to provide around the clock communication surveillance. Monitored by the National Security Agency, SIGINT was instrumental in providing one of the first warnings that an Iraqi invasion of Kuwait was likely.

When the ESO surfaced, the United States had her position almost instantly. She was situated off the coast of South Africa almost 1,500 miles due west of Luanda. She was not sitting still, however. On the surface, ESO was moving in a zigzag formation at about 10 knots. This placed her approximately 1,300 miles southeast of Porto Novo where the USS Anzio was stationed. The Tomahawk missile the Anzio would aim at ESO had a top speed of 550 mph. It would take almost two hours for the launched Tomahawk to reach ESO. Once initial coordinates are placed in the Tomahawk's computer, adjustments would then be made based on the distance from the Anzio to the target, the speed of the target and the direction it was moving and current wind speeds in the target area. Even though the Tomahawk is capable of receiving mid-course updates, which counteract drift inherent in gyroscope inertial navigation systems, the Tomahawk was only accurate between 12 and 120 yards. They would have to get extremely lucky to make a hit.

Knox had hoped they could scramble a few Harrier FA2s at them once they knew their location. It wasn't to be. The location of the ESO, some 1,500 miles off the coast of South Africa prohibited a reconnaissance with the Harriers. There simply wasn't enough time to scramble the jets. Too bad, Knox thought. Had they known where the ESO was, they could have solicited the help of the British Royal Navy and their Harriers. The Harrier is equipped with anti-ship missiles called Sea Eagles. The Sea Eagle is a sea-skimming missile with active homing radar. It has a range of 50 miles and can travel at Mach 1. If the Harriers were available, the ESO would have been a dead duck.

Knox knew the Anzio was a long shot. The odds of a direct hit some 1,500 miles out in the Atlantic were not good. It was precisely for this reason that they must intercept any communication from the K-387 in hopes of determining where the ESO was headed. The USS Woodbridge would have a much better chance of chasing the sub down if they knew where in America the ESO intended to release the anthrax canisters.

After the conference call with the White House, Knox called John into the office to give him the news about the Woodbridge. He also wanted John to get him the documentation on the new sonar she was testing. Knox was not familiar with the LAF/72 Series sonar the CNO had mentioned. The Navy had done a good job keeping this one under wraps. Although Knox was encouraged by the capabilities of the sonar, he was also skeptical. It is rare, he thought, that any initial test of any new technology went as planned. He was sure this would be no exception. If anything went wrong with that sonar, they would have to do everything humanly possible to fix it. If they were not successful in their attempt to destroy the ESO with the Tomahawks, the sonar would probably be their last chance to stop the delivery of the anthrax on American soil.

179

USS Woodbridge

George left the bridge and went to control. They still had not resumed communications with COMSUBLANT or CINCLANTFLT. His radioman was working diligently trying to raise CINCPACFLT but that endeavor also remained unsuccessful. By now, his cruise guests were taking everything in stride and seemed to be enjoying being on the surface. In an effort to provide a diversion from last night's turmoil, George permitted bridge visits, one-at-a-time, limited to no more than 10 minutes. Seas were calm and the view spectacular. He also had ordered a pizza party in the crew's mess. The cook on board Woodbridge made some of the best pizza he had ever eaten. He would stand it up against any commercial pizza available. With the flood of pizza and the bridge visits, his guests seemed to have forgotten what happened during the night.

George had not yet announced to the crew or guests what they had learned from the MARS ham operator. He knew the internal communication that existed on any ship would ultimately get the word out so for the time being he would leave it at that. Once he made official contact with the Navy and had more specifics, he would get on the 1MC.

Although George was concerned for the Woodbridge, he was equally concerned for his wife and son he left behind in Norfolk. Somehow he found solace when he thought about his two sons that were on board. But it was short-lived. Not knowing what had actually happened back in the Norfolk area didn't help his piece of mind one bit. The messenger from radio, stumbling into the control room, interrupted his train of thought.

"Captain, sir, I have a Flash (Z) message we just received."

Whenever a Flash (Z) message is received on a ship, it is always delivered to the Captain regardless of the time of day. The radioman messenger has access to every part of a ship including all officer's quarters and the wardroom.

George looked at the message. It was from the Secretary of the Navy and routed through CINCPACFLT. Finally they made contact with them, he thought. His sense of relief quickly vanished when he read the message.

FLASH(Z)
113500Z***********298773
TO: CO USS WOODBRIDGE
CNO BULLETIN
FM: SECNAV
MESSAGE FOLLOWS:

YOU ARE ORDERED TO PROCEED TO 28°40′N, 54°12′W AND MAINTAIN POSITION / /
ENEMY CONTACT AT 8°25′S, 3°40′W / /
CONTACT IS A NUCLEAR SUBMARINE EQUIPPED WITH BIOLOGICAL WEAPONS AND IS OF IRAQI ORIGIN. CONTACT IS STEALTH DESIGNED / /
UPON ARRIVAL, MAINTAIN SURVEILLANCE OF AREA / /
AFTER SUBSEQUENT EVALUATION FURTHER ORDERS WILL BE ISSUED / /
SECNAV REQUESTS IMMEDIATE CONFIRMATION OF SONAR STATUS / / - STOP
XXXXX END MESSAGE 113510Z

George looked up after reading the message and was numb. He read it again. The messenger waited for the required signature that the Captain had received the message. "Captain, I need you to sign the message, sir," the messenger said.

George signed the message and called the bridge.

"Bridge, control."

"Bridge, aye."

"Bill, secure the bridge. We're going to battle stations."

He turned to the OD. "Come to battle stations!"

"Is this a drill, sir?"

"This is not a drill," George said.

The OD briefly gave him a blank stare and sounded the order. "Come to battle stations. This is not a drill. I repeat. This is not a drill. Man your battle stations."

George wrote the coordinates down on a piece of paper and gave them to the quartermaster of the watch. The navigator helped with the calculation and gave the headings to George. George turned to the OD. "Come right two three degrees, all ahead full. You have the conn."

"Aye, sir."

"When Bill gets down from the bridge, tell him I want to see him in the wardroom."

"Aye, sir"

George calmly walked to the wardroom. As he walked he read the message again. He would like to submerge, he thought. Riding on the surface would slow them down considerably, but he had to keep communications open in order to receive further instructions. He sat down at the head of the table in the Captain's chair and picked up the phone and called sonar. "How we doin' Chief? Any improvement?"

"I'm afraid not, sir, we're still getting all kinds of screwy readings down here. I don't think we're going to see any improvement until we can get a software fix on this baby. What's with the battle stations announcement? Is this for real?"

"I'm afraid it is Chief. I'm afraid it is."

George picked up a pad of paper and started penning a reply when Bill walked in.

"What in the hell is going on, George?"

"Take a look at this!"

Bill read the message, and looked up at George. "What the living hell is this all about?"

"I don't know Bill. But for damn sure it isn't good. I just checked the coordinates where they're sending us and we're looking at 1,100 miles southeast of our current position. It sure as hell doesn't look like we're heading back to Norfolk. We're sitting here with a third of our crew missing, screwed up sonar, orders to proceed 1,100 miles out in the Atlantic and an enemy contact. That's not what I would call a rosy situation. Would you?"

Bill looked at George and they both came to the realization that what was transpiring before their very eyes was what they had trained for throughout their navy careers.

"Bill, this message is from the Secretary of the Navy. Something big is going on and I'm afraid we are squarely in the middle of it. Biological weapons! Just what in the hell are they sending us into anyway? Don't they realize we don't have full crew onboard?"

"I have this sinking feeling George we're the only game in town. My bet is, this is going to get a lot worse before it gets better."

George started writing the reply. "Bill, call a meeting in the wardroom at 1200 hours. Tell the officers to quietly question the guests on board and see if any of them are computer programmers or have any experience at all with programming."

George quickly penned the reply.

FLASH(Z)
113525Z***********298773
TO: SECNAV
CNO BULLETIN
FM: CO USS WOODBRIDGE
MESSAGE FOLLOWS:

PROCEEDING TO 28°40′N, 54°12′W AND WILL MAINTAIN POSITION / /
UPON ARRIVAL, WILL MAINTAIN SURVEILLANCE OF AREA / /
SONAR IS NOT OPERATIONAL— REPEAT SONAR IS NOT OPERATIONAL. APPEARS UNIT WAS DAMAGED FROM SHOCK WAVE. PROBLEM APPEARS TO BE SOFTWARE RELATED. TECHNICIAN ONBOARD IS NOT, REPEAT, NOT SOFTWARE ENGINEER / /
REQUEST SECNAV CONTACT DARRICH FOR FURTHER INSTRUCTIONS / /
AWAITING FURTHER INSTRUCTIONS / / – STOP.
XXXXX
END MESSAGE 1132610Z

George took the reply down to the radio room for transmission and returned to the wardroom for the meeting.

He passed out copies of the message they had received and began the meeting.

"Gentlemen, it looks as though our tiger cruise has been extended. As you know, we are missing almost a third of the crew. I would like to go around the room for your opinion as to where we are most in need of help and what you think we can do to get by. Until we receive further orders, I will assume we are operating under wartime conditions. The Woodbridge will remain in battle stations. This is not going to be easy especially operating without a full crew complement. Sonar is not working properly and is our highest priority at this moment. If CINCPACFLT cannot patch us into Darrich and get a programmer online, we might be in a world of trouble. I asked Bill to see if any of our guests onboard…"

"Captain, we have a guest onboard who says he's done some programming. It's Chief Tanandra's brother-in-law. I don't know what language he's programmed in but he says he has some programming experience," Lt. Berlin said.

"I assume you're talking about Scott Schneider?"

"Yes, sir. I was asking around in the crew's mess and he overheard me. He offered to help in any way he could."

"We'll take all the help we can get. While we're sitting here, go see if you can find him and also check with the technician from Darrich and see if he has any tech manuals with him that might possibly help us out."

Lt. Berlin left and George continued. "Out of the 14 guests we have on board, we just might have to use 12 of them to help us out. I don't want to extend the crew too much, especially since we are in battle stations. Of course, Matthew and Willy are out of the question. Although Randy Geshire is only 15, he's probably old enough to pitch in, perhaps in the mess hall. As far as the others are concerned, see if any of them have prior military experience and, if so, what it was?"

"Captain, my father was in the Navy during WWII. He was a quartermaster. I'm sure he could be of assistance in control," Lt. Archibald said.

"OK Lieutenant. I'm sure he can. I think it's time to get together with our guests and go over the situation. For right now, let's just say we have been ordered to do more tests on our sonar and will not be returning as scheduled. It might be a good idea to go over the disaster that struck the coast. I'm sure everyone is wondering just how things are back home. Lieutenant would you please set up a meeting in the crew's mess in about 15 minutes?"

"Aye, sir."

"By now, most of you have read the orders we received. I know as much as you do, which isn't a whole lot. None of us have served in a combat situation but I am confident we can and will rise to the occasion. I expect when we receive additional orders, we'll know more. But for right now, like I said before, we are going to operate this submarine under wartime conditions. Considering that we received our orders from SECNAV, I don't think this is an overreaction on my part. Something big is brewing and we have been called on to help rectify the situation. Our Iraqi friends are heading this way in a submarine that is a stealth design and I'll bet the farm they're not on a tiger cruise." George heard a slight chuckle around the room.

"I suspect our job will be to catch her before she unloads her payload. A payload, I might add, we'll probably be seeing a lot more of as time goes on. America welcomed in the nuclear age in 1945. Let us hope Iraq is not successful in welcoming in the biological warfare age. Our job will be to prevent that."

Lt. Berlin returned with Scott and the Darrich technician.

"Come on in gentlemen. Scott, Lt. Berlin tells me you have some programming background. We have new sonar that's on the blink and we seem to think it's some kind of bug in the program. It was working fine until our little mishap last night. The chief seems to think that something got fried when we lost power temporarily and had to go on battery power. The sonar is extremely important to us, Scott, so anything you can do to help would be greatly appreciated."

"I'll do whatever I can, Captain. I am not a programmer by trade. I have worked in systems for the past 25 years but primarily from the analytical side of it. I have

186

done some programming in several languages but mostly as a hobby. I just want you to know up front what my qualifications are."

"That's good enough for me, Scott. Based on what you just told me, you've got more qualifications than anyone else has on this submarine. As of now, consider yourself working for the Navy."

George turned to the technician who had been silent up to this point. "What can you tell us, Jack? Do you have any specs that can help Scott?"

"I have a copy of the systems specs that Steve left behind. He left them with me just in case something went wrong. Frankly, I don't know why, because I have never worked on the software side of the project. But anyway, here it is. I hope it helps?"

George took a quick look at the specs and handed them to Scott. "Scott, I hope this can be of assistance to you. If you need anything else, please let me know immediately. You have full access to sonar. I'll tell the chief to give you a set of keys."

Scott, looking somewhat sheepish, took the specifications. "I don't know what to say, Captain, other than I will do my best. I'll review the specs as quickly as possible and see what I can do." With that, Scott and Jack left the wardroom and headed for sonar.

"OK, gentlemen, let's hope Scott can help us out. It's about time to go down to the crew's mess and discuss the situation with everyone. As soon as we finish, I'd like to come back here to go over a few more things."

K-387

As soon as the K-387 surfaced, Andrei made contact with the ESO. They were right on schedule. He would waste no time communicating coordinates to the mini-sub. Andrei was well aware that once he tried to make contact with ESO, the Americans would realize the K-387 was not alone in this venture. It's possible they already knew, he thought. Perhaps the corrupt Russian government told them the K-387 was carrying a mini-sub when they realized what he had done. Andrei wasn't at all concerned if that was the case. If the Americans knew about the mini-sub, he was certain they didn't know where he deployed it. They would be looking for a needle in a haystack and the odds of them finding that needle were slim indeed. The ESO was almost impossible to detect with conventional sonar and, because of its small size, it was difficult to detect when surfaced. He picked up the mike and called the ESO. Within seconds he was speaking with Abdulla.

"Comrade Abdulla this is Andrei. I would like to congratulate you on your mission thus far. We are proceeding as planned and are on schedule. What is the status of ESO? Has she performed adequately?"

"Oh yes, Comrade Captain. The little sub is everything they said she would be. The autopilot feature is most enjoyable and enables us to tend to other duties. We are very pleased."

"Good! We are, my friends, about to finish our war with America. It is what we have been dreaming about and planning since the beginning of the Gulf War. It is now time to win that war. And we will. I will say this only once Abdulla. Are you ready?"

"Yes Captain, I am ready."

"You are to proceed to 24°48′N, 49°1′W. You are to remain submerged until you reach this position. You will then surface to receive your final deployment orders. Is this understood?"

Abdulla repeated the order to Andrei. "I have placed the order in the log and we will proceed immediately. Comrade Andrei, where will we be when we reach this position?"

Although Andrei knew precisely where this would place them, some 1900 miles southeast of Washington, DC, Andrei would not reveal this to the ESO. Andrei's vast experience as a sea captain had taught him over the years not to divulge information to subordinates. They simply didn't have a need-to-know. "That is not your concern my friend. Your only concern is to arrive at those coordinates on time. Is that understood?"

"I understand Comrade Captain. We will be there."

Andrei terminated the communication and called the control room.

"I will take the conn on the bridge."

"Aye, Captain, transferring the conn to the bridge," the OD replied.

Andrei climbed the ladder to the bridge confidant the ESO would succeed. He wanted to wait until ESO was in position before issuing the final instructions to the little sub. There was another reason he wanted to wait. He had not decided where they would attack. He would make this decision at the last possible moment to perhaps capitalize on any unforeseen circumstances that might be beneficial to their effort. Unbeknownst to Andrei, those circumstances had already taken place. The K-387 had not heard the earthquake news and the destruction that had occurred on the East Coast of the United States. A mistake he would later learn to regret. Had he known about the tsunami disaster he could have issued orders to the ESO with his latest transmission. The K-387 was not aware of the extensive damage to the U.S. because he had ordered radio silence. Even though they were equipped with the latest jamming technology, Andrei was from the old school. After receiving the message from the La Salle earlier, he had ordered all communications equipment shut down until they were ready to contact ESO. Had it not been for his radioman who left the line open after their ESO transmission, the K-387 might never had known about the disaster that struck America and the opportunities it would provide.

"I see our American friends are staying with us, Sergio."

"Yes, sir. They continue to maintain pace with us, although it appears they no longer have their weapons locked on us."

In the excitement about contacting ESO, Andrei had forgotten about that little problem. It was unlike him to disengage himself from something as important as that, he thought. A mental lapse he would not tolerate. Andrei, like most of us, was exceptionally hard on himself whenever he made a mistake. He was, after all, a trained submarine commander who was not supposed to make mistakes. He would not, however, reveal this weakness to Sergio.

"That is good Comrade. I think they were trying to scare us before. If it happens again, I want to know about it immediately."

"Aye, sir."

While Andrei and Sergio talked on the bridge, the radioman below was facing a crisis of his own. The news copy that came over the wire told of devastating damage to the United States. He knew Andrei would want to know about this. It was the type of information Andrei could use in deciding where to attack the Americans. He also knew that, by leaving the lines open, he had violated Andrei's orders to maintain radio silence. If he delivered the news to Andrei, he surely would be incensed that he had disobeyed orders. On the other hand, if he didn't deliver it, Andrei would not know of the American disaster. The young radioman was well aware of what happens to those who disobey orders in the Soviet Navy. He had seen summary executions take place within minutes of disobedience. He really hadn't disobeyed the order; he had inadvertently left the radio on after their communication with ESO. This surely would make a difference in the eyes of the Captain. Especially since the news he would deliver would be most welcome. He reached for the bridge phone.

Sergio answered on the first ring.

"Comrade, this is the radioman. I have received a message the Captain should see immediately."

Sergio handed the phone to Andrei without saying a word.

"This is the Captain."

The radioman decided to tell as much as he could and as fast as he could. "Comrade Captain, sir, I have received a message that indicates America has suffered terrible destruction as a result of a major earthquake. Their entire East Coast has been struck hard by tsunamis. I will bring it to the bridge if…"

Andrei cut him off. "I'll be right there."

The smell of fresh brewed coffee permeated Knox's office. To this day, Knox would grind his own coffee beans. It rekindled those pleasant memories of the weekly A&P visits. The first thing he would do when he walked in the store was to go over to the coffee grinder and smell the fresh ground 8 o'clock coffee. He drank it non-stop from the minute he awoke and until he went to bed. And he slept like a baby.

"Knox, we've got the K-387 on the surface and CINCPACFLT made contact with the Woodbridge. We've got the two cruisers standing by. NSA is monitoring SIGINT but has not detected any communication between the two," John said as he entered the office.

"No communication? What's the K-387 doing?"

"Just sitting there dead in the water," John said.

"Then she must be trying to connect with the ESO." He yelled for Madge. "Madge, see if you can get me a direct patch into the NSA. I want to monitor their surveillance efforts."

Knox walked over to get another cup of coffee. Before he could return to his desk, Madge had the NSA on a secure line.

"This is Knox, what's going on over there?" Introductions were no longer necessary. By now, everyone knew who Knox Jones was and what was at stake.

"Mr. Jones, it's the strangest thing. Initially we thought we had intercepted their communications. But when we downloaded the connection from SIGINT, we had a message that originated in Australia and received in New Zealand. The message appeared to be some sort of communication between two weather stations. As a result, we again keyed in the coordinates for the two submarines, made a connection and downloaded immediately. I'm afraid the results were the same. Only this time we picked up a television broadcast out of Sweden. We're looking into the matter now. Perhaps there has been some recent solar activity that might be interfering with the SIGINT satellite network."

Knox knew what it was. What he didn't know is how they were doing it.

"They're scrambling their transmission and somehow decoying it. We have got to intercept their communication. If we don't find out ESO's destination, our chances of finding the sub are slim to none," Knox said.

"Mr. Jones, we don't believe that's possible, sir. Our GPS Digital Tracking System is state-of-the-art and is configured with the latest up-to-date surveillance software. As you know, we are using the MERCURY signal intelligence spacecraft that is equipped with the latest encryption and de-scrambling technology. The bottom line is there just isn't a communication out there that we can't pick up."

"Sir, quite frankly, I don't care what kind of goddamn fancy equipment you are using. I do know this. It isn't properly detecting the communication between the K-387 and ESO. Those two submarines are talking to each other and we need to know what they are saying. Is that understood?"

"Yes, sir. I'll relay your concerns to the front office. We are still analyzing the two transmissions we intercepted. If you are correct, we'll figure a way out to decipher their transmissions. That I guarantee you, Mr. Jones."

Knox turned his attention to the USS Woodbridge. The Woodbridge had been ordered to its new location using the coordinates Knox had supplied. The reply they received from the Woodbridge concerned him greatly. They had reported their sonar was not working properly as a result of damage the submarine sustained when struck by the earthquake shockwave. The Woodbridge indicated they thought it was a software problem and they did not have a software engineer onboard.

Knox was now faced with two very serious problems. First, they had not been successful in intercepting and deciphering communications between the K-387 and ESO and now, the submarine Knox was counting on to seek and destroy the ESO, reported malfunctioning sonar. Again, he yelled to Madge.

"Let's get Darrich on the secure line also. Let me know when they're connected. I want a three-way between Darrich, CINCPACFLT and the USS Woodbridge."

Within minutes, Madge had the conference call hookup he requested. Knox was now talking direct to Darrich and CINCPACFLT. They were in the process of trying to raise the Woodbridge. As soon as they made the connection, they would join the conversation.

"Gentlemen, we have to move very fast on this one. To whom am I speaking with at Darrich?"

"Mr. Jones, my name is Steve Wilson. I am the Program Director for the LAF/72 sonar project."

"Mr. Wilson, we need to get a programmer from your group to link up directly with the USS Woodbridge. Something's gone wrong with the LAF/72's software and the Woodbridge is without a programmer."

"I've got one coming over as we speak, Mr. Jones. We think the best way to approach this problem is to step through the program line by line until we find out where the problem is. Our hardware technician on the sub should be able to do this along with the programmer here. Once we find the damaged code, it will be a simple matter of uploading the fix directly to the Woodbridge. We will need a direct line to the Woodbridge and that line will have to remain open until we find the problem. It can be a time consuming process but we should be able to find out where the error is."

The Woodbridge was now connected to the call. "This is Captain Owens. We have a civilian onboard who has limited programming experience. I've asked him to try and determine where the problem is. Do you recommend we wait until your programmer is ready?"

"Captain, we do not recommend anyone other than a skilled Darrich software engineer attempting to resolve the software problem. An inexperienced programmer could cause more damage and make things worse than they already are. Our programmer should be here any minute now and we can get started," Wilson replied.

"Knox Jones speaking here. Mr. Wilson, we will keep the line open to the Woodbridge indefinitely. Mr. Owens, I agree with Mr. Wilson. Pull your novice programmer off now before we really screw up the stuff. Gentlemen, let's get this done as soon as possible. It is imperative we have that sonar working properly to have any luck at all in finding the ESO. Captain Owens, you are to remain on the surface until we get the software fixed. What is the ETA at your location?"

"If we can maintain 22 knots, we're looking at a little over 42 hours. It is difficult to maintain that speed on the surface. Submarines travel faster submerged. In addition, on the surface we are much more vulnerable to attack. As soon as we get the sonar repaired, we can submerge and max our speed to 24 knots.

Regarding the programmer, I'd like to have my volunteer sit in while the Darrich programmer is attempting to resolve the problem. It may help if we lose communications to have someone familiar with what they are doing. Does anyone object to that?"

"That's fine, Captain," Wilson said. "Good idea Captain," Knox replied.

"OK, gentlemen, until we get the sonar fixed, we will maintain these open lines. Mr. Wilson, as soon as your programmer arrives on site you are to let me know immediately," Knox said.

Knox got up, stretched and walked over to Madge's desk just outside his door.

"Madge, I'm going to take a quick break down the hall. Buzz John and tell him to meet me in my office in ten minutes. Do we still have an open line with the Normandy and the Anzio?"

"Yes, Mr. Jones. All lines are open and will remain so, just like you ordered."

Madge was used to Knox and his worrisome habits. He knew the lines were open but he somehow needed that little extra comfort just hearing her say so. Knox continued down the hall and Madge started to call John when he turned the corner.

"Where's Knox headed?"

"I think he needs to make a pit stop. Probably had two pots of coffee already today and it's not yet 10 o'clock. He wants you in his office in ten minutes."

John went in and sat down. Working for Knox Jones was better than working for the President of the United States, he thought. His energy was endless and his work habits exceptional. If there was one man who could help the country out of this mess, it was Knox. John teased him occasionally about entering politics. John would say something like, "Ya' know Knox, you would make a great President. Ever think of running?" And Knox always had the same reply. "Sorry old bean. That's not for me. I'd rather push marbles around the parking lot with my nose than put up with that abuse." John would laugh and go about his business all the while thinking how great he would be for the country.

Knox walked back in and went right for the coffee. "Want a cup John? Nothing like a fresh pot!"

"No thanks, Knox. I've had my limit for the day. How can you drink that much coffee? If I drank as much caffeine as you do, you'd have to peel me off the ceiling. I don't know how you do it."

"Practice my man, practice. John, I wanted to talk some more with you about my plan of attack. I want your honest opinion, John. No bullshit, OK. What do you think our chances are at nailing the ESO?"

John was used to the routine. He had reviewed the plan with Knox over and over again. But that's how Knox was. He needed that reassurance.

"I think we've got a chance to get her before she gets too close."

"How much of a chance?" Knox interrupted.

"Well Knox, if we get lucky with the Tomahawks and…"

"Damn it, John, I said no bullshit. How much of a chance?"

"At best 50/50. You know as well as I do the Tomahawks don't do that well on moving targets. The best computer programs in the world can't take into account all the variables we're dealing with in trying to hit a moving target from over 1,500 miles away. We can calculate down to a square inch on a coordinate that isn't moving. But add in a target that's moving in a zigzag pattern, variable sea conditions and wind speed, and we're going to have to get real lucky."

"I agree. Although I think we're looking at something more like 30/70. Our only real hope lies with the USS Woodbridge and the sonar she is carrying. I did a little reading last night on our current sonar capabilities and neither the active or passive variety has much of a chance of detecting a submarine in 50 million miles of ocean. A nuclear submarine moving at 18 knots radiates about 28 decibels at 180 feet. About the same as a utility vehicle would on a highway. The noise from the submarine is easily drowned out by other factors in the ocean. Factors like waves, whales, schools of fish, etc. If the ambient noise is louder than the radiated noise, conventional sonar won't pick it up.

"Also, a sub's stealth is greatly increased by underwater acoustics. Our best submarines can go as deep as 3,500 feet. At that depth, the ocean is comprised of three thermal layers. The shallow layer is relatively warm. Then there's the thermocline layer, which is colder as depth increases. And finally, at the lowest layer temperatures level off."

"Knox, where we going with this?" John asked.

"Hold on John, you'll see." He continued.

"The noise a submarine makes as it's moving through the water can propagate in several different paths. If a submarine is in the surface layer, the sound waves she radiates can stay at that level and never get down to a deep-running submarine that is running passive sonar. Therefore, unless the attacking submarine's sonar is active in the first and second levels, they will never detect their target.

"The LAF/72 sonar the Woodbridge is carrying is the biggest improvement in sonar technology in the last 20 years. The sonar operates at a very low frequency, which enables it to cover a much greater distance. Also, and here's the best part, it has a superior signal processing computer that is capable of identifying variant sounds that distort conventional sonar. In other words, you can't hide from it. Not in the shallows or in the deepest part of the ocean. It's like comparing a modem to a T1 Fiber-optic connection. The LAF/72 would be the equivalent to the T1 but only better.

"John, our only hope is that sonar on the Woodbridge. We've got just one chance to nab the ESO and it lies with an attack submarine that, although missing a third of its crew, is equipped with the most technologically advanced sonar known to mankind. A sonar, I might add, that is broken."

198

Madge stuck her head in the door. "Mr. Jones, Darrich reports their programmer is in touch with the USS Woodbridge."

"Thanks Madge. And stop calling me Mr."

Knox picked up the phone and joined in the conversation. "This is Knox, how we doing gentlemen?"

"Mr. Jones, this is Steve Wilson at Darrich. We are now communicating directly with the Woodbridge. We are patched into their sonar room. We have one of our best software engineers that will step through each line of code with our technician on the sub. Our engineers helped design the LAF/72 and have a copy of the specifications they will use to verify the code."

Knox couldn't get used to the term, software engineers. He never could quite understand how programmers evolved into engineers. Knox was also well aware that systems specifications rarely reflected what was actually in the code. There was only one organization that he knew of that had Capability Maturity Model (CMM) Level 5 compliant systems specifications. And those specs were written at Goddard for the Space Shuttle. No other business or government agency in the United States was CMM level 5 compliant. Most of them couldn't even qualify for level 2. So, Knox was well aware of the problems they would face trying to compare specifications to what was actually coded.

"How long will it take to step through the code, Mr. Wilson?"

"Mr. Jones, you must realize that a system this large can run..."

Knox did not do well when he did not get a direct answer.

"Mr. Wilson, I don't realize shit, sir. I don't want a lot of who-struck-John. All I want to know is how long it will take to go through the code?"

199

After a brief period of silence, Mr. Wilson attempted to answer the question. "We suspect the problem might be in the software that handles the low frequency transponder. There are over 7,000 lines of code that control this area. It will take as long as it takes to step through the code and compare the specifications to that code."

"How can you be sure your specifications reflect what's in the code, Mr. Wilson?"

"I can't, Mr. Jones. We'll just have to do the best we can and hope we come up with the problem."

Knox appreciated an honest answer. "Thank you, Mr. Wilson. Please let me know as soon as you come up with something."

USS Woodbridge

All attention on the Woodbridge was now turned toward sonar. The little room wasn't much bigger than a broom closet but seemed much smaller because of the crowd that was constantly hanging around. Scott was sitting in while the technician talked with the Darrich programmer, Bill Dixon. The conversation had been going on for over an hour now. The task was slow and tedious. After they received the password to access the compiled code, Jack asked Scott to print out each line of code for review. After almost 35 minutes, it was still printing. Although they would concentrate on the low frequency portion of the program, they decided to print out the entire program just to make sure.

Already Scott could tell that most of the task would fall on his shoulders. Jack, the technician left behind when Steve Harmon decided cramped quarters on a submarine were too much for him to handle, didn't even know how to log onto the computer. Scott could sense the Darrich tech on the other end of the phone was becoming more and more frustrated. Each time he would tell Jack to do something, Jack would turn to Scott and ask, "Do you know how to, or do you know where the…" Finally, sensing things weren't going so well, Jack turned to Scott and asked if he would talk to Bill. From that point on, it would be Scott and Bill doing the grunt work.

As luck would have it, the program for the sonar had been written in Visual C++ with some ANSI "C" thrown in. Scott's experience in programming had been limited to some COBOL and Visual Basic. Before the advent of the Visual programming tools, programming was much more labor intensive not to mention time consuming. Although the C language and Basic language are different, all programming languages have one thing in common.

They don't make any sense and seem to be based on reverse logic. So, if you were the type of person that easily understands nonsensical, illogical data you'd make a great programmer.

After the code for the low frequency module had been printed out, all 7,134 lines of them, Scott would read each line of code to Bill who would then confirm its correctness. They had examined 230 lines of code in the first hour looking for something that didn't look right. At this rate, it would take them 31 non-stop hours to check each line of code.

Captain Owens walked into sonar. Returning from the briefing for the crew and guests, he wanted to see how they were progressing. You could tell he didn't like what he saw. "I want everyone out of this room with the exception of the Chief, Jack, the sonarman on duty and Mr. Schneider. Is that understood?"

It's amazing how fast an irritated Captain can clear out a room. Within seconds there was breathing room again. Before the Captain came in, everyone was tiptoeing around and just standing there trying to see what was going on. In the middle of all this was a computer printout that continued to grow by leaps and bounds. Scott breathed a sigh of relief.

"Sorry about that fellows. Chief, you know this is a restricted area. I don't want to see that happen again."

"Aye, sir!"

George hadn't noticed when he first came in the room that Scott was on the phones. He glanced down and looked at the Chief with a questionable stare. The Chief looked back and rolled his eyes. For the time being, George decided to ignore it.

"What's the prognosis? We having any luck?"

"They're stepping through the code. Looks like it's going to be a long drawn out process," the Chief said.

"Scott, you OK?"

Scott pulled the phones off temporarily to speak with the Captain. "I'm OK, Captain. Glad to help out. We're going through each line of code to see if we can find the problem. So far everything looks like it should. I'm afraid this is going to take a while though. It's very tedious and time consuming."

Scott was sitting at the console, the phones on his head and reading back line for line of boring monotonous code. "Jack, can you take over for Scott for a while. I'd like to talk with him briefly. Also, I'm sure he'd like to grab a bite to eat. Chief, I'd like you to join us."

"Sure, no problem, Captain."

Scott and the Chief followed the Captain to the wardroom. The Chief hesitated at first. The wardroom was not a place he frequented often.

"Come on in Chief and have a seat. You guys want a cup of coffee? How about a bite to eat?"

They ordered dinner and grabbed a cup of coffee from the urn in the corner that was always full of fresh brewed coffee.

"Chief, it was my understanding that Darrich wanted Jack to handle the back and forth with the computer code and that Scott was supposed to listen in. No offense, Scott but when I walked into sonar and saw Jack sitting on his ass and you up to your ear lobes in printer paper, it struck me that...."

"Captain, to put it bluntly, Jack doesn't know shit from shineolla! Didn't even know how to start the damn computer. The Darrich programmer on the other end was gettin' real frustrated with him. He asked Scott to sit in."

"I don't mind at all, Captain. Jack has never worked on the software end of the sonar project so it really isn't his fault. This is going to take a while though I'm afraid. What I'd like to do, if it's OK with you, is take the printout of the code back to my stateroom at night. I won't have the luxury of reading the code back to Bill Dixon but it might save us some time. And who knows, I might get lucky and pick up something."

"That's OK with me Scott. I do appreciate you helping us out. It's extremely important we get that sonar back online as fast as we can."

"Captain, what went on at your briefing?" Scott asked.

"There was an earthquake out in the Atlantic. That's what caused the little mishap with the submarine when we were submerged. I'm afraid the quake created some rather large tsunamis that struck the East Coast. Significant damage resulted."

"I heard rumors to that effect, Captain, but what else is going on? Why are we not heading back to Norfolk as planned?" Scott knew that something big was going down but he wasn't sure what it was.

"Well, we've been ordered to a new location to help out with a little problem that has developed. I'm afraid that's about all I can…"

"Captain, I've been around a long time. I'm an old navy veteran and know full well that when a sub goes to battle stations it's serious. I would appreciate knowing just what it is we're up against?"

George didn't hesitate. "We've been ordered to intercept an Iraqi submarine that is headed for the States. She's carrying biological weapons. It's our job to stop her."

Andrei opened the door to the radio room and walked over to the message box. This was what he had been waiting for. He read the news about the demise of the American East Coast. He was most interested in the report on Norfolk and Washington DC. It would be much easier to deliver his cargo now that the American coast had been severely damaged by the tsunamis.

"How long was the radio left open?"

"Not long sir. Only a few minutes at most. When you were here before, I forgot to shut it down after you left. Comrade Captain, please forgive my indiscretion."

"Do not be concerned my friend. Your blunder enabled us to receive great news. Our task will be much easier now. This is good news indeed."

The young radioman breathed a sigh of relief. He knew he had done the right thing when he notified the Captain of the news. He was glad now that he hadn't thrown the message away. He had guessed correctly. The Captain was pleased. His leaving the receiver on was good for the mission. Surely, he wouldn't be punished. Perhaps even a commendation would come his way.

Andrei picked up the phone and called the bridge. "I am returning to the bridge. Call the OD in control and tell him I will need the new flag on the bridge immediately. I have selected our comrade from radio to raise it to celebrate our victory."

Sergio had raised the flag for Andrei before. He knew exactly what to do. Sergio reached in a small toolbox just inside the hatch opening and removed a wrench and some deck rope. He walked over to the snorkel tube and tied the rope to it. He then swung the rope over the periscope, made the short climb up the superstructure to the top of the scope and secured the line. He made the familiar hangman's loop at the end and climbed back down to take his seat on the bridge.

Andrei turned to the radioman. "Secure the radio room and meet me on the bridge. You will have the honor of raising our new flag for the first time."

After Andrei left for the bridge, the young man quickly secured the equipment. He removed his work jeans replacing them with his dress blues, grabbed his camera, locked the door and headed for the bridge. I hope they will take my picture, he thought!

The radioman started the climb up the 20-foot ladder leading to the bridge. It was an honor indeed that the Captain had selected him to raise the new flag for the first time. He didn't know what was louder, his heart beating from anticipation or the clank of his heavy work boots on the gray rusty rungs of the bridge ladder. As he cleared the hatch, he could smell the sweet aroma of sea air. He hadn't seen daylight since they deployed the mini-sub. The glare of the sun and fresh air was a welcome relief.

Sergio reached down and grabbed him under his shoulders to hoist him the remaining few feet to the bridge deck. He saw Andrei holding a flag. Snapping to attention, the radioman saluted the flag and his Captain. Without saying a word, Andrei started to hand the flag to the young man. Still at attention and reaching for the flag, he never felt the blow from Sergio's wrench. As he slumped to the deck, Sergio picked him up by the seat of his pants. To brace the doomed radioman for his final act of service, Sergio placed his belt loop on a small flange protruding from the snorkel. Sergio again climbed the small superstructure leading to the periscope, reached down and grabbed the radioman by the collar and lifted his head into the noose.

Andrei picked up the bridge phone and gave the order. "Up scope."

For the next three hours at 30-minute intervals, Andrei would parade his crew, two at a time, to witness the hanging of the radioman. As each set of crew arrived on the bridge, Andrei would read the same speech. First he would preach the official Russian equivalent to the Navy's BUPERS manual citing all of the sections pertaining to dereliction of duty and the importance of following orders. He would then read the charges that were filed against the radioman and pronounce the guilty verdict. He would stress his utter dislike for having to carry out such an order but his duties as commanding officer of the K-387 demanded that he follow the letter of the law. Dereliction of duty was a serious crime and must be dealt with accordingly. As the Captain of the K-387, his primary concern was for the welfare of the submarine and his crew. He would not tolerate any form of dereliction of duty that jeopardized his command.

During the five-minute or so speech, Andrei would raise and lower the periscope repeatedly. After every crewmember had witnessed the execution, Andrei ordered Sergio to remove the almost decapitated radioman from the periscope. Although the young man had died in disgrace, Andrei would see to it that he received the traditional burial at sea once they reached the North Atlantic. He ordered the conn transferred to control and all-ahead full. He would remain on the surface for a brief period to see if the American ship continued its pursuit. Shortly thereafter, Andrei would order the K-387 to submerge until it was time for the final contact with the ESO.

The K-387 was now without a radioman. Andrei was not at all concerned. The K-387 would be making but one more radio transmission and it would be a short one. Relying on his military instincts, Andrei would assume their communications had been compromised. He would assume the enemy knew the location of the ESO and were waiting for his next transmission. Andrei would protect the

ESO at all costs. Even to the extent of not issuing final orders for the deployment of the anthrax.

Knox started for another cup of coffee when Madge came in. "Mr. Jones, I have NSA on Line 2. They say it's extremely important they talk to you now."

"This is Knox Jones."

"Mr. Jones, we cracked their communications. You were correct sir. They were using a scramble we've never seen before. It was extremely intricate and cunning, I might add. They were actually using our damn satellites to disguise their transmissions and then would add a decoy header that made it look like the message originated elsewhere. We were very fortunate. After their initial communication with each other, we had no idea what type of scramble they were using. The K-387 kept their end of the line open for a short time giving us an opportunity to latch onto it and run it through our system. It was a stroke of luck on our part and a crucial mistake on their part. We are faxing the text of the messages to you now."

They move quickly at NSA, Knox thought. Damn good thing too. "You've made my day. I appreciate the quick turnaround," Knox said. Before he could get up to ask Madge if she had received the fax, she walked into his office and laid it on his desk. He read the message. It was what he had been hoping for.

Comrade Abdulla this is Andrei. I would like to congratulate you on your mission thus far. We are proceeding as planned and are on schedule. What is the status of ESO? Has she performed adequately? - BREAK

Oh yes comrade Captain. The little sub is everything they said she would be. The autopilot feature is most enjoyable and enabling us to tend to other duties. We are very pleased. - BREAK

Good! We are about to finish our war with America. It is what we have been dreaming about and planned for since the beginning of the Gulf War. It is now time to win that war. And we will. I will say this only once Abdulla. Are you ready? - BREAK

Yes Captain, I am ready. - BREAK

You are to proceed to 24°48′N, 49°1′W. You are to remain submerged until you reach this position. You will then surface to receive your final deployment orders. Is this understood? - BREAK

I have placed the order in the log and we will proceed immediately. Comrade Andrei, where will we be when we reach this position? - BREAK

That is not your concern my friend. Your only concern is to arrive at those coordinates on time. Is that understood? - BREAK

I understand comrade Captain. We will be there. – END TRANSMISSION

Knox now knew where the little sub was headed. In addition, the K-387 would be contacting ESO again to send final instructions. Just as Knox had suspected.

Knox sat down at his computer to do a few calculations. He quickly calculated the coordinates for the ESO to see how long it would take for the mini-sub to travel to its new destination. They first tracked the ESO on the surface at 8°8'S, 3°49'W. The coordinates she had been ordered to placed her roughly 3,800 miles to the northwest. At a speed of 24 knots, it would take her almost five days to reach her destination. Knox then turned to the Woodbridge and recalculated her ETA to the new location. The Woodbridge could be on location in less than three days. Now they were getting lucky, he thought. They now had a chance to move the Woodbridge in position and wait for the mini-sub to arrive. This time, they would be ready for them and the Iraqis would not be so lucky.

Knox quickly issued new orders to the Woodbridge to proceed to 24°49′N, 49°1′W that would place them just a little over five miles due west of the ESO when she arrived on site. The USS Woodbridge would be waiting for the mini-sub when she surfaced.

He then picked up the line to the Anzio. He had time to move the Anzio out of Porto Novo and closer to the ESO. He ordered the Anzio to 14°50′N, 28°19′W. When the ESO arrived at its new location, the Anzio would be approximately 1,461 miles to the southeast and within striking range. He picked up the phone and called John.

"John, the odds just swung in our favor. We cracked their communication and know where the ESO is headed. We can have the Woodbridge onsite waiting for our little friends a full two days before she arrives. Even if we don't get the sonar repaired, we stand a good chance of picking her up on the surface and sinking her. In addition, I've moved the Anzio into a better position if we need to use the Tomahawk. I'm raising the odds to 70/30 in our favor."

"That's great Knox. Glad things are finally looking up. If the Woodbridge and Darrich can come up with a sonar fix, our chances will be even better. It's looking more and more like we're getting the situation under control."

"Hold on John, Madge just walked in."

"Mr. Jones, the Captain of the La Salle wants to speak with you."

"John, I've got the CO of the La Salle on the other line. I'll get back to you."

"Captain, this is Knox. What are our friends up to?"

"Well, Mr. Jones, they just started moving again but are still on the surface. There is a rather strange occurrence going on that I thought you'd like to know about. One of our lookouts picked up what looks to be like someone hanging from the periscope. Every 30 minutes, the scope is raised and lowered continually for five minutes and then left in the raised position until the next little exercise 30 minutes later. They have been doing this for the last couple of hours. Our photographer is in the process of developing some pics' he took with the telephoto lens. With the bigeyes we can't tell if it's a dummy or for real. Strangest damn thing I've ever seen. Could this be some Russian Navy tradition equivalent to King Neptune and the crossing of the equator?"

"If it is, I've never heard of it. Did you say it looked like someone was hanging from the periscope?"

"Yes, sir. Right from the damn scope. And each time they raise the scope you can see the dummy or body go up and then back down again.

"Hold on a minute, Mr. Jones, we've got our first photos coming in now."

Knox thought about getting another cup of coffee while he was on hold but he didn't have enough time.

"You are not going to believe this sir but they are hanging one of their crew from the periscope. It is definitely an execution. It's a very gruesome sight."

Knox was not surprised. Military justice in the Soviet navy, especially the old Soviet navy, was swift and usually brutal. Something must have happened on that submarine that greatly disturbed its captain. Knox had the feeling it had something to do with the NSA intercepting and deciphering the communication between the K-387 and the ESO.

"Captain, can you make out the rank of the sailor from the photograph?"

"He does appear to be dressed in his navy blues. I'm not sure if they wear their ratings on their sleeves like we do but there does appear to be some sort of insignia on his left sleeve. He wasn't exactly standing still for us when we took the photograph so it's a little blurry but there is definitely something there."

"Can you send me over a copy of that photo? Whatever it was that sailor did must have been serious enough in the mind of their Captain to warrant the execution. If that's the case, I'd like to find out what it was."

"It's on its way, Mr. Jones."

Knox went to get that cup of coffee that was still calling his name when John walked in.

"How's things with the bad boys over in the Mediterranean?" John asked

"They're on the move again. Still on the surface though. I just got off the hook with the La Salle. They've photographed the K-387 executing one of their crew. They hung the poor bastard from the goddamn periscope. Kept raising it up and down as a little show for the rest of the crew. Damnedest thing I've ever seen and I've been in this business a long time. They're sending us a photo over now."

"No shit. Wonder what the hell is going on?"

"I suspect it might have something to do with us cracking their communication with the ESO. If that's the case, they probably killed their radioman as an example for the rest of the crew. I'm hoping the photo will show his rating. If it was the radioman, then they must suspect we're listening to them."

Madge walked in with the photo and laid it on his desk without saying a word. Knox could tell she was upset.

John and Knox looked at the gruesome picture, first out of morbid curiosity, but then in an effort to determine the rating on his sleeve. Having been with the CIA for some time now, Knox had seen his share of gory pictures, but this was one of the worst. No wonder Madge was near tears. From the raising and lowering of the periscope, the neck of the sailor had been stretched to a grotesque proportion. They had not used a hood so the bulging eyes and extended tongue were clearly visible. The executed sailor's bowels had given way and were splattered over the deck mixing with the steady stream of blood running from the almost decapitated corpse. It was one of the worst Knox had seen.

"Man, they are some sick bastards," John said.

"Yes they are, John. Yes they are!"

Knox went over to his file cabinet and walked back with a magnifying glass. He thought of scanning the photo and magnifying it on his computer, but his trusty old glass would do the job. Getting as close as he could, he strained to see the enlisted rating on the sleeve of the deceased sailor. It was indeed the Russian insignia designating the rating of radioman. He looked at the photo again and then at John.

"John, as soon as they contact ESO on their next stop, we will give the K-387 and this Captain a taste of their own medicine."

It seemed like George spent most of his waking hours in sonar. Scott was working diligently on the damaged code but so far found nothing. George looked at the sonar screen. In its current state, the sonar was very unreliable. "Any luck with it Dennis?"

"Not really, sir. Earlier, we picked up what we thought was a whale that turned out to be a large mass of seaweed. The sound waves were so garbled we couldn't even determine a proper bearing for the floating sludge. It's really not much use to us in this state. If we had to pick up another submarine with this stuff, he'd have to be right on top of us before we'd pick up the screw."

"Sonar, control."

"Sonar aye, go ahead control."

"The Captain down there?"

"Aye control, he's here."

"Jessie's looking for him. He's got another Zulu he needs to see."

While waiting for the message, George continued looking at the sonar screen as if, by some miracle, it would start gracefully scanning the ocean detecting anything in its way.

Jessie walked in with the message. "Another Flash (Z), Captain."

George signed for the message and read the copy. They had new orders. George looked at the new coordinates and knew immediately they were being sent much farther out in the Atlantic.

"Control, radio."

"Control aye." It was the OD, Lt. Tom Berlin.

"That you Tom?" Before Tom could answer, George issued the new orders.

"Tom, we have new coordinates. We're going to 24°52′N, 49°3′W."

"Aye Captain, 24°52′N, 49°3′W. We're on our way."

George turned to Dennis before he left for control. "Dennis, I'll be in control. If anything develops with the sonar, let me know ASAP!"

"Aye, sir."

George walked into control and went straight to the navigator. "What's our ETA?"

"We're looking at another day to reach the new location."

"Thanks. I'll be in the wardroom for a while."

"Aye Captain."

George grabbed a cup of coffee and sat down at the head of the table to finish reading the rest of the order. Once they arrived at the new location, they would be within five miles of the target. The Iraqi submarine was expected to surface some 22 hours after their arrival. The Woodbridge was to arm her torpedoes and await further orders. He knew what those orders would be. If they had a shot at the Iraqi submarine while on the surface, they were going to take it. If it turned out that way, the sonar problem wasn't as serious as it seemed. If they didn't get the opportunity to kill the submarine while surfaced, then it was a whole new ballgame without working sonar. The Woodbridge would then become the hunted and the Iraqis the hunter. The USS Woodbridge was one of the best Los Angeles class attack submarines in the Navy but without reliable sonar, they would be a sitting duck out in the middle of the Atlantic. A scenario George didn't like to think about. It would be bad enough with a full crew, but he was missing a third of his and had a boatload of civilians along for the ride.

To get his mind off what might happen, George started reviewing the guest assignments that had been made after they went to battle stations. The Woodbridge had been operating under battle stations now for almost 14 hours. Already George could see its effects on the crew. Maintaining and running a nuclear submarine under battle stations with its 12 on, 12 off schedule took its toll after a while. The guests were pitching in as best they could to help relieve some of the watches. John Archibald had volunteered to help with the quartermaster watch; Scott was reviewing code; Tom Kahl and Kevin Dunn were currently volunteering their services at the helm; Sean Berlin had graciously offered to help in the engine room with the diesel and all its noise and David and Paul had volunteered as lookouts. Matthew and Willy Carlos were still running around the boat having a good time.

Before George could get another cup of coffee, Matthew ran into the wardroom with Willy close behind.

"Whoa fellows. Slow down. What's the rush?" George snapped!

"Hi Dad. We're playing wolf-wolf and Willie's It. Can we have a donut?"

George briefly reminisced about his grade school days at St. Anne's and the daily wolf-wolf games on the playground. All the boys would stand in a circle and one would spin the stick. Whoever it pointed to would quickly pick up the stick and the chase was on. The first kid touched with the wolf-wolf stick was "It"! The game usually continued until one of the nuns either got knocked down or recess was over.

The tray of pastries that always sat in the middle of the wardroom table didn't go unnoticed by the two at play. "Yea, go ahead. You too Willy. You can have one."

"Thanks Dad."

Willy and Matthew sat down at the table and dove into the tray of donuts. Amazing, George thought, what a little sugar will do to two running wolf-wolf players.

"What ya' reading Pop?"

217

"Just going over a few things before I have my next meeting."

Matthew, already chomping on his second donut kept looking at George's waist. George, noticing his continuing stare, realized Matthew was looking at his badge.

"That's my radiation badge, Matthew. Everyone has to wear one."

"I know Dad. They told us what it was when that chief talked to us before we left. I was just wondering why yours was a different color."

George looked up at Matthew. "What do you mean a different color?"

"Well, when we were playing in the diesel room, Mr. Fred's badge was red. Yours is green. Is that because you're the Captain?"

George jumped up from the table yelling as he ran. "Matthew, you and Willy stay right here. I don't want you leaving this room. Do you understand me?"

"OK Pop."

George immediately ran to the radiation division officer's stateroom and knocked on the door. He had just finished his 12 hour watch and wasn't real happy at the intrusion. "Who is it?" He snapped.

"It's the Captain. I need to see you."

LT-CDR J.D. Danforth was the radiation division officer. The division was primarily responsible for radiation monitoring and control. Once a month, the division would examine everyone's radiation badge for contamination and replace those badges that were out of date. In addition, those working in areas designated as radiation areas also wore a pocket dosimeter. The pocket dosimeter requires no processing and keeps a running check on radiation levels throughout the submarine. Finally, the division was responsible for testing air samples on a 24-hour basis.

His tone changing dramatically, JD opened the door. "Yes Captain, what is it?"

"When's the last time we did a radiation check?"

"You mean the badges Captain?"

"Yes, the badges JD! When did we last check them?"

JD walked over to his wall calendar. "That would have been three weeks ago. We're due for the next one a week from yesterday."

"What about air samples? When's the last time you checked it?"

"Just yesterday. Everything was fine. What's this all about Captain?"

George walked over to JD's phone and called the engine room. He recognized Fred's voice on the other line. "Fred, this is the Captain. You wearing your radiation badge?"

"Sure I'm wearing it Captain. I don't leave home without it."

"Look at it!"

"Jesus, my damn badge is red. Captain, what the hell is going on?"

"Meet me and JD in the Demineralizer room. We'll be waiting there for you."

The Demineralizer room contains the cooling tank that is used to cool the "rods" in the reactor. It is routinely inspected and tested for any leakage.

George slammed the phone down and looked at JD. "Fred's got a red badge. He's meeting us in the Dem room."

JD didn't say a word. He put on his pants not even bothering to put on his shoes and followed the Captain out and down the corridor. Fred was waiting for them. Fred's complexion was usually bright red in color from working in the heat of the engine room. This time he was pale as a

219

ghost and seemed to be shaking. JD opened the locked door as Fred handed him his badge.

"You got your dosimeter with you?" JD asked.

"Yes sir, right here in my top pocket."

JD took the badge and the pen-shaped dosimeter and went in the dark room. He looked at the dosimeter first. The dosimeter's small sensor has a direct reading monitor that operates on a scale of 0- 200 mR. Its carbon filter, consisting of liquid polymer, had been calibrated before they left. Fred's read 60 mR. JD then took the badge, turned it over and scanned the barcode into the computer to check its identification and when it was issued. The issue date was correct. JD then calculated the readings from the glow curve and entered them into his computer. The badge's readings were identical to the dosimeters. Walking out of the dark room, he looked at Captain Owens.

"Captain, we've got to shut down the reactor. We've got a radiation leak. I will need to see every crewmember immediately to check their badges. Fred, who else has been standing the watch in engineering?"

"Just me and the Chief, sir. Oh, and one of the guests has been helping us down there also. Sir, how bad is it?"

"You're only at 60 rads Fred. Not much more than a bad sunburn. You'll live. But we need to find out where that leak is coming from before it gets any worse. Captain, I want to look at these three fellows first and anyone else who's been in that room since we left, before I check the rest of the crew. It's a good bet the leak is somewhere in engineering."

George walked over and called control. "Control, radiation."

"Control aye." Tom was still on duty.

"Tom, we're shutting down the reactor and going on diesel."

"Captain, did I hear you correctly? Did you say we're going to scram the reactor?"

"You heard me right, Tom. We're leaking. Call the senior chief and tell him to fire up the diesel on the double. I want to lose as little time as possible."

"Aye Captain"

When the reactor is scrammed the submarine draws its electrical power from the diesel and the storage batteries combined. When the submarine is operating under nuclear power, the reactor produces heat that generates steam, which drives the turbine. The turbine drives the propeller and the electrical generators. The diesel can perform this task but its output is considerably less than nuclear power and, as a result, has much less capacity. As a result, the submarine's maximum speed is reduced considerably.

Reactor leaks on ships are much more serious than that of a commercial reactor. The reactor in a nuclear ship uses a highly enriched uranium fuel, which allows it to deliver a large amount of energy from a rather small reactor.

Combined with the stressful conditions of battle stations, the deafening sound of the diesel only made things worse aboard Woodbridge. Top speed was reduced to 16 knots, down from 22. George decided it was time to contact command and let them know they now had a new problem on board. A problem that not only could seriously contaminate the crew with radiation but one that would degrade the submarine's operation considerably.

George walked into radio and called London.

"Mr. Jones, this is George Owens. We've got another problem that is potentially more serious than the one we have with sonar."

Knox did not want to hear of any additional problems. Within the last 24 hours, things had turned their way. "What's wrong now, Captain?"

"We just detected a radiation leak and had to shut down the reactor. We're running on diesel. We are in the process of determining where the leak is and how serious it is. Hopefully we can pin it down, fix it and get back on nuclear."

"What's your top speed Captain?"

"16 knots, sir, and that's pushing it. In order to maintain that speed for any length of time, we'll have to shut down everything electrical on the submarine except for essentials. We're doing the best we can, Mr. Jones under some very trying circumstances."

"How bad's the leak?"

"Right now it doesn't appear to be that bad. One of our machinist mates came up with a color change on his radiation badge. When we analyzed it, the badge was reading 60 mR on the scale. We're in the process of checking the whole boat right now. I shut down the reactor until we can determine where we're leaking and whether we can fix it. I suspect we sustained some damage when the earthquake hit.

"Keep at it, Captain. Let me know as soon as you find the leak. What's the status of the sonar?"

"Still down. We're working around the clock to try and determine where the damage is. So far, all the code looks normal."

"OK Captain. Keep me posted."

George went back to the Dem room to see how things were going. Under normal circumstances, anytime a nuclear sub reports a leak, they're ordered back to port. But this wasn't normal circumstances. First the sonar and now the reactor. On top of that, George was missing a third of his crew, had 14 civilians onboard and orders to hunt down an Iraqi submarine carrying biological weapons. It doesn't get much better than this, George thought!

"How we doin' JD?"

"So far only Fred and Sean show any sign of contamination. The Chief checked out OK. I've looked at half our guests and they're all clean. I checked the boys first. They're OK. Even though they were playing in the area they showed no signs of contamination. I suspect the rest of the crew will also test negative. It's looking more and more like the leak is restricted to engineering. And it must be slow as well. Perhaps the only reason Fred and Sean have some contamination is because they spent extended periods of time in the area."

"What about the air and the cooling tank?"

" No sign of any contamination in the air monitor. We checked the cooling tank right away and it too is clean. We're in the process of checking out the rest of the equipment now."

George was starting to feel a little better. Small radiation leaks on nuclear submarines were not that uncommon. If the air is clean and the rest of the radiation equipment checked out OK, there was a good chance they could fire up the reactor again.

"OK JD. I'm heading back to sonar. If you find anyone else with contamination or locate the leak, call me immediately."

"Aye, Captain."

When George walked back into sonar, Scott was still reading code back to Darrich. Since the recovery effort started, Scott had looked at over 5,000 lines of code and still no luck.

"I bet when this is over you won't want to look at any more "C" code, hey Scott?"

"Captain, I won't want to look at any computer code. After a while, the stuff seems to run together. I can see why programming can tax the brain. Bill, over at Darrich, seems to think whatever it is we're looking for must be real small. He was telling me how it doesn't take much to damage code. An extra space here or a misplaced hyphen there can cause the program to crash. We'll find it Captain."

ESO

ESO was right on schedule. Actually, she was ahead of schedule. Ocean currents exist as large-scale horizontal water movements. They can be quite fast and just as complex as the winds that circle the earth. Although oceans can be very cold, they can be quite warm in certain areas. As the warmth increases, the currents move faster. The speed of ocean currents is measured in knots. One knot is equivalent to 6,076 ft. an hour. It's not unusual for large ocean currents, such as the Gulf Stream, to move 164,042 feet of water per hour.

The onboard computers had selected the optimum water temperature that enhances ocean currents and had steered the ESO into a fast moving current moving at 8 knots. In doing so, the ESO was being swept along not unlike that when an airliner catches a tail wind in a jet stream. Consequently, the little sub was moving close to 32 knots, 8 knots faster than she was rated. If she could maintain this pace, the additional 9-mph would enable her to arrive onsite a full day ahead of schedule.

Although the trip thus far had gone without incident, the cramped quarters on the sub were beginning to take a toll on its inhabitants. The three men lived in an area not much bigger than a small bedroom with very little headroom. They were only able to stand erect when they opened the hatch that provides passage from the reactor room to the crews quarters. Each would take turns standing, when they were off watch, and would run in place to exercise. In addition to looking forward to this rather awkward form of relaxation, they would eagerly stand their watch when that job entailed driving the submarine. The ESO was equipped with a canopy and when the waters were clear and calm the driver was able to see underwater, sometimes at great distances. Equipped with a powerful headlight in its nose cone, the ESO was quite capable of viewing marine life and light reflections as she cruised beneath the Atlantic. Although the driver of the little sub sat in an area no bigger than 3 feet by 4 feet requiring a shift in position every so often to avoid leg cramps, the beauty of the sea passing by at 32 knots would transform the tedious task into an adventure.

Abdulla had been driving for almost four hours now and, although he slept at times, showed no inclination of leaving his post. His next watch would be inspecting the diesel, taking battery readings and checking the reactor for any signs of leaks. That watch requires the inspector to move about the small sub in a prone position for nearly three hours. A job that Abdulla detested.

"Abdulla, your time is up comrade. Engage the autopilot and meet Mahmoud and me in the crew's quarters. Mahmoud has recalculated our ETA," Mustapha said.

Reluctantly Abdulla engaged the autopilot, crawled down from the canopy and went to meet his comrades.

"Comrade Abdulla, we are moving much faster than anticipated. We are in an ocean current that is sweeping us along like birds in the sky. If we can maintain this pace, we will arrive at our destination 23 hours ahead of schedule," Mahmoud said.

Abdulla already knew they were moving faster. The view from the canopy had been breathtaking and almost hypnotic. The ocean was quite clear and very blue in color. He had noticed how sea matter and an occasional large fish would pass very quickly. At one point he thought they would hit a large squid that seemed to be coming right at them. At the last moment, the squid released its defensive ink, which seemed to congeal into a squid-like shape. Suddenly, the squid turned from a dark green to a pale opaque color and quickly moved away from the submarine.

"That is good news my friends. We will certainly be on time for the rendezvous with Andrei."

Although all three crewmembers enjoyed equal rank, Abdulla had emerged as the leader on the small sub. As such, Mustapha and Mahmoud were hesitant to approach him with their idea. Mustapha spoke first. "Comrade, Mahmoud and I have been talking and we thought that perhaps, since we are way ahead of schedule, we could surface for a brief time to replenish our air and see the light of day again?"

"Yes comrade, it would be nice to visit the surface briefly to help break the monotony," Mahmoud added.

Abdulla looked at both of them in astonishment. "Our orders are specific. We are to remain submerged until we reach our predetermined rendezvous point. Then and only then are we to surface. The answer is no!"

"Comrade Abdulla, what are we to do when we arrive at our destination a full day ahead of time? Sit on the surface like sitting ducks waiting for the prescribed time to talk with the K-387? That would be even more foolish."

"Mustapha is correct comrade. We are making exceptional time. It would make more sense to surface now for some much needed fresh air and arrive at or near our designated time. We are a small target my friend. With just a few minutes on the surface, I do not think the enemy will detect us way out in the middle of the ocean. Once we submerge again, we can easily rejoin the swift moving current and still arrive in plenty of time."

Abdulla was more disciplined than the other two. If they surfaced now, they would be disobeying specific orders from Andrei.

"Comrades, you know Andrei's orders. We cannot disobey him. What if something went wrong? What if Andrei were to learn of our disobedience? I would like to smell the fresh air again as you do. But I am not ready to put this mission in jeopardy by surfacing just for fresh air."

Mustapha grew impatient. "Comrade, we are all of equal rank. All three of us are commanding this submarine, not just you. We think you are overreacting. This is our last mission in the service of our great country and our last tribute to Allah. A few sorely needed minutes on the surface will not unduly put us in harm's way. Comrade, we're going up."

The change of command had just taken place. And, without pomp and circumstance.

Abdulla was not surprised that his two comrades had decided to overrule him. He was surprised how easily they had done it. Perhaps it was the right thing to do.

"OK comrades, let's take her up. But if we see any sign of trouble, or if the weather is bad, we come back down immediately. Is that understood?"

"Aye, Captain, understood."

John ran into Knox's office. He didn't usually react this way but this was something they hadn't expected.

"Knox, AWACS has the ESO on the surface. She just came up within the last two minutes and, get this, she's at all stop like a sitting duck."

As soon as the AWACS located the ESO, her coordinates were immediately compared with the 24 GPS satellites circulating the earth in polar orbit. The network ground stations then took the readings and translated the satellite data into precise positional information. The system then used this data to obtain latitude, longitude and vertical fixes on the ESO. All three provided for a complete three-dimensional position of the little sub. The three-dimensional position for ESO was then entered into ground station mainframes and translated into course acquisition code. The code was processed again using selective availability, which degrades the signal somewhat but provides for a 90% accuracy rate in most circumstances.

When all final calculations were finished, the GPS inaccuracy rate of not striking the ESO was 4 dRAMs. One dRAM is equal to a 2.5% probability of inaccuracy. The bottom line: if the ESO remained stationary, they had a 90% chance of hitting her from over 1,500 miles away.

The nice thing about the cruise missile is that no one knows how to shoot the things down. Cruise missiles fly below most radar systems and maneuver at high speeds. Bringing down a cruise missile is a lot like trying to dodge a speeding bullet. In addition, these bullets can track you when you move. No air defense system in the world had the means to protect against a missile as agile as the cruise. Technology breeds technology. As the free market in the computer industry lowers the real cost of cruise missiles down to about $15,000 apiece most countries will obtain them in great numbers. The smart weapons of today will become smarter as chip densities double every 12 months. The battle cry of future wars will be attack, as it will become more and more difficult to defend!

Knox immediately contacted the USS Anzio and had her target the ESO. The Anzio loaded the coordinates into the Tomahawk's computer and in less than five minutes, they had their target marked. Knox knew it was a long shot but one they had to take. The odds of the little sub remaining on the surface long enough for the Tomahawk to reach her were slim indeed. But perhaps she surfaced because she was in trouble. Since she was sitting dead in the water it might be an indication she had surfaced for some type of repairs. If that was the case, she might still be there after the two hours or so it would take for the cruise missile to reach her.

A few last minute calculations were made and Knox gave the order to fire the cruise missile. Immediately the Anzio reported that the Tomahawk was airborne and all systems were go. When first launched, the missile seemed to hang in the air for a brief moment before its propulsion system propelled it to its proper altitude. The force of the launch would rock the Anzio and move her laterally a full five feet. A rather large distance for a heavy cruiser. Within 30 seconds of launch, the inboard guidance system, programmed to hit a target in the ocean no larger than a bus some 1,500 miles away, would steer the weapon toward its ultimate destination. Every 20 seconds the GPS satellites circling far above would adjust its course. The ultimate in smart weapon technology, the Tomahawk was a born killer. Its only goal was to seek and destroy. Within five minutes of launch, the missile had reached its maximum speed of 550 mph.

The waiting was the worst part. If the ESO would remain stationary, they had a good chance of ending this threat to the United States once and for all. If they got lucky and made a direct hit, the problem with the defective sonar on the USS Woodbridge would be one they could address when she returned to port. The threat of a biological attack on the United States would have been averted with one Tomahawk missile.

USS Woodbridge

After discovering the radiation leak, only two of the crew had shown any signs of contamination. As a precaution, George had JD check the air monitoring systems every two hours. Still, it showed no contamination. George had the crew check every nook and cranny throughout the Woodbridge for any signs of radiation contamination, with not one positive reading.

Ordinarily the lack of additional readings would be a good sign that perhaps what had happened was an anomaly, a one-time happening, that would not be repeated. Maybe when the submarine was rocked as a result of the earthquake, a valve temporarily opened releasing a minute amount of radiation and that was it. George knew better. In nuclear power training they were taught that there was no such thing as a little leak. A radiation leak, no matter how small, is equivalent to a slow hanging; the outcome is always the same. Although he was tempted to reactivate the reactor, he would not do so until he found that leak.

In the Nucleonics room JD was busy checking specimens using radiochemistry. Before washing the clothing of Fred and Sean in the decontamination washer, JD would first take samples from 30 different parts of their clothing and run them through Nucleation. Each fiber of clothing would be analyzed to determine density, length of contamination and the type of contamination in order to help pin down where the leak might have originated. The tests are time consuming but extremely accurate. Radiation contamination is not unlike a fingerprint. Its mark is distinctive and cannot be duplicated. After almost 16 hours of continuous testing, JD had his answer.

The footprint on each piece of clothing indicated the leak originated as radioactive waste. The next chemical analysis confirmed JD's worst fears. The leakage was High

Level Waste —HLW. HLW is highly radioactive material produced from the reprocessing of spent nuclear fuel. The spent nuclear fuel can produce liquid waste, and/or solid waste. HLW contains radioactive elements that decay slowly and can remain radioactive for hundreds or thousands of years. Nuclear reactors burn uranium fuel creating a chain reaction that produces energy. Over time, as the uranium fuel is burned, it reaches the point where it no longer contributes efficiently to the chain reaction. Once the fuel reaches that point, it is considered spent. Spent nuclear fuel is thermally hot and highly radioactive.

JD turned his attention to the waste system pumping station located beneath the reactor. First he would check the pressure readings to ensure they were within tolerance. They were. He then located the entry valve and, using a needle insertion tube, injected a tracer into the pumping system. If there was a leak in any of the 14 valve connections, the tracer would attach itself to it and, at the point of the leak, emit a fluorescent glow of bright amber. The next step would be to simply turn the lights out in the reactor room and, using night vision goggles, look for any infrared light. He found the leak at valve 12 at the connection point. It was possible, he thought, that a slight twist of the wrench might be enough to stop the leak but of all the valves in the system, number 12 was the most difficult to reach. In dry-dock it would be a simple matter of evacuating the system and then dismantling the network of pipes and valves until the 12th valve could be reached. They were not afforded that luxury at sea. He called control.

"Control, radiation."

"Control, aye."

"This is JD down in the reactor room. The Captain up there?"

"He's on the bridge, JD."

"Bridge, radiation."

"Bridge, aye."

"This is JD. I need to speak with the Captain."

"Go ahead JD. This is the Captain."

"Captain, I found the leak. The pumping station has a leak at valve 12. Can you come down here? I think it would be easier if I showed you what we're up against."

"I'm on my way."

George walked aft through the crew's mess, down two levels reaching the first door to the reactor room. He entered his password on the touch pad and opened the door. At the second door, George reentered his password and also placed his hand on the scanner. The door opened.

"What have ya' got for me, JD?"

JD handed the Captain a pair of goggles and turned out the lights. George saw it immediately. "Where do you think its leaking?"

"My guess it's leaking at the pressure valve. More than likely all it needs is a turn with the wrench."

"Just how in the hell are we going to get in there to turn it?"

Valve 12 was clearly visible but it was all the way at the back of the pumping station. In order to reach the valve, someone would have to crawl over a pipe maze cluttered with valves that was only about a foot high. The skinniest guy on the submarine wouldn't have a chance of squeezing through such a small area.

At first JD didn't say what he was thinking. But it was their only chance. It might just work. "Captain, I think we have someone on board who can squeeze through the area."

George looked at JD. "What'd we do? Smuggle a midget on board!"

"Not exactly. We invited him!"

"You're not thinking what I think you're thinking, are you?"

234

"Captain, it might be our only chance to stop the leak."

"Damn it, JD, he's only 10 years old. I don't want to expose my son to a high-level radiation leak. I can't do that."

"Captain, I understand your concern and realize how difficult it is for you to do that, but the welfare of the crew and this submarine is at stake. If he were not your son, would you do it?"

George started to answer immediately but then thought about what JD just said. George was too close to the situation to make an objective decision. "What do we need to do, JD?"

"There are two types of anti-contamination suits used by radiation personnel who work in and around areas suspected of contamination. One for "wet" contamination and the other for "dry" contamination.

"We can outfit Matthew in our smallest wet suit to protect him, give him a wrench and show him where to go. When he reaches the valve, we'll have him turn it one-quarter-turn clockwise. While he's at the valve, I'll inject another tracer, turn out the lights and see if we're still leaking."

"Do you think he's strong enough to turn it?"

"Frankly, I don't know. It's possible he won't be able to budge it."

George picked up the phone.

"Control, radiation."

"Control, aye."

"This is the Captain. I'm down at the pumping station. Somewhere on this submarine my son Matthew is probably running around playing wolf-wolf. See if you can find him and bring him to control. I'm coming right up."

"That's easy Captain. He's standing right here next to me looking through the periscope."

George felt sick to his stomach.

235

For the next hour, JD and his team cautiously outfitted Matthew in a wet decontamination suit. The smallest size they had covered Matthew from head to foot with two feet left over. Eventually Matthew was encased in what looked like a gray snowsuit that included a hood that had a large yellow plastic visor from ear to ear.

"Matthew, how does it feel in there?" JD asked.

"This is fun. Can I keep this for Halloween?"

"Wiggle your fingers for me."

Matthew moved his small fingers in the oversize gloves. JD handed him the open-ended wrench. "Can you hold this OK?"

Matthew grabbed the wrench and squeezed. The gloves were over an inch too big for his small hand, and the fingers bent backward as he grabbed the wrench.

They showed Matthew where he had to go and the fitting he was to try to tighten. JD then had Matthew place the wrench on a fitting on one of the valves up front and explained to him which direction he was to turn it. "Matthew, when you put the wrench on the fitting, like this, you have to turn it clockwise. Clockwise is to the right. You need to turn towards your right. Hold up your right hand for me."

Matthew quickly raised his right hand.

"Good, now tell me which way you need to turn it to tighten it."

Matthew, holding the wrench, pointed with his left hand. "This way. Right?"

"I think we're ready, Captain."

George didn't say a word. He just looked at JD and nodded.

"Matthew, when you get to the valve fitting and are in position, as soon as you turn the wrench, we are going to turn out the lights. It will be very dark in here but only for a few seconds. We need to turn out the lights to make sure the valve isn't leaking anymore. Are you afraid of the dark Matthew?"

"No, sir. I play in the dark all the time. I can even play wolf-wolf in the dark."

They were ready. Slowly they lifted Matthew up and into the tiny crawl space. Without hesitation, Matthew started crawling back to where the valve was located. Kids are amazing, JD thought. As soon as it looked like Matthew might get stuck on a protruding valve stem, he would just wiggle a little this way or that way and was on the move again. Matthew was at the valve in less than a minute.

"Matthew, you did great. You're the best crawler I've ever seen. Now take the wrench and put it on the fitting we showed you. Don't turn it yet," JD said.

Matthew placed the wrench on the nut and waited.

"I think we've got a natural here, Captain."

George did not reply.

JD reached over and picked up the needle insertion tube and threaded it onto the entry valve. "OK Matthew we're ready. See if you can turn it to the right."

When Matthew had practiced the turn procedure earlier, he was standing and looking at JD. But now he was laying down facing a valve nut on a pipe that ran horizontally in front of his head. George, sensing he was confused, spoke for the first time since they started.

"Matthew, push up on the wrench to turn it."

"But Mr. JD told me to turn it to the right. How can up be to the right?"

"Your father is correct Matthew. I know it's confusing but when you push up on the wrench you will be turning it to the right. Give it a try."

Matthew pushed up on the wrench and the nut didn't budge.

"I think it's stuck," Matthew said.

"Push harder Matthew. Push real hard."

237

Matthew pushed on the wrench and still it didn't budge.

"Matthew, there is a black pipe next to your right foot. Pull your leg up and put your foot on the pipe, then push again on the wrench," JD said.

Matthew pulled up his foot, moved it slightly to his right, and braced it against the pipe. He pushed on the wrench and the nut moved slightly clockwise.

"OK Matthew. That's enough. I'm going to turn out the lights. You just stay there OK?"

JD opened the insertion tube and injected the tracer into the pumping system. He then reached over and turned out the lights. For a moment there was nothing. And then they saw the infrared light at the valve stem. JD turned the lights back on and turned towards the Captain.

"Captain, it's still leaking but not as bad. The infrared light was considerably less than the first time we checked. I think we can get it."

"Try it again," George said.

"Matthew, you need to push the wrench again. Push a little harder this time."

Matthew, with his foot still braced against the pipe giving him the leverage that he needed, pushed the wrench with a loud grunt. This time it moved a full quarter turn.

"That's great Matthew. OK, we're going to turn out the lights again."

JD again turned out the lights and injected the tracer. They waited, for what seemed like an eternity, and saw no infrared leakage.

They immediately took Matthew into the decontamination room and disposed of his wet suit. Matthew was then given a decon' shower and checked for signs of contamination. The tests were negative. The oversize wet suit had done its job.

JD would continue to monitor the valve for the next 12 hours to ensure the leak didn't return. It did not. Little Matthew Owens had performed his task flawlessly.

What started out to be a few minutes of relaxation turned into one-and-a-half hours on the surface. The weather was perfect. Seas were like glass and the temperature ideal. The three Republican Guards had even opened the canopy and, one at a time, climbed out on top of the sub to bask in the sun and take a short swim. After almost three days in the cramped little sub, the fresh air and wide open spaces of the Atlantic were a welcome relief.

Each knew this would be their last assignment. They would not be returning. Although Abdulla had objected strongly to this blatant disobedience of orders, he remained on the surface longer than the others and never once suggested they leave. After all, they were still way ahead of schedule and only an hour away from their rendezvous with the K-387. So why not enjoy this last measure of relaxation before they embark on their final journey. Andrei would never know, and even if he did, what could he do about it. They would never see him again.

Before they surfaced, they took extra precautions and made sure the radio transmitter was turned off and temporarily shut down the reactor. While on the surface, they would replenish the little sub's air supply, not with a snorkel, but by simply opening the canopy. Opening the canopy was risky. A large wave could easily swamp the small boat and sink them. But because the ocean was so calm they all agreed it posed no threat. So, for some time now they had been enjoying a much needed break that would revitalize them for the final leg of their journey.

Mustapha poked his head up through the canopy opening and looked at Abdulla lying on top of the submarine. "Comrade, I think it's time we closed things up and continued on with our mission."

"Five more minutes comrade. Why don't we do a little fishing before we leave?"

Of course they didn't have any fishing equipment on board but it would have been nice indeed to eat some fresh fish instead of the freeze-dried rations they had been consuming since the trip started. Jokingly, Mustapha threw out a piece of string coming to rest on Abdulla's nose.

"Here you are comrade. Tie it to your big toe. Or even better, just dangle your cruddy feet over the side. Maybe some poor fish that can't smell might decide to take a bite."

Abdulla sat up and took one last look at the beautiful day that surrounded them like the white of a yolk. "Anyone else coming up for one last fling?"

"No my friend, Mahmoud has already gone down to turn the reactor back on, and I just finished removing the last drop of sea water from my skin. It is time Abdulla."

As Abdulla stood to take the short walk over to the opened canopy, an eerie high shrill pitch began to break the deafening silence they had enjoyed while on the surface. Abdulla, turning in the direction of the noise could see nothing.

"Mustapha, you still there?"

Poking his head up once more to answer, he too noticed the unusual noise. "What's that noise Abdulla?"

"I was about to ask you the same thing. Whatever it is, it's getting louder. Maybe it's visitors from outer space. That would be…" Mahmoud, breaking through the opening almost jamming Mustapha up against the console, started yelling.

"Get in here now. I just turned the radar back on. We have contact at bearing two-six-five, range 1800 yards and closing fast. Hurry comrade, we don't have much time."

Traveling at 550 mph, the Tomahawk would reach them in 7 seconds.

Mustapha turned white as a ghost. In his hurry to get out of the way so Abdulla could reenter the sub, he almost wedged both himself and Mahmoud in the canopy opening. Mahmoud grabbed the rung below him and pulled himself down. As Musatpha started down he saw it. Instinctively he closed the canopy.

The Tomahawk cruise missile, with its 1,000-lb. bomb, struck the ocean less than 30 yards away, just north of the ESO and detonated. The same swift current the ESO had ridden under the ocean was enough to move the submarine laterally, confusing the missile's guidance at the last minute. Abdulla was at the canopy just as Mustapha latched it down. Looking up, Mustapha could see the horror on the face of his comrade, but only briefly. The shockwave from the exploding missile and the resulting swell lifted the submarine and tossed it almost 50 feet crashing it to the surface. ESO rolled another 80 feet before finally coming to rest.

Mustapha weathered the brunt of the shock rolled up in a ball in the canopy area. Mahmoud was tossed around the engine room like a rag doll, coming to rest on top of the diesel, unconscious. Abdulla was gone.

Mustapha crawled from the canopy area. He quickly opened the small hatch to the reactor area, climbed down and looked for any signs of reactor damage. He then checked the gauges. All readings were normal. Satisfied the reactor was OK, Mustapha then moved to the crew quarters and opened the hatch to the engine room. Mahmoud lay on top of the diesel. Mustapha climbed on top and felt for a pulse. He was alive. Carefully he lowered his comrade to the deck and tried to revive him. Slowly, Mahmoud opened his eyes. "That was a close call comrade," Mustapha said.

Mustapha started breathing again. With the exception of a broken forefinger on his right hand and a multitude of bruises, Mahmoud was OK.

"We lost Abdulla. I could not wait for him to close the canopy."

"You did the right thing comrade. Had you waited one more second, we would have been swamped for sure. You are a hero Mustapha. You've saved the mission. Abdulla is now with Allah. He is at peace and will watch over us."

"We must hurry comrade. They may have another one coming at us. We must submerge immediately."

"Contact. We have contact!" The voice from NSA shouted over the phone. The Tomahawk is down. We're looking at the AWACS readings now in conjunction with GPS data to determine if we've made a hit. The ESO was still stationary and on the surface when we reached the area. It's a good chance we got her."

Knox rocked back in his chair, looked at the ceiling and prayed. "Just once, dear God, just once." He waited patiently. Finally, the voice cracked again.

"AWACS reports no surface contact. Considering she was still on the surface when the cruise hit, it's a good assumption we got her. It's highly unlikely she could have submerged that quickly."

"Can AWACS detect debris, oil slicks or anything like that?" Knox asked.

"AWACS can detect anomalies on the surface. In other words, something unusual or out of the ordinary. It's difficult, though, to say for sure if we detect insignificant data that it is debris from the submarine."

Knox was quickly growing impatient. "Well, did we detect any insignificant data on the surface after the missile hit?"

"We're still checking, sir. So far we don't see anything of intrinsic value. That's not unusual though. If a cruise missile scored a direct hit on a little submarine like the ESO, it's quite possible the submarine was literally vaporized. As soon as I get more data, I'll let you know."

"You do that!"

It's possible, Knox thought, that a direct hit would so destroy the ESO that nothing of significance would be left. Perhaps after things settled down something would show up on the surface indicating they got the little bastards. He called John.

"John, they don't know if they hit them or not. The ESO was still on the surface when the missile arrived. It's possible we got them but we're not showing anything on the surface. If they were disabled, and that's possible since they remained stationary for so long, we just might have scored a lucky hit. But it concerns me that we can't locate any debris."

"It is possible, Knox, there isn't any. That little sub is just a tad over 20 feet. If we hit them direct, she just might be part of the atmosphere by now. We'll find out for sure real soon. The K-387 is due to surface for their final contact with them."

In all the confusion, Knox hadn't realized how much time had gone by. John was right. All they had to do was wait for the K-387 to surface and attempt to make contact with ESO. If they did, they sure as hell would know they weren't successful with the Tomahawk.

"You're right John. We'll know shortly. If we missed them, once the K-387 talks to her, we'll at least know where she's heading."

Knox poured himself another cup of coffee. It suddenly dawned on him that he hadn't heard from the Woodbridge since they reported the radiation leak. He picked up the phone and rang Madge. "Madge, connect me with the Woodbridge."

"That won't be necessary, sir, they're on Line 2 holding for you."

"Mr. Jones, this is Captain Owens. I'm happy to report that we're back on nuclear. We isolated the leak at one of the valves on the waste pumping station. Although it was a high level leak and in an almost unreachable location, we managed to get to it and tighten the valve. We were fortunate we had someone on board small enough to fit through an opening no bigger than 12 inches high and crawl through a maze of pipes and valves some 10 feet away to reach the valve. So far it's holding."

245

"Good work, Captain Owens. You must have some damn skinny sailors on that submarine. That's quite a feat, maneuvering through all that."

"No skinny sailors here, Mr. Jones. My ten-year-old son did the work for us. He's quite a kid. Real proud of him."

"As you should be Captain. Sounds like your tiger cruisers are pitching in during our time of need. Speaking of that, how we coming on the sonar? Any luck with the software?"

"I'm afraid not, sir. We're still checking it line by line. The problem wasn't where they originally thought it would be. Darrich started checking the low frequency transponder code first. Since the sonar wasn't operating at all within the low frequency range, they assumed the problem was in that module. So, after checking over 7,200 lines of code, they've moved on to other modules within the program. We're keeping our fingers crossed."

"Keep me posted, Captain. If we got lucky about 15 minutes ago, we won't need your services. I'm hoping for the best."

"What's that, Mr. Jones?"

"We fired one of our cruise missiles at the Iraqis that are, or were, heading in your direction. They surfaced some two hours ago giving us a chance. We're checking AWACS readings now for verification. Keep your fingers crossed."

"That would be great, Mr. Jones. My crew and guests would love to head home. We'll keep plugging away at the sonar just in case."

No sooner had Knox hung up the phone, he was on it again. He would find out shortly if the ESO survived.

"Mr. Jones, this is the La Salle. The K-387 is back on the surface."

"Knox, NSA reports the K-387 back on top. They're ready for any communications from them," John said, strolling into his office.

"Hold on gang." Knox picked up Line 3 and immediately was connected with the USS Normandy. "What's your ETA?"

"We've got her arriving on site in 16 minutes."

"Good, I'll let you know if there's any change so you can divert."

Knox had taken a chance. Over two hours ago, he had ordered the Normandy to fire her cruise. He knew when the K-387 was scheduled to surface and contact ESO. If the two didn't communicate as planned, he would order a course correction at the last minute to divert the Tomahawk.

Knox picked up the NSA line. "I want a live feed on this one. As soon as we have confirmation that the two have resumed communications and we have received and deciphered that communication, I want to see it flashing before my very eyes. Is that understood?"

"Yes, sir. Understood."

Knox then picked up the La Salle's line. "Is the K-387 moving or stationary, Captain?"

"She's dead in the water, sir. Not moving an inch."

He went back to the NSA. "Do we have any signs of the ESO on the surface?"

"Not as yet, sir. It's looking more and more like we might have hit her."

It was now a waiting game. If the K-387 opened up her transmitter and tried contacting ESO they would know immediately if the little submarine had survived. AWACS was positioned to detect her as soon as she broke the surface and GPS, using the MERCURY signal intelligence spacecraft, was ready to detect and de-scramble any communication between the two.

Knox didn't have to wait long.

247

"We've got the ESO on the surface," NSA shouted.

"Shit!" Knox yelled. The Tomahawk had missed its target. "OK, gentlemen, I'm watching my monitor. Are we ready?"

"Yes, sir. As soon as they start, you'll see their transmission on your monitor."

After the execution, the K-387 submerged. They were now on the surface preparing to make the final communication with the ESO. When finished, they would again submerge and head for the Atlantic.

The crew went about their business as if the execution had never happened. Most were veteran Soviet sailors and had witnessed at-sea executions before. Just as a precaution, Andrei interviewed each member of the crew to ensure that they understood why the execution was necessary. It was a ritual all had been through before and, when interviewed by their Captain, offered their condolences to the Captain for the painful but necessary order he had given. Each would tell the Captain how they respected his supreme authority and, had they been in his position, would have done the exact same thing.

Before they surfaced, Andrei ordered a special meal for the officers and crew. They all ate together in the crew's mess, officers included, and dined on the best prime rib cut available. A vodka toast was offered for their fallen comrade. Afterward, each senior officer made a brief speech highlighting the success of the mission and how important it was to follow orders. Finally, Andrei closed the dinner with a special service for the radioman. Holding up his picture, he read the various service commendations he had received during his short career. Andrei then passed around for all to see a copy of the letter that he would personally send to the young man's parents advising them that their son had died in the line of duty. Finally, he held high the special plaque that would be placed on the Wall of Valor for the young man on the K-387.

By the time the ritual was over, each crewmember not on duty, was up to their gills in vodka. Some even looked forward to the executions. As long as it wasn't theirs, they provided an opportunity to eat steak and drink good Russian vodka. It is rare indeed that Russian sailors are given the opportunity to eat fine western beef. Some good comes out of everything, they thought. So hell, because the poor dumb bastard make a mistake, they were afforded the luxury of fine food and plenty of booze.

Andrei and his officers had accomplished what they set out to do. And that was to ensure the solidarity of their crew for the rest of the mission. Once completed, he didn't give a damn what happened to them. But they were vitally important now and he would make sure they stayed committed to his endeavor. Having conducted one-on-one interviews and lavishing them with food fit for a king and good ol' Russian vodka, he was satisfied they would perform.

Andrei had not had one drop of vodka. Unlike his officers and crew, he was always on duty. He always had the watch. He was the consummate professional!

Andrei was now in the empty radio room. He checked his watch, reached down, and turned on the transmitter. He then turned on the encryption device that would scramble the outgoing message. Once contact was made with the ESO, the equipment would no longer be needed. This would be their last radio transmission. He picked up the mike.

"ESO, K-387."

"This is ESO. Reading you loud and clear."

"Mainframe!" Andrei said

And that was it. Andrei immediately shut down the equipment and picked up the phone.

"Control, radio."

"Control, aye."

"Take her down. Level off at 300 feet, and set our course at two-six-nine. Full speed ahead."

"Aye Captain."

Andrei would not issue the final orders to the ESO. Because their radio had been left on during their last transmission, he assumed their communications had been compromised. Instead, the ESO would rely on the default plan that was designed for situations like this. The ESO had been instructed that in the event communications were interrupted or rendered unusable, they would open the sealed black box located beneath their mainframe computer and proceed to a predetermined location in America. Andrei had just given the order to do just that by simply reciting the code word they previously agreed upon.

Knox saw the word come across his monitor. He waited for more. There would be none.

"That's it Knox, they've shut down their transmitter," NSA reported.

Knox immediately picked up the line with the Normandy. "Splash the K-387," he said.

"We're less than a minute away from impact. Stay tuned!" The Normandy replied back.

Knox looked back at the monitor. "Mainframe" was the only communication sent by the K-387. Knox immediately knew what this meant. The Commander of the K-387 was on to them. They had a fallback plan in the event their communications were compromised. He would not tell the ESO the final destination for delivery of their payload. As a result, they now had no idea where the little sub was heading. They would, broken sonar and all, now have to depend on the Woodbridge to intercept the ESO and destroy her before she reached the coast.

"Status please?" Knox asked.

"T minus 30 seconds and counting," the Normandy replied.

Knox was determined to destroy the K-387. After seeing what they had done to one of their own, he wanted nothing more than to blow them out of the water. What's more, they were no more use to the United States. They were expendable! Knox had a good feeling about this one. The Anzio had been much farther away from the ESO than Normandy was from the K-387. They would get what they deserved, he thought. The Commander of the K-387 would never have the satisfaction of knowing if his planned attack on America was successful. After the demise of the K-387, America would have only one vessel to worry about. Although small in stature, the ESO carried a huge biological payload. If allowed to deliver its weapon, the United States would suffer tremendously. Knox would do everything in his power to prevent that from happening.

"We have impact. We have impact," the Normandy reported.

"That's confirmed. We have definite impact with this one," NSA replied.

And finally, the one Knox had been waiting for. The USS La Salle, onsite and only 500 yards south and east of the K-387 got on the horn. "That's a direct hit. No doubt about it. You got her. She is sinking fast at the stern. Wow, I've never seen anything like it. One second she was there and the next, bango – gone! Nice job fellows."

Knox didn't feel one ounce of remorse. Briefly for the crew maybe, but not for long. After all, they all knew what the K-387 was doing. They surely had been recruited for this mission knowing full well that their government did not support it. Once Knox saw the hideous photo of the execution, he decided he would kill the K-387. It needed killing! He now turned his full attention to the ESO and the USS Woodbridge. They must do whatever they could to get the sonar on the Woodbridge operational again. This episode that started, what seemed like an eternity ago, was now down to two players; the Woodbridge and the ESO, and Knox was determined the good guys were going to win this one.

Although she had lost some valuable time when her reactor went down, the Woodbridge was still scheduled to arrive on site and close to where the ESO had surfaced for her last communication with the K-387. From now on it would be a cat and mouse chase between the two of them.

The Woodbridge had the advantage, Knox thought. Even though she was still operating with defective sonar, the Woodbridge knew they would be looking for the enemy once they arrived on site. The ESO did not. The ESO had no idea the Americans had a nuclear attack submarine heading in their direction.

Nine

Race for the Coast

After repairing the radiation leak, the Woodbridge resumed normal operations. To make up for lost time, George requested permission to submerge for the last leg of the trip. Since Scott had gone over every line of code with Darrich and found nothing, George persuaded Knox that making up time was probably more important at this stage than continuing to read code line for line. George assured Knox that Scott would continue to analyze the code while they were submerged. Mr. Jones was specific in granting the request. If at any time the Woodbridge identified or somehow managed to fix the sonar, they were to surface immediately and contact him.

Before they finished talking, Knox issued an order directly to George. Once contact was made with the Iraqi submarine the USS Woodbridge was to destroy it at all costs. Knox also told George what the Iraqis were carrying. It was imperative that the Woodbridge sink them in deep water. If that submarine made it to shallow water carrying the anthrax payload, a torpedo attack was out of the question.

The Woodbridge finally arrived on location. But they arrived late. Originally scheduled to arrive almost two days before the ESO, running on diesel had slowed them considerably. George gave the order to periscope depth. As soon as he gave the order, the only noise heard in control was that of the humming monitors. Silence is mandatory when a submarine is ordered to periscope depth. Although we live in an age of technological revolution, the fact of the matter is when a submarine begins to surface, they simply don't know what's on the surface. Extreme caution is the rule of order. Because the USS Woodbridge was in battle stations and ordered to seek out and destroy an enemy submarine, this order to surface was anything but routine. Lt. Berlin, the OD, was glued to the periscope looking for whatever he could see while the submarine was surfacing. He would continue to search the ocean for signs of anything that might prevent their surfacing. This time he was looking for the hull of a submarine. Even though the Woodbridge was not yet on the surface, Berlin's job was to make sure there wasn't any surface vessel near the vicinity of the Woodbridge.

"No close contact," Berlin reported.

Within a minute, the Woodbridge was at periscope depth. The OD was now scanning the ocean surface for any signs of the Iraqi submarine. He did a complete 360 twice before he was satisfied it was OK to surface. "Prepare to surface," Berlin ordered.

The USS Woodbridge was now on the surface. "I'll take the conn on the bridge."

"Aye, Captain, transferring control to the bridge," Berlin replied.

George and the XO climbed the ladder, opened the hatch to the bridge and stepped out.

"Damn nice weather. Don't think I've ever seen the ocean this calm this far out in the Atlantic," Bill said.

"Yes, it is nice, Bill. Probably the lull before the storm. Somewhere out there heading in our direction is an Iraqi submarine that we need to stop. We'll stay here for a few minutes so we can make radio contact with command. Then I want this boat submerged as soon as possible."

Sitting on the surface they were vulnerable. Especially since they would soon be in earshot of an enemy submarine that would try to sink them. George would waste no time submerging once contact with London was complete.

"Bridge, sonar"

"Bridge, aye."

"Captain, we've got a contact bearing two-nine-one, range 1,200 yards. We can't determine what it is but there is definitely something there. If only we had this damn sonar fixed."

"Control, bridge."

"Control, aye."

"Dive, dive!" George yelled.

They would not have time to contact London. Although the defective sonar may be picking up nothing more than a whale or school of fish, George would assume the worst and hope for the best. As far as he was concerned, the sonar contact was the enemy. And he would prepare for it.

ESO

ESO arrived onsite 30 minutes before the Woodbridge. That was enough time to make the brief contact with the K-387 and submerge for the rest of the journey. They wasted no time going back under. As soon as they heard the one word command from the K-387, they filled the ballast with seawater and submerged. The two remaining Iraqis were scared. They had lost a comrade and an important member of their crew doing something foolish. Had they listened to Abdulla he would still be with them. His loss would make the remaining and most important part of the mission, that much more difficult.

And now, after receiving the abbreviated transmission from the K-387, they knew something was wrong. Before embarking on their revenge toward America, all three were specifically reminded of the orders sealed in the black box attached to the side of the mainframe computer. These orders were to be used only in a time of emergency. The box was not to be opened unless the code word was transmitted or communications with the K-387 rendered impossible.

Mustapha opened the gray metal box. Inside was a small container no bigger than a cigar box. On the front were two inset locks. Mustapha inserted his key first and turned; Mahmoud inserted his key in the remaining lock, turned the key and the box opened. Inside were the sealed orders. Mustapha opened the silver-coated envelope and read the orders. After quickly glancing over all the official headers he finally came to the portion describing where they were to deliver their payload. The coordinates were listed first and then the literal translation identifying their destination. They were ordered to proceed to the mouth of the Potomac River, anchor and immediately embark for deployment. Once all weapons had been released, they were to place the ESO on autopilot, set the timer for reactor detonation and head straight up the river. They were to remain with the ESO until the end. Neither one of them realized the importance of the Potomac. In fact, they had no idea where it was.

Mustapha walked over to the keyboard sitting in front and to the left of the mainframe, entered his password and keyed the coordinates into the ESO's navigational system. Immediately the small submarine made a slight course correction pointing it in the direction of the Capital of the United States.

Because of the encounter with the missile and a lost comrade, the aborted communication with the K-387, and now the reading of their new orders, they were not paying attention to the sonar readings that were currently displayed on the small monitor in control. Ordinarily this would have been Abdulla's job on this shift and already the two-man crew, because of his absence, had carelessly ignored the readings. Consequently, neither one of them were aware that an American attack submarine was heading straight at them.

Mahmoud saw it first. Having not been formally trained as a sonar technician, he called for Mustapha. "Come quickly! We have a sonar contact, bearing two-six-nine, range 1,100 yards."

Mustapha, looking at the scope, picked up the earphones and immediately recognized the distinctive identifying sounds of a submarine. "We have company, my friend."

Mustapha immediately disengaged the autopilot and took control of the small sub. His first act of defense was to slow to a speed of 8 knots. At this speed, the huge propeller turned one complete revolution every 30 seconds. The slow awkward revolution of the propeller, emitting very little noise, rendered the ESO practically undetectable with conventional sonar. Next he turned the submarine headfirst into the sonar reading of their visitors and descended to 150 feet. He turned to Mahmoud. "Prepare the Mod 14 Torpedo Tube for launch!"

"Comrade, are you sure? It might not be wise to give away our position so easily."

"Now, comrade, now! It must be the Americans. We cannot take any chances. We must destroy them. Do it now."

Mahmoud ran over to the small computer console and entered the command. Just above were the two levers. He lifted the red lever on the left and pushed the button. He lifted the black lever. "Armed and ready."

When Mustapha turned the small sub in the direction of its target, onboard computers immediately programmed the Mod 14 torpedo's with the same coordinates. Once fired, it would seek the target using these coordinates and automatically change course based on any additional instructions from the ESO.

"Where are they now comrade?" Mahmoud asked.

"Range 800 yards. We will fire when they are within 200 yards of us."

"Two hundred yards! Comrade, that is much too close. We must fire now."

"Mahmoud, we will wait until we reach 200 yards. I want to make sure we hit them. Remember my friend, they don't know we're here."

They had fifty yards to go. Surely the submarine that was heading right at them had no idea they were there. This was going to be easy, Mustapha thought. Their small stealth designed submarine was capable of moving to within 200 yards of an enemy submarine without being noticed.

"Range, 200 yards. Fire one," Mustapha shouted. Mahmoud reached over and gently pushed the black button. "One fired."

"Control, sonar."

"Control, aye."

"Captain, whatever it was, it's gone. Strangest thing. One second it was there and then it was off the scope. Must have been a school of fish that dissipated."

"Keep an eye on it. Any changes let me know immediately."

"Aye sir."

George didn't like sonar he couldn't trust. It reminded him of the trip he and his wife took right after he graduated from the academy. It was supposed to be their honeymoon. They had decided to drive to the Grand Canyon. They didn't make it. Knowing everything there is to know about life, and because they didn't have two nickels to rub together, they bought the dealer's special off a small used-car lot in Baltimore. The car was 14 years old and only had 56,000 miles on it. After breaking down eight times, they finally gave up in Cleveland.

"Control, sonar."

"Control, aye."

"Captain, we have a weapon lock. Range 150 yards and closing."

Although the sonar was not working, the anti-submarine warfare system onboard Woodbridge was operational and state-of-the art.

George reacted immediately. They didn't have much time. He turned to the weapons officer.

"Ready scutter. Launch when ready!"

The weapons officer reached over and turned a small dial and immediately lifted the lever located to the right of the dial.

"Aye, sir, scutter ready and launched."

Scutter is a self-propelled torpedo countermeasure system designed specifically for submarines. Highly effective, it provides an optimal directional coverage and enables a submarine to deceive and escape acoustical homing torpedoes.

The Woodbridge was equipped with the standard four-foot signal ejector tube that was mounted externally just beneath and two feet in front of the submarine's rudder. Scutter is able to detect and analyze acoustic transmissions of torpedoes and immediately simulate the Doppler effect and noise radiated by a submarine.

Within seconds of launch, the scutter detected the oncoming torpedo and immediately established itself as a decoy, emitting a noise identical to that of the Woodbridge. The small expendable torpedo, using the algorithm contained in its data bank, then veered sharply right and away from the Woodbridge at a 90-degree angle.

"Emergency dive, take her to 500 feet."

"Aye, sir, diving to 500 feet."

The Woodbridge immediately pitched forward and began her descent. This was no ordinary dive. In addition to the customary filling of the ballast with water, which literally sank the submarine, an emergency dive also used the boat's propulsion to assist in the dive. The result was a much quicker and steeper dive. If the scutter was successful in deceiving the torpedo that was coming at them, the Woodbridge would reach 500 feet in just 40 seconds.

Twenty seconds into the dive they heard and felt the explosion. The scutter had done its job perfectly. At 500 feet, George ordered all stop. The Woodbridge sat silently waiting for any signs of their attacker. You could hear a pin drop throughout the submarine. Control was packed with crew and guests, each doing their job flawlessly and very quietly. It was extremely important to maintain total silence when under attack. A dropped wrench is enough noise for a trained ear to detect a submarine's position.

262

As soon as they reached 500 feet, George went to sonar looking for any further signs of attack. While glancing at the screen only one thought possessed him more than any other: the Woodbridge must do whatever it can to repair the damaged software. Otherwise, they might not be so lucky next time.

Mustapha detected the course change almost as soon as they released the torpedo. Instantly he relayed the new course readings to the Mod 14 through the small tracer wire it carried behind it. The onboard computers immediately altered the torpedo's course to follow the distinctive acoustical submarine sound it needed to find its target.

"We got them comrade. That's a hit," Mustapha said.

Mahmoud leaned over and looked at the visual display on the small screen in front of Mustapha. "Are you sure, comrade?"

"Yes, my friend. Look at the diffusion displayed on the sonar screen. You don't miss and display particles like that. We definitely got them."

The two Iraqis continued to monitor sonar readings for the next hour and heard or saw nothing. Satisfied they had killed the enemy they submerged to 300 feet, reset the autopilot and steamed full ahead in the direction of the United States. Mustapha maneuvered the small sub several times before it sensed another swift moving ocean current allowing it to reach a speed of 28 knots. If they could sustain this speed, they would reach the coast in two days.

The ESO carried only one Mod 14 torpedo. The Iraqis would now have to face any new unforeseen adversaries without any additional torpedoes. Although both were well-trained Special Forces soldiers in the Republican Guard neither one was proficient in military planning or possessed the wherewithal of military strategic analysis. Still two days away from deployment, they had used their only torpedo to destroy a target that, they believed, was unaware of the ESO's presence.

Convinced they were now alone, the crew of the ESO went back to business as usual. They would closely monitor sonar as they approached the coast of the enemy. But for the next 24 hours they would rely on the autopilot for navigation and settle back for what would be their final sacrifice for Allah and the motherland.

USS Woodbridge

The anxiety of the wait when an enemy has fired a torpedo at you from less than 200 yards away is overwhelming. It is a state of mind that cannot be described nor taught. Not knowing whether the metal cylinder you inhabit will survive or implode from the direct hit of a torpedo can do strange things to your head. Seasoned veterans have been known to crack as soon as the command is given to launch a scutter.

The crew of the Woodbridge had been exceptional during the attack. When Captain Owens gave the order to launch the scutter and then ordered an emergency dive, no one in control displayed any sense of panic or sudden sense of doom. Even more astonishing was the reaction of the guests standing watch at the time. Although most probably didn't know what the scutter was or what it's used for, they surely knew they were in trouble when the Woodbridge tipped its nose and dove at a 30 degree angle to avoid the hit. At this angle, not only is it difficult to stand, but anything not tied down is immediately on the deck. George, standing in the middle of control when he gave the order, instinctively took a quick panoramic glance at the crowded control room.

"Chief, is Scott still looking at the sonar code or have we given up entirely trying to find whatever it is we're looking for," George said.

"Yes, sir. As far as I know, he's in his stateroom looking over the same code he and Darrich previously analyzed. He thought it might be a good idea to look it over again, just in case they missed something."

George thought of going up to talk with Scott but his presence in sonar was much more crucial at this point. The Woodbridge was still sitting at 500 feet and, with the exception of the activity in sonar, shut down.

"Captain, we've got activity on top of us. I think our friends are heading out. The readings aren't good but we can still detect movement at close range. And they are definitely at close range. Right now, they are only 200 feet above us moving at 28 knots in a northwesterly direction."

George, looking at the screen, picked up the earphones to listen. What he heard was not your normal submarine acoustics. It sounded more like a muffled whoosh. Nothing like the distinctive mark of a submarine. "Chief, listen to this. What do you make of it?"

The chief picked up the phones. "Don't know, sir. Never heard a sound like that. Whatever they're driving, it's nothing like I've heard before."

"Chief, get these acoustics into our ASW databank immediately. Make it the highest priority for the Mark 48. Let me know as soon as they're ready."

"Aye, Captain."

George followed the erratic display on the monitor. It wasn't long before the image began to fade. Soon it would be unrecognizable. "Chief, what's their range now?"

"80 yards off our starboard bow, sir."

"Jesus, and we're losing them already?"

The Woodbridge was armed with 28 Mark 48 torpedoes. The Iraqi submarine would be a difficult target to hit. With the sonar in the condition it was and the speed at which the enemy sub was traveling, the odds were slim. George would love to end this now but the odds of doing so were too great. An errant torpedo would give their position away and invite another attack. The Iraqis must have assumed they made a hit with their torpedo and were apparently proceeding full speed ahead toward their destination. For now, George would like to leave it that way. He would wait until the Iraqi sub was well out of range but still detectable with his weak sonar and start moving again. George decided the Woodbridge would follow the enemy sub until their sonar was operating

267

normally. If the Iraqis got too close to the U.S. and sonar was still down, he might then decide to go out on a limb and attempt a kill. But until then, he was not about to jeopardize his crew.

George waited until he could barely see a sonar reading and called control.

"Control, sonar."

"Control, aye."

"All ahead one third. Come to course two-six-four."

"Aye, sir. All ahead one third, course two-six-four."

At this speed, the Woodbridge would progressively fall behind the fast moving enemy submarine. George would give it an hour. After that, he would order all ahead full and do the best he could to remain on their tail. George knew what his orders were. He knew how important it was to destroy the Iraqi submarine while it was still in deep water. George knew time was running out to get his sonar back in working order before the Iraqis arrived at the continental shelf. If he couldn't kill them before then, he quite frankly didn't know what in the hell they would do to stop them.

Slowly the Woodbridge trailed the small submarine without any additional confrontations. They were quickly approaching their drop dead point and George still didn't know how he would stop the ESO.

It was time to visit Scott.

George politely knocked on the door.

"Who is it?" Scott replied.

"It's the Captain, Scott. May I come in?"

Scott quickly jumped up and opened the door. The stateroom floor was covered with printed code extending to each wall in the small room. In addition, Scott had taken the liberty to cover each rack, in the room that accommodated eight officers, with additional output.

"Any luck?" George asked.

"Sorry to say, sir, but not as yet. I'm just about finished with the low frequency module for the second time. I can't really tell you why Captain, but my gut tells me the problem is in that module. I've got about 800 lines remaining. Maybe I'll get lucky."

"Scott, you know we can't surface right now. So any additional help from Darrich is out of the question. Can anyone else here help you out?"

"Not really, sir. It's just a matter of reading through it line by line looking for anything that looks unusual or out of place."

"OK. Before I leave I need to tell you something. We are now in a position where it's crucial we get our sonar back online. If there's anything at all that looks suspicious or that you'd like to try, call me immediately."

"Yes, sir. I hope I can just come up with something."

George left for control and Scott went back to reviewing each line of code looking for anything that might be the problem. He returned to finish the low frequency module. He started at line 6,241. Placing the system output across his mattress, he began reading it out loud. Up to this point he had read it to himself. Perhaps if he read it out loud something might stick out. Only five minutes into the exercise, he read a line and, almost going to the next, saw something he hadn't noticed before. He read it again. Could this be the problem? Scott was very familiar with Visual Basic (VB) programming and how code is commented out. In VB, when a programmer wants to add a comment about a specific line of code, he or she would simply key an apostrophe in front of the line and the program would not read that line of code. Programmers routinely comment their code to add descriptions so someone else reading or using it later can more easily follow the logic.

In C++ code, two back slashes are used to comment out code or add any incidental instructions. Throughout the code, Scott had seen thousands of commented lines. All of which seemed to be some sort of definition of the routine. On the line for the ipp frequency, he noticed two slashes in front of the code. The coded instruction clearly had something to do with frequency. It was not an incidental comment made by the programmer but appeared to be legitimate instructions for the frequency module. And then he saw the commented line just below line eleven describing its function.

```
#define SAT_BIT 0x01
channel = channel_ID_table[buffer_index].ID - 1;
ipp_width =
(num_pts_adc_data/channel_ID_table[buffer_index
].IPs);
tx_width = ipp_width/10 + 1;
for (j=0; j<num_pts_adc_data;
j++) // This routine doesn't know pulsewith, so
assume //
if (j%ipp_width >tx_width) // 10% duty cycle to
determine sat check start point //
satcount[channel] += adc_data[j] & SAT_BIT;
//ipp frequency = (1-0; f<num_pts_adc_data;
// perform low frequency modulation for one CPI,
one channel //
for (j = 1; j < num_pts_adc_data; j += 4) {// negate
proper a* values //
adc_data[j] = -adc_data[j];
adc_data[j + 1] = -adc_data[j + 1];
```

Scott's heart started pounding as he reached for the phone on the wall. Christ, he didn't even know how to call someone on the damn boat. Instead, he grabbed the output and ran to control.

"Where's the Captain?" Scott yelled.

The OD, looking at Scott, started to chew him out for the outburst but the look on Scott's face stopped him. "He's in sonar."

Scott walked through the small doorway leaving control, turned right and opened the door to sonar. "Captain, I might have something here. I started reading the code out loud as soon as you left and noticed a line of code that appears to be commented out. It's possible it's supposed to be that way but I think it has something to do with the low frequency operation."

George looked at the line. "You mean here?"

"Yes, sir. See those two slashes in front of that line? They tell the program when it's running to ignore that line of code. If that line is significant to the rest of the program, the system isn't reading it."

George was skeptical but at this point he would try anything. "Can you fix it?" George asked.

"Yes, sir, Darrich gave me the password to open the module. All I have to do is find that line, remove the two slashes and recompile the code. If it's the solution, we'll know right away."

George didn't hesitate. If the change screwed things up more than they already were, Scott could just go back in and put the space back in. "Do it," George said.

Scott sat down at the small console just to the left of the two sonar screens and opened the LAF/72 program. He then opened the low frequency module and paged down until reaching the line of code. Placing the cursor just in front of the two slashes, he hit the delete key twice and they were gone. He then saved the change and compiled the software. In a little over a minute he was finished. Scott placed the cursor on the newly compiled software's icon and opened it. Almost instantly, the images on the two sonar screens came to life.

The captain, chief and sonarman on duty looked at the monitors in disbelief. They could clearly see the Iraqi submarine that earlier tried to kill them steaming along 950 yards off their starboard bow.

"Well, I'll be goddamned," Captain Owens whispered.

"Two little stinking slashes shut down a multimillion-dollar sonar program and an old rag-tag of a tiger cruiser fixed it," the Chief yelled.

George reacted immediately.

"Control, sonar."

"Control, aye."

"All ahead full, come right one-six-zero."

"Did you say all ahead full?"

"All ahead full, Lieutenant."

"Aye, sir, all ahead full, right one-six-zero."

George knew the target was small. But he also knew the sonar he carried was capable of hitting them. The Woodbridge would trail the small submarine slightly below and to its right. George took the short walk to control.

"The Captain has the conn," George ordered as he walked in the crowded room.

"Aye, the Captain has the conn," the OD replied.

"Sonar, control."

"Sonar, aye."

"Where are they now, Chief?" George asked.

"Bearing five-two-nine, range 850 yards."

"Let me know when they're at 500."

"Aye, Captain. Will report at 500."

"Dive officer report," George ordered.

When a submarine prepares for a shoot, the Chief of the Boat automatically becomes the dive officer, the navigator assumes the duties of the "Deck" and has control of the boat and the Captain is in charge of the fire.

"28 knots and closing," the dive officer shouted.

George would fire when they were within 500 yards of the target. He had maneuvered the Woodbridge about 50 yards to the right of the ESO and directly behind her. Just before he would issue the fire order, he would swing the Woodbridge hard left at a 45 degree angle and fire.

"Control, sonar. Approaching 500 yards. On my mark and...Mark."

"Come left nine-two-zero" George immediately ordered.

"Aye, Captain, left nine-two-zero."

"Fire one."

"One fired, sir," replied the weapons officer.

ESO

The two Iraqi Republican Guards soon discovered that operating the little sub with a two-man crew was not that difficult. Actually, they found it less stressful. Because there was one less person that stood the canopy watch, each crewmember rotated more frequently making the trip more bearable.

Since the encounter with the enemy submarine, the ESO was making good time. Their speed had increased to almost 30 knots, thanks to the ever-present ocean current that helped carry them on their way. They were now just a little over a day away from where they would deploy their weapon against the great Satan. A sense of gentle euphoria with the two remaining crewmembers seemed to be ever present the closer they got to America.

Mustapha decided to check and see just where the Potomac was. After all, if they were about to give their life for the cause, it would be nice to know where they were going. He logged onto the computer and opened the Atlas program it contained. Not knowing where to start, he searched on "Potomac River." He now knew where they were headed. Mustapha printed out a copy of the map showing the river and went to see Mahmoud.

"Comrade, look where they are sending us?"

Mahmoud glanced at the map and smiled. "We are going to sail right up their imperialist ass. This is going to be exciting, indeed. Before they even know what's hit them, their central government will be dead. Maybe even their political dictator President will fall as well."

"Yes, comrade. This plan was well conceived. I've checked the depth charts for the river and we will be able to sail right up to the Pentagon. See it here on the left. We can hit their military at its heart. We will devastate America."

Mustapha started back down the small opening from the canopy when the submarine suddenly veered sharply downward and the engine shut down. A loud, two-second, deafening, warning sound permeated the small submarine. Mustapha immediately knew what it was. Looking down at the console that displayed the ASW data, he saw the weapon lock flashing bright amber. Almost instantly, the ESO was totally silent. They had dropped from 300 feet to just under 600 feet in 30 seconds and the large awkward propeller was no longer turning.

Leaning down from the canopy, Mahmoud panicked. "Comrade, what has happened? Are we sinking?"

Mustapha didn't say a word. Reaching up into the small opening of the canopy, he grabbed his comrade by the throat and squeezed as hard as he could. Mahmoud's blood engorged face looked down at Mustapha who, holding his finger over his mouth, released his death grip. Mahmoud got the message. Silence was mandatory.

The ASW systems aboard ESO were completely controlled by computer. Because of its size, the ESO was not equipped with a decoy ASW device like the scutter. There just wasn't enough room. What the ESO could do, however, was project its acoustical identification away from the submarine much like a ventriloquist throws his voice. When the ESO detected the weapon lock, it automatically extended a shunt wire from a small exhaust hole located near the stern. Propelled by a small conventional powder blast, the wire was much like a radio transmitter. At full length, the wire extended one hundred feet away from the submarine. It then began emitting a low but distinguishable acoustical sound remarkably similar to the ESO's propeller noise. At precisely 30 seconds before impact, the wire would be released and the transmission stopped. The last sound waves sent from the small wire would reach the approaching torpedo just 2 seconds before impact. Just at the right time to confuse the torpedo's onboard navigation system into exploding without impact or simply continuing on its journey until its propulsion was exhausted.

USS Woodbridge

The ESO proved to be an elusive target. For the next eight hours, the Woodbridge fired ten Mark 48s at the small submarine without a hit. They were quickly approaching the coast and were unable to strike the sub with the most sophisticated torpedo known to man. After ten attempts, George was facing the stark reality that the Woodbridge could not kill the submarine.

George found it interesting that the Iraqis had not taken another shot at them. Perhaps the small sub only carried one ordinance. If that was the case, the Iraqis could not hurt them. They could not go on the attack. Their only defense was to run and continue heading for the coast. Which is exactly what they were doing. And it was working.

George decided it was time to surface and contact London to apprise them of the situation. Perhaps the Navy had recovered enough from the tsunami disaster to provide additional support at the coast.

"Come to periscope depth."

"Aye, Captain. Coming to periscope depth."

"No close contact," the OD reported

"Prepare to surface."

"You have the conn, Mr. Berlin. I'm going to sonar."

"Aye, Captain."

"Radio, sonar."

"Radio, aye."

"Patch us through to London and transfer the call to sonar."

"Aye, Captain."

George did not want to leave sonar while on the surface. He would remain at periscope depth just long enough to report in and receive further instructions.

"Sonar, radio. I have Mr. Jones on the line."

George picked up the wall phone.

"Mr. Jones, a lot has transpired since I last talked with you. We managed to fix our sonar and are fully operational. Before the sonar was repaired, we sustained an attack by the Iraqi submarine that was not successful. Consequently, we remained submerged to best avoid further attack." Knox interrupted.

"Captain, where are they now?"

"They are at 1,000 feet moving at 10 knots. They slowed considerably after we…"

"Did you say they fired a torpedo at you?"

"Yes, sir, that is correct."

"Captain, that little submarine only carries one torpedo. You need not worry about any additional attacks."

"I suspected as much, Mr. Jones, when they didn't attempt to go after us again. Sir, we have fired ten of our Mark 48s at them and haven't come close to a hit. The Iraqi submarine is obviously equipped with a very sophisticated ASW device. I am concerned we won't be able to stop them from entering coastal waters."

For the first time Knox was speechless. The USS Woodbridge just reported that their torpedoes were not capable of breaking the defense system of the ESO, and time was quickly running out. The Iraqis were approaching the coast and it was appearing more and more likely that the Woodbridge would not be able to stop them.

"Mr. Jones, do we have any support on or near the coast that can be of assistance to us?"

"I'm afraid not, Captain. We're in pretty bad shape militarily right now. I'm afraid you're all we've got at the moment. Where is the Woodbridge in relation to the ESO?"

"We are currently at periscope depth approximately 100 yards astern of them. As soon as we terminate this communication, we will again submerge. Once we're down again I might try…"

278

Matthew came crashing through sonar with Willy Carlos in close pursuit.

"Matthew, sit down now!" George snapped.

"Sorry, Mr. Jones. Some of my more rambunctious guests just crashed the party. As I was about to say, as soon as we submerge I might try another shot at them. Frankly, sir, I don't know what else to do. The Mark 48 has not been able to penetrate their defense."

Matthew, sitting in the corner and listening intently to the conversation his father was having, jumped in front of his father. "Hey Dad, why don't you crash into 'em?"

"Matthew, please sit down. Now!"

Matthew retreated back to the corner. He had seen that look on his father's face before and was not about to test him anymore.

"What did he say?" Knox yelled.

"What's that, sir?"

"That's it, Mr. Owens. That's it."

"That's what, sir?"

"Captain, it might just work. Did you say the ESO was sitting at 1,000 feet?"

"Yes, sir, that's correct. I'm, sorry, sir but I'm not connecting here. Just what are you talking about?"

"Captain, I'm not sure who spouted those words of wisdom a few seconds ago but it might be our only chance. I want you to ram the ESO, Captain. I want you to ram her and sink her now."

George quickly glanced over at his son and returned to the conversation.

"Go ahead, Mr. Jones."

"The ESO is equipped with conventional passive sonar. It's one of the few things they didn't improve upon when they built her. If you maneuver the Woodbridge directly over her and slowly sink your sub in the ESO's direction any sound waves you radiate will stay at that level and never get down to a deep-running submarine that is

279

running passive sonar. In other words, Captain, she won't know you're there until it's too late. Hold on a minute while I look at the ESO's layout."

Within a few minutes, Knox returned.

"Captain, the ESO is carrying her biological cargo in the forward section. Immediately to the rear of this section is the reactor area. We want to steer clear of both of these areas. From what I can see, she's most vulnerable in the canopy area. If we can ram her there, since most of her weight is in the diesel area, she should quickly sink by the stern. At a depth of 1,000 feet, the Iraqis would die immediately and the ESO would collapse or implode from the sudden pressure loss and sink to the bottom."

George paused for a few seconds to gather his thoughts.

"Mr. Jones, we've done nothing but the unconventional on this submarine since this episode started. I don't see why we should change now. We will proceed as ordered and attempt to ram the ESO."

"As soon as you're finished, surface and contact me."

"Aye, sir."

"Control, sonar."

"Control, aye."

"Dive, dive. Take us to 150 feet. At 150 feet, all ahead one third."

"Aye, Captain, diving to 150 feet, all ahead one third."

At this speed, the Woodbridge would be moving at exactly 10 knots. The same speed the ESO continued to maintain.

The Woodbridge leveled off at 150 feet and began moving slowly. George ordered a slow descending dive with ballast only. The diving officer issued the order to the plainsman who slowly pushed the wheel until reaching a 5°

angle. At the exact same time, the helmsman did the same and the Woodbridge slowly began to sink.

"150 feet," the Chief of the Watch reported.

"Count 'em down Chief. When we reach 700 feet bring her to a stop."

"Aye, Captain, coming to 700 feet."

Slowly the Chief counted out the depth as the huge attack submarine gently sank toward the ESO. "400 feet. 550. 675."

At 675 feet both wheels were pulled up gently to even out the ballast. The chief made a few slight adjustments and the Woodbridge settled in at 700 feet.

"We're at 700, Captain," the Chief said.

The Woodbridge was now sitting just 300 feet over the ESO moving in tandem with the small submarine.

"How we looking sonar?" George asked.

"Got 'em on the scope just fine sir. When this baby's working, you can almost count the bolts on her hull. She's real clear."

"Come to 8 knots. Bring her down to 850."

"Aye, Captain. Coming to 8 knots down to 850."

"Sonar, control. Can you make out the canopy area on top of the sub?" George asked.

"Control, sonar. You betcha we can Captain. I could draw a picture for you."

"How good are you, Chief, at darts?"

"I can throw 'em with the best of 'em, Captain."

The Woodbridge carried a 33-foot beam. At 50 feet, that would leave a 17 foot clearance over the ESO.

"Sonar, control. When we reach 950 feet, we're going to tip the bow at her. At that point we'll have about 17 more feet to go before we strike her. You'll have to take us in from there."

"Control, sonar. Aye, Captain, we'll take control at 17 feet."

The Woodbridge was now slightly behind the ESO. "Bring her back to 10 knots and level off at 950 feet," George ordered.

"Aye, Captain. Coming to 950, at 10 knots."

The ESO still did not know they were sitting right on top of them.

The next maneuver would be a tricky one. George took a few minutes to take a deep breath and surmise the condition of the crew in control.

"Sonar, control. You've got the conn. In a few seconds I will give the order to increase to 12 knots to maximize the impact when we ram them. When I give the order, you are the dive officer from there on in."

"Aye, Captain, we're ready."

George took another deep breath. "Come to 12 knots."

"Coming to 12 knots and mark," the OD reported.

Instantly the Chief in sonar spouted his command. "Come down 2 degrees."

There was no repeat of the order. There wasn't time. Again sonar issued a command.

"Left rudder, down 3 degrees."

Seconds later they felt what seemed to be nothing more than a slight vibration.

ESO

After ten torpedo attempts by the enemy, the two Iraqis were confident they could not be sunk. Somewhat surprised that the Americans were able to locate their stealth-designed sub, they were not surprised they were not able to hit them. Andrei had informed them of the ASW system the ESO contained and had all but assured them an attacking enemy would not be able to hit them with conventional torpedoes.

Even though they had slowed considerably to keep noise level at a minimum, they were now only hours away from entering coastal waters. From there they would casually steam toward the Potomac and, when ready, simply exit the submarine with the launchers, swim to the beach and fire away. It all seemed so simple. They regretted they would not be able to see the ESO explode at the end of the river. After delivering the deadly anthrax, the final blow would come when they spread their radioactive core in the heart of Washington, DC.

Mustapha checked the sonar. Strange, he thought, how the Americans were able to fire torpedoes at them and yet they couldn't detect them on sonar. Must be some new long-range torpedo. It didn't make any difference anyway. They hadn't been able to hit them with ten attempts. It must be very frustrating for the imperialist pigs to have the best technology in the world and have their weapons fail so miserably.

Mahmoud had the canopy watch. The ocean was completely different at 1,000 feet. Traveling at a slower speed enabled him to view the strange marine life that thrived at that depth. The large headlight on the ESO illuminated life forms he had never imagined. As he concentrated on the beauty in front of him, he did not notice the terror above him.

The bow of the Woodbridge struck the canopy dead center. At first Mahmoud thought it was just some curious sea creature attempting to enter the transparent top of the submarine. The blow from the Woodbridge was almost subtle. The four-inch Plexiglas canopy seemed to absorb the blow bending somewhat inboard and then retracting to its original shape. The normally clear canopy now had somewhat of a milky look to it. Mahmoud, realizing for the first time that something was terribly wrong, felt an unusual pressure in his forehead.

"Mustapha, come quickly. Something has struck us. I think we might have sustained some damage to the canopy."

Mustapha didn't have time to answer. The small hairline crack extending the length of the canopy finally gave under the immense pressure. Collapsing inward with a force of 500 pounds per square inch, the small submarine imploded immediately. Its two inhabitants never knew what hit them. Death was instantaneous.

Within seconds, the once stubby rounded shaped ESO was literally flattened like a pancake. And then, as the pressure equalized, the little sub resumed an almost normal shape. Slowly she sank by the stern coming to rest just off the continental shelf in over 15,000 feet of water.

Within two weeks, the United States located and recovered the ESO using the Nautile, the famous submersible used to explore the Titanic. Capable of diving to 20,000 feet, the small undersea research vehicle had little trouble locating the ESO, recovering all 30 canisters intact.

The White House

Standing tall and erect and with a smile from ear to ear, the President of the United States walked out of the south portico and up to the podium. He looked over at the distinguished guests sitting directly to his left. Before he began the presentation, he placed his prepared remarks aside, turned to the American heroes they were honoring and began.

"I am extremely proud to be standing here with you today. Not as your President but as a fellow American. You are what makes this wonderful country of ours stand out amongst all the rest. I am truly humbled to be in your presence. You are America!"

The President then proceeded to present the Presidential Medal of Freedom to each tiger cruise guest. The President awards the Presidential Medal of Freedom, the nation's highest civilian award, annually to those individuals who have made outstanding contributions to the security or national interest of the United States or to world peace.

"As President of the United States and as Commander in Chief of the armed forces of the United States, I hereby:

Present this medal to you for outstanding service to your country. Your bravery, courage and determination aboard the USS Woodbridge prevented a national catastrophe, saving millions of Americans from the devastation of biological warfare. Had it not been for your presence as tiger cruisers aboard the USS Woodbridge, we would not be standing here today. America will forever be in your debt."

Today's ceremony was also historic. It would mark the first time that 14 awards were bestowed simultaneously, and the youngest American to ever receive the award, ten year old Matthew Owens!

I hope you enjoyed the book.

Sincerely,

Made in the USA
San Bernardino, CA
27 June 2013